Proximate
Causes

Proximate Causes

Lyndsay Smith

HARBOUR PUBLISHING

Published by
HARBOUR PUBLISHING
P.O. Box 219
Madeira Park, BC Canada
V0N 2H0

THE CANADA COUNCIL | LE CONSEIL DES ARTS
FOR THE ARTS | DU CANADA
SINCE 1957 | DEPUIS 1957

Cover design by Warren Clark
Printed and bound in Canada

The characters and events described in this book are fictional, products of the author's imagination. Any similarity between them and real persons or events is purely coincidental.

The epigraph is from *Black's Law Dictionary*, 5th ed. (West Group Publishing Co., 1979), p. 1103. Quoted with permission.
"Here's to Life" written by Artie Butler and Phyllis Molinary © 1992, 1993, Artie Butler Music (ASCAP), Dominant Jeans Music and Live Music Publishing (BMI). All Rights Reserved. Used by Permission.

Harbour Publishing acknowledges the financial support of the Government of Canada through the Book Publishing Industry Development Program (BPIDP) and the Canada Council for the Arts, and the Province of British Columbia through the British Columbia Arts Council, for its publishing activities.

Canadian Cataloguing in Publication Data

Smith, Lyndsay, 1963–
  Proximate causes

  ISBN 1-55017-214-X

  I. Title.
PS8587.M5529P76 1999   C813'.54   C99-910905-7
PR9199.3.S55165P76 1999

Acknowledgements

This book is a collaboration . . . I received input and ideas from so many people—in and out of the legal/policing world and amongst my family members—that it wouldn't be possible to name every contributor. So thanks. You know who you are.

On the technical side, thanks to my sister, Kelly, for her creative and technical support, and for coolly retrieving the manuscript from cyberspace numerous times while I panicked at her side.

Finally, thanks to Harbour for taking a chance.

● ● ●

This book is for Fred, and for the Invisible
Enemy and the Pink Anemone.

With all my love.

L.

Proximate cause. That which, in a natural and continuing sequence, unbroken by any efficient intervening cause, produces injury, and without which the result would not have occurred.

—*Black's Law Dictionary*

They skied fast, with the urgency of painters racing the light. Neither wanted to prolong the task by missing this chance: they had been waiting for the weather to break and the mountains to clear for three days now, and the forecast was for clouds tomorrow.

It was the end of the season and the last run of the day. There were few other skiers around. Lauren Grey led, tucking down tight to reduce wind resistance as they traversed the side of the mountain, and crossed to the far edge of the ski run called Seventh Heaven. It had been her husband's favourite run.

She had been widowed twenty-eight days.

She looked to her right, to the coastal mountain range. The sun was just touching the highest peaks, turning them a blazing pink orange. The sky above the sun was a deepening blue. Stars would be soon. It was perfect.

She reached the end of the traverse, straightened up and

dug her ski edges into the snow, stopping expertly. Seventh Heaven fell below her to her right, bumps and moguls and groomed snow. To her left lay untouched snow and the odd rock. A rope sporting an Out of Bounds sign was strung across the end of the traverse. Lauren ducked under it and skied out onto the snow toward a crop of rocks.

Moments later Rick Parker reached the sign. He looked across the snow and saw that Lauren had reached a rock bluff, mid-mountain face, and was bent down taking off her skis. He ducked under the rope to follow her as she crossed her skis in an upright X in the snow.

Lauren climbed the black volcanic rock and stood above the white-blue snow, feeling the wind on her cheek. It was coming from the east, flowing invisibly across the diamonding snow toward the sun's evening warmth. Perfect. Transfixed by the magic of the approaching evening, she had almost forgotten about Rick. It was as if the night had been made for this.

She heard him now, as he cut sharply to a stop behind her. She pulled herself away from the horizon and the first star, turning to him.

"We need to hurry," she whispered. "We're losing the light."

Parker nodded in understanding. He had been her husband's business partner and friend, and by default had won the position of sole pall bearer. He skied up next to the rocks, sidestepping to get close, and took off his backpack and handed it up to her.

Lauren bent down to take it. "Thank you so much for helping," she said quietly. "We need to be alone for this."

He nodded. "I'll wait back on the run," he said firmly. "I'm not going to leave you on the mountain at this time of day to ski down alone."

"Fine," she said.

He pushed off and skied back across the mountainside, thinking about her. Lauren Grey was remarkable—strong, beautiful and smart. He recalled Martin occasionally bragging about her business savvy and independence, traits Parker wouldn't have expected in an artist. While Martin hadn't liked mixing business with his personal life, Parker had socialized with him and Lauren often enough to have learned that although she was well connected to the art world through the gallery she owned, she had no family except her husband.

When Martin died, she had turned to Parker, entrusting him with decisions ranging from how long to close the gallery, to how to break the news to Martin's relatives. It had been Parker who had held her as she cried inconsolably for hours that first night.

Since then, she had just been going through the motions. Parker knew it would be a very long time before Lauren got over the loss of Martin Grey.

Lauren waited until she felt alone again. Then she opened the pack and took out a book, leather bound with thin pages. She laid it on the black rock beside her. Next she took out a stainless steel cylinder nine inches long and five inches wide and placed it carefully on the rock next to the book. She kissed the fingertips of her right glove and bent down to touch them to the cylinder. She then picked up the book and stood tall on the black rock against the dying sun and the wakening stars, and opened the book to the marked spot.

She spoke in a wavering voice, speaking to the wind and the sun and the snow and the stars, for there was no one left alive who mattered to listen. "Love is patient, love is kind, and it is not jealous." She read the words carefully, one by one into the cold air. "Love does not brag and is not arrogant, does not act unbecomingly; it does not seek its own, is not proved, does not take into account a wrong suffered, does not rejoice in unrighteousness, but rejoices with the truth." Her voice shook.

"Love bears all things," she continued, "believes all things, hopes all things, endures all things." Her voice trailed off.

She gulped in cold air and spoke the final words. "Ashes to ashes. Dust to dust."

The stars were out for real now, icy sparkling rents in the blackening sky. Lauren placed the book on the rock and picked up the cylinder, spun flat grey steel. She tried twisting the lid, her gloves slipping on the smooth metal. She would have to do it with her bare hands.

She nipped the end of her right glove and pulled it off. The easterly wind had picked up. Its cold bit her hand. Lauren held the cylinder in her left hand and gripped the top, turning it hard with her right. It felt colder than the air. Her grip held this time and the lid gave. She pulled it off, leaving the mouth of the cylinder open and black.

Ashes to ashes. Dust to dust.

Standing straight in the night and the wind, she cradled the upright cylinder in her arms, swaying back and forth. A moan escaped her lips. The wind was starting to lift the skiff of fresh snow off the frozen crust below, raising whirlwinds of white powder around the rock. It was bitterly cold now. It would be dangerously so soon.

Lauren looked one last time at the western horizon, where a melting crimson strip outlined the black mountains of the coast. She stretched her arms out as far as she could, holding the cylinder out to the wind, and turned it until his ashes began to spill out of the black hole into the night and the swirling snow below.

She shook the cylinder until there was nothing left.

Feeling as though she were watching someone else's actions, Lauren recapped the cylinder and placed it next to the Bible and the pack. She didn't want them any more.

She slid off the rock to where her skis stood crossed in the snow. She put on her glove, snapped her boots into their bindings, picked up her poles and pushed off, back toward Parker.

When she reached him, she turned back for one last look. She could barely see the rock through the snowy whirlwinds skittering across the face of the mountain now. In her mind the snow had picked up his dust and his ashes, and was dancing them out into the cold night.

VANCOUVER, BRITISH COLUMBIA
October 11, 1997

"What the fuck are we doing here?" Dovee spoke quietly in Latvian, almost to himself.

It was 8:10. He and Oskar had been parked in the shadows for fifteen minutes and the waiting was making him edgy. He had a feeling about tonight.

"You'll be happy enough when you get your split," Oskar replied impatiently, never taking his eyes away from the parking lot.

They waited at the far end of the main lot. This spot, at the top of Queen Elizabeth Park on Little Mountain, was the highest point in Vancouver. By daylight it allowed a 360-degree view of the cityscape: to the north, Burrard Inlet and the North Shore mountains; to the east, the lush Fraser River valley and Mount Baker; to the south, the lowlands of the delta and spine of the Gulf Islands; to the west, the city's high-end residential neighbourhoods and, beyond them, the Pacific Ocean.

In the morning the plaza beyond the parking lot would be filled with early risers practising Tai Chi, and people would begin arriving to visit the tropical conservatory in the glass dome on the hilltop. But now it was dark; the dome had been closed for more than two hours. The park was deserted, and the black car was well hidden in the sheltered darkness of huge evergeens with low-hanging branches. From this vantage point they would see anyone approaching from any direction. It was an ideal meeting place.

Neither man spoke. 8:14.

The cellular phone resting on the dash rang. Oskar reached across from the driver's seat and flipped it open.

"Uh huh. Okay." These words were in English. In Latvian he said, "Let's get it done and get out of here." He terminated the call. "They just passed Andris and Yuri," he told Dovee. "They will be here in moments."

It was as if his voice had unstopped a cork: words came spilling out of the dark-haired man beside him. "I've got a bad feeling about this, Oskar. Let's call them back and call it off. How many times can we do this and get away with it? We don't need the money, you've said so yourself."

Oskar grunted. Dovee had always been the weak link in the chain, uptight about the guns and the odd hit, uptight about the police and Customs. Oskar shook his head unconsciously at his cousin's failings. Dovee hadn't liked it when they were importing and distributing, and now he didn't have the stomach for the rips. Too bad he liked the money.

"You'll have your wish after tonight," he said.

Dovee slumped down in his seat.

Oskar tried to hide his annoyance. The four cousins had made over a million dollars in the last year doing rips. Nobody was a hundred percent sure it was them: they hadn't left many live witnesses. Still, their luck wouldn't hold forever, and tonight, before splitting into their two cars, they had agreed that this would be their last rip.

It was a cocaine buy from the Red Dragons. Oskar had arranged it through his middlemen and their mutual associates. One buy, thirty kilos. The Red Dragons expected them to be bringing money. Surprise.

A moment later, a pair of headlights turned in to the dark parking lot. Oskar could not make out the model, but guessed the car to be an Acura or a Honda Prelude, the car of choice for snot-nosed gangsters, it seemed. The car stopped in the middle of the deserted lot, engine running, lights on.

Oskar recognized the low, sleek shape of his cousin's high-powered Lotus as it turned into the lot fifty yards beyond the first car. Andris drove it slowly toward the waiting car, just as planned. Oskar wished that he had pushed harder to ride with Andris, close to the action, instead of letting his brother Yuri take the passenger seat and the fun. He watched as the Lotus pulled up to within twenty feet of the first car, facing it, the two engines still running.

Two slight figures got out of the first car. Andris and Yuri got out of the Lotus and stood behind the flare of its headlights. Oskar knew their guns, silenced Uzis, would be shoved down the waistbands of their jeans at the back. It would be a matter of confirming that the dope was there, and then *spfft, spfft,* and away they would go.

The passenger of the first car appeared to be holding something but Oskar couldn't make out what it was. A moment passed without Yuri or Andris moving.

"What do you think is going on?" Dovee asked.

"I don't know. But something." Oskar paused, watching. He picked up the cell phone and pressed in a one-digit code. He could hear his brother's phone ringing across the lot.

"Yes." It was Yuri's voice, tense.

"What's going on?"

"We may be in trouble," Yuri responded in Latvian. "One of these assholes is Chris Wong's brother. It looks as though the Red Dragons did him a favour letting him in on this deal. The other asshole has us covered with an automatic Gloc."

"Fuck."

Oskar remembered Wong, a cocaine trafficker who they had ripped off several months ago, and not quite killed. Obviously the bullet in his head hadn't erased his memory of who'd shot him.

"What do they want?" Oskar's question was cut off by two flashes of light twenty feet in front of the Lotus. Both head-lights had been shot out.

The cousins watched as Wong bent into his running car and turned off the headlights. The parking lot went black.

Oskar was about to turn the ignition key and drive to Yuri and Andris when he heard a third car, loud and powerful and approaching fast. It came from the west—from the plaza, where no cars should be. Wong quickly got into his car while his associate covered Yuri and Andris with his gun.

The third car closed in fast, its headlights cutting through the black night. Andris and Yuri reached behind their backs for their guns. Wong's companion shot Andris in the right arm before Yuri sprayed him with bullets, tearing into his chest and throat.

Wong aimed through the flying glass of his car window, pointing his weapon at the two figures outside his car, but Yuri's shots quickly peppered his face and shoulders with blood. The speeding car was fifteen feet away from the Lotus when the passenger leaned out the window and aimed at the falling cousins, finishing them off in a flash of yellow light and bullets.

Andris and Yuri lay collapsed against each other at the side of their car. The third car tore away. 8:17.

Oskar waited several minutes, then turned the powerful engine over and eased the Porsche out of the shadows and across the black parking lot toward his fallen brother.

As they came abreast of the two cars, Dovee realized that Oskar was not stopping. He was accelerating.

"What are you doing?" he yelled. "Why aren't you stopping?"

"We can't do anything for them," Oskar replied calmly, "and they can't do anything for us."

"But he's your brother." Dovee sounded desperate.

"He's dead, Dovee. And there is no money or drugs in either car, so there's no point in stopping unless you want an unnecessary meeting with the police." Oskar stomped on the brake and clutch, stopping the car with a jolt. He looked at his cousin. "You want to go back and watch Andris's corpse go stiff? Get out, then." His voice was cold stone.

Dovee sat in the passenger seat squeezing back tears for his brother and cousin. He finally shook his head.

"Okay, then."

The car picked up speed and flew down the dark winding drive leading away from the parking lot.

Jackson Cole was a legend.

When he walked into the classroom at the Training Academy of the Royal Canadian Mounted Police, Vancouver, at 08:59 hours, every one of the twenty-three men and seven women watched each move he made. All were experienced members of the Mounties, all were in Vancouver to be trained, all had hopes of becoming some of the most effective undercover operators in the world.

It was the start of the third and last week of the course. They had spent the past two weeks role-playing and listening to lectures by a judge, a defence attorney and a prosecutor, about weaknesses and strengths observed in undercover cases. Today they were to begin a five-day immersion in the field with a man whose reputation was peerless. He was a chameleon with an incredible memory and an uncanny ability to persuade strangers to discuss intimate details with him, almost immediately upon meeting. His huge presence of expertise and integrity made him formidable on the witness stand.

Cole had not lectured at the undercover course for many years, mainly because of his schedule and his reluctance to be seen. Everyone on the course knew they were lucky to be in his audience.

Superintendent George Lawson took the podium, greeted the students and introduced Cole. "For those of you who don't know our next trainer," he said, "Jackson Cole has been with our outfit for twelve years, having been with the British SAS intelligence section for two and on loan to Scotland Yard for six. He has spent most of his Mountie time stationed in Vancouver, but moving from place to place to perform undercover operations. In the last twenty months he has done twenty-eight undercover operations, ranging from an internal theft to murder. Twenty-seven have resulted in convictions; twenty-one of those were guilty pleas." He paused, looking out at the trainees. "Listen to this man and learn from him. He's the best there is." He turned to the man seated to his left and said, "Without anything further, I give you Sergeant Jackson Cole."

Cole rose and walked to the podium. He was impressive: six-foot-three, two hundred pounds of muscle and bone, a handsome man in his late thirties, wearing a wide-shouldered navy blue suit, white shirt and black tie. His hair was dark, collar length. Below his high cheekbones he sported a neat beard, grown for the role he would perform in this course. Tanned and relaxed, he grasped the podium with his two strong hands and smiled a broad smile. Laugh lines creased the corners of his eyes and mouth.

To look at him, no one could guess that the reason he was available for the training course was that he was the subject of an internal investigation for shooting a man dead six weeks earlier. He had time on his hands because, officially, he was suspended. The course was a favour to the superintendent.

Leaning forward, Cole spoke in a deep voice that carried a hint of his time in England. "I have two rules for this type of work. The first is you must be having fun. If you're not, get out of undercover work—it's lousy hours, hell on marriage, and gets you to rubbing shoulders with murderers, dopers and skinners. The second is, if you ever stop caring about whether or not you get out alive, get out." He looked at them. "You might not care, but the people working with you and relying on you do."

Cole knew what he was talking about. He had reached that point himself, five years earlier, when he was working in Bolivia with the DEA, posing as a cocaine broker from Canada. The targets he was dealing with had forced him into a Mercedes outside his hotel and driven off. As he rode through La Paz, blindfolded, on the way to an unrequested meeting with the cartel's boss, Cole lost track of the number of left and right turns they had made, and he realized that he really didn't care: he didn't care whether he could get back to his hotel on his own, or whether he could describe the route and guide the DEA to the meeting place afterwards. All of which meant he didn't care enough about important things.

He had been fortunate. There really had been a meeting and he was returned to his hotel, alive. But he knew it was time to get out of the game for a while. After six months' leave, life seemed more worthwhile. So he had jumped back in.

Now Cole surveyed the eager faces before him. "That concludes the theory part of my lecture," he said. There was laughter in the classroom. He flashed his smile. "Now, down to business. Your notebooks for the next five days are in here," he said, pulling a small spiral-bound pad from a box, tossing it in the air and catching it. "You've been told the drill: as operators, you leave your notebook somewhere safe." He pounded the table with his fist, making the table and several of the trainees jump. "Safe," he repeated. "That means not your car trunk. Not your briefcase in your car when you're just running into the store for a pack of smokes. Not your girlfriend's apartment. Is that understood?" He waited a moment. "Lost notes, stolen notes, can get any one of us killed. I, for one, would be a very pissed off corpse if I knew that I'd been killed by someone's sloppiness.

"All right then." He was smiling again. "That's your lesson in notebook security. Now, this week, as you know, is about putting into practice the concepts you've been taught, and honing skills. Tonight I'll be the UC operator and," he pointed to three men in the front row, "you three will be my cover team. As such, I expect you to groom so that you won't be 'made' as cops; to observe me so that you could testify to facts, so as to corroborate my evidence about what went down, and finally, I expect you to keep me safe."

The three men nodded.

Returning his attention to the rest of the group, Cole said, "Observing this should not be absolutely dull for the rest of you. I am going to bodypack a recording device, so that even if you aren't close enough to the action tonight to hear the conversations, we'll be able to review my approach later—how I respond if the target initially rejects my approach, how I try to get the target to make statements that will prove his knowledge of the crime he's committing. We'll listen to the tape recording of the approach tomorrow night before you start your own operations.

"Tonight we'll just do a straight dope buy. If it feels right I may try to score from the level above my first target, to try to engage that person in conversation that incriminates him. We'll just see how the time goes." He looked at his watch.

"The target location is the bar at the Hotel Columbian." The students knew the place, a skid road flophouse with a bar on the main floor that was notorious for drug trafficking. "Be in position, dressed appropriately, by nine o'clock tonight. I'll be near the pool tables."

He stepped away from the podium. "Between now and then, grab yourself a notebook and try to get some sleep. It'll be a long night."

With that, he turned and walked off the low stage. He shook hands with the superintendent, then strode quickly out of the classroom.

Cole had a busy day ahead of him. At 11:30 he was scheduled for a workout at his dojo. He tensed the muscles in his chest and shoulders and then relaxed them. A good workout was overdue. Before that, at 10:00, he had to meet with his lawyer to discuss the shooting and any possible criminal charges. Cole wasn't too worried about it—it was more a nuisance situation than anything. He knew that he was on good ground for discharging his firearm. If he hadn't, instead of investigating Cole they'd be investigating the other guy for Cole's death. All in all, he didn't mind the way things had turned out. Then some zealous reporter had got bits on Cole's background, so the internal investigation had dragged on. Now that there was a public element to it, the force had to make the investigation look purer than pure. Never mind that the victim had had a record for kidnapping and attempted murder, and a loaded gun drawn at Cole when he died.

Cole had been relieved of his duties, with pay, except for this training stint, which George Lawson had asked him to do. So the effect of the suspension was that he stayed in his waterfront flat for more than two weeks at a time, instead of rushing off to some town to sit on a bar stool next to some thug and try to get him to explain the whys and hows and whos and the location of the body. It felt just fine.

After the dojo, he had a hair appointment starting at 2:00. He knew from experience that he would be there for at least three hours. That would take him to five. A run and a meal and it would be time to go.

He parked the beat-up Land Rover in a spot reserved for clients of Lundford and Simpson, Barristers and Solicitors, and headed for his appointment. Thirty-five minutes later he was moving again, comfortable with the way his lawyer was handling things and confident that the whole thing would blow over.

He walked into the dojo twenty minutes early and dressed in the uniform of the art. In the main room he stretched his ropy muscles and then began his kata, a familiar routine of kicks and punches and blocks.

"Looking good." The words came from behind Cole.

He turned to see his sparring partner, Don Edwards, smiling his usual cock-eyed grin. He and Cole had met at the London School of Economics during their first year of undergraduate studies. Edwards had ended up with an MBA and an investment banking position in London, and Cole had managed to put up with one year of sedentary theory before being recruited by the SAS in one of their quiet campus approaches. Neither man had looked back. And eight years later, when they both wound up back in Canada, their friendship had picked up easily where it had left off.

The two men bowed and squared off, and for the next forty minutes Cole's natural agility and speed showed itself. Edwards found it difficult to remain serene internally when Cole was dancing circles around him.

"No mas," he said finally, holding his hands up. "What's eating you?" He wiped his forehead with the sleeve of his gee. "That was not a fun practice."

"Yeah, sorry," Cole said as they headed for the locker

room. "I have more on my mind than I realized. I didn't mean to get you in the middle of the release process."

"No problem. You can make it up to me by joining Liz and me for dinner Friday night."

Cole stopped stripping off his clothes and looked at Edwards, eyebrows raised. "Just the three of us?" he inquired. Liz was not above matchmaking attempts when it came to Cole.

"Well, actually . . ." Edwards seemed slightly uncomfortable. He knew that as a rule Cole did not date, preferring solitude to a relationship which, in his words, could only end up disappointing someone. His erratic comings and goings had certainly disappointed his ex-wife Kate. "There is someone Liz thinks you should meet." Edwards hurried on before Cole could interrupt. "I've met her, Jack. She's a knockout—smart, good-looking. I don't know why she's on her own." He paused and added good-naturedly, "I sure don't know why she'd be interested in you. Come on, it could be fun."

Cole thought about the coming week—very late nights tonight until Thursday, then on Friday morning a wrap-up critique of the week's undercover performances. And he thought about Liz's friend. He had not dated much at all since leaving Kate; he had believed her when she said that if she could not stand his absences and unpredictable schedule, no one could. Still, there were times when he had to admit to himself he was lonely. His disappointment in the end of their marriage, and his separation from their son Michael, made his heart ache when he let it. Only recently had he allowed for the possibility that he'd be good for someone.

"All right, I'll come. But tell Liz the only reason I'm doing it is because she is so damn good to me and you're so damn ugly that I feel sorry for her." He walked naked toward the shower, then paused. "What's her name?"

"Janine Wright."

"Okay, page me with the time and place and I'll be there."

They discussed the market as they showered and dressed.

The salon was the perfect place for what Cole wanted. It was tucked away on a street with cracked pavement, just steps away from the cobblestones of Water Street in Gastown, the oldest part of Vancouver. A narrow alley ran next to the salon, serving as a delivery lane for the area's cafés and souvenir shops, and as a shooting gallery for local junkies. The shop had no sign and no street number, and the windows were painted over so no one could see in and find that there was, in fact, an active salon there.

None of this seemed to concern the owner of the shop in the least. The first time he went, Cole—known to the two stylists as Mr. Jackson—had pointed out these marketing deficiencies to the owner, whose response had been, "But you found us, didn't you? All our clients do." After he had spent time in the salon, hearing the telephone ring incessantly and seeing the results, Cole understood what the owner had meant: they didn't have to advertise because they didn't need more clients. They were masters.

For today's appointment, as usual, Cole had booked both chairs in the salon, paying a premium to ensure complete privacy. It also speeded up the process by permitting both stylists to work on him at once. He stepped through the nondescript door into the funky studio.

A slight man with close-cropped blond hair stood behind a high desk just inside the threshold, adjusting the shade on a small Tiffany lamp. He looked up from his task when Cole walked in. "Hello, Mr. Jackson," he said enthusiastically.

"Hello, Nathan," Cole smiled.

"It's great to see you. Let's have a quick look at you before you robe." Nathan came around the table to where Cole stood and gently pulled the hair around Cole's neck. "Well," he said, "I'm certainly glad it isn't any shorter." He pointed to a corner of the salon. "If you just want to put on a robe, we're ready for you."

Cole nodded and walked into the changing room, sectored off from the rest of the salon by heavy chartreuse velvet curtains. He stripped off his T-shirt and slipped on one of the short silk kimonos, then gave himself one last look in the mirror, knowing that when the glass next reflected his image he would look very different indeed.

The stylists stood on either side of the antique barber's chair, each ready to take a side of Cole. Two assistants were present, one for each stylist; once the gluing got going, it would be difficult for the stylists to handle the strands.

Two trays, identical in setup, stood by the chairs, one on either side. In each one the assistants had laid scissors, razor, comb, glue and hundreds and hundreds of dark brown strands of human hair, about eighteen inches long, woven at one end into half-inch strips. Each strip would be tucked under Cole's own hair, woven and glued into his natural hair, with the flowing strands extending his hair by a foot and a half by the end of the afternoon. The weaving and gluing process would take about three hours. Then there would be a dye job, so that Cole's own hair and the extension strands matched exactly. Then a cut and a hack job on his beard, and that would be that. The well-groomed man would be gone.

Cole said his hellos and sat down in the overstuffed chair. The process began. Each assistant took a hair extension strip from the tray, placed a small dab of glue on the strip and passed it to his respective stylist. The stylists started at the back of Cole's neck, pinning up his hair to the left and right of an imaginary part down the back of his head, and placing his hair over and under and into the woven glued strip.

Cole closed his eyes. This was the only opportunity he would have to sleep until the early morning hours of the following day. He pictured a clock in his mind and mentally swept the hands around its face until it read 5:00. Three hours. He fell asleep.

He awoke exactly three hours later, opening his eyes to a completely different image of himself in the mirror: his hair had been parted down the middle and fell over his shoulders, reaching past his midriff. They were doing a great job.

"We're almost finished the extensions," Nathan said. "It's really looking fabulous."

It was true. The long hair suited him, framing the high cheekbones and strong face.

"You guys are pros," Cole acknowledged.

He endured the rest, opting for a darker brown than his natural colour for his hair and beard. He had them give him an uneven trim and, looking at the result in reflecting mirrors, nodded his approval: he looked completely different than when he had walked in.

He paid them eight hundred dollars and left. It was 5:45.

· · ·

The message had said to meet at six.

When Danny Fox first got the message and figured out who it was from, he managed to convince himself that he would not go. Meeting another con on parole, while you're on parole, is strictly bad news. If you get caught.

As the days passed, he began to consciously allow for the possibility that he might go. Just for a few minutes. Just for old time's sake. By the time Monday afternoon rolled around, he had accepted the inevitability of his going as he accepted the inevitability of his next fix.

As he walked down Cambie Street he realized that he had never really had any choice at all. He headed for the North Cambie Inn with his head on a swivel for cops and noticed a tall, well-built guy with long hair walk out of an unmarked storefront. Fox had walked by the place before and wondered what the hell it was. The guy leaving it didn't give much in the way of clues. Fox stepped out of his way when they passed on the crumbling sidewalk.

He was going to meet Roger-the-Dodger Morrit, who hadn't dodged so well as to avoid getting caught holding the bag just over eleven years before. Unfortunately for Roger, the bag had contained over twenty pounds of heroin. He had been sentenced to twenty years. Three weeks ago he had been released on early parole, and two weeks later he had contacted Fox, a person known by him to be a criminal, contrary to the terms of his parole.

Morrit knew that Fox was a criminal because they had worked together a few times over the years: robberies, drug deals, enforcements. Not often, as Fox had always been pretty much a loner and Morrit had lots of work from the bikers, his baby sister having married a member. But often enough to be a problem for both of them, if a cop saw them having a beer together.

Fox walked into the beer parlour a few minutes early and chose a small table in the back, in the shadows. He hoped being the first to arrive wouldn't make him look too eager. Shooting the shit with Morrit would be fine, but he knew that the real purpose of the get-together was business, and he was just hoping that it was big business. Everyday shit he didn't need anyone for. A big score was what he wanted, and that usually meant at least one partner. Fox wanted to get in and get out in a big way and be left alone with his cash and his habit.

He spotted Roger walking into the dim room and waved him over.

It didn't look as though the joint had been too unkind on Roger—he looked his sixty years but not much older, with a comfortable-looking paunch above his spindly legs. Fox had seen him since his sentencing, when Fox was doing a little pen time for his latest robbery conviction. They both shook hands hard.

"Good to see you when we're both breathing free air, Danny," the old man said. "But kid, you're lookin' like shit. You gotta get off that stuff."

Both men knew he never would.

"Ya, ya." Fox waved, bending forward to light Morrit's cigarette. "And these things are so good for you."

"So, we both have our vices."

The two men sat in comfortable silence, waiting for the waitress to bring them their beer.

For the first half hour of their visit they discussed mutual friends and associates, Morrit updating Fox on those inside the joint, Fox updating Morrit on those out.

"So," said Morrit, finally turning to business. "How are you living?"

"The usual," Fox responded. The usual, in his case, consisted of welfare and small-time crime. "It's enough until I come up with a kill."

Morrit nodded thoughtfully.

"Hey, talking about big deals, do you remember that hit you approached me on the last time I was in?"

Morrit nodded again.

"Well, I read about his death. It was a good job; maybe as good as I'd have done."

Morrit laughed. "Yeah, Jesus, didn't they do a bang-up job. You really walked away from easy money that time—a hundred grand, Danny. Jesus." He shook his head in disbelief. "Yeah, it was Wesley who ended up doing it, the brains and the brawn with a little help with the brawn from one of the hangers-on." He laughed again. "They found out where the guy was eating—some high-class wop joint—with a couple of mucky-mucks and they just bought off the car hop with a couple of lines of coke and gave the man the ride of his life." Morrit took a pull on his beer and raised his glass in Fox's direction. "A little of this, a tap in the head, a solo drive down a cliff. What cop's gonna care about one more dead drunk driver?"

Fox nodded. It was a clever hit that probably would never get investigated from the right angle. Smart.

"I'm hoping *this* deal," Morrit emphasized *this*, "you'll take." He leaned across the table toward Fox, so that they were less than a foot apart. "I need you to move some stuff for me, Danny." He was almost whispering.

"What do you mean?" Fox was sure that he knew, but wanted to be completely clear.

"I mean, they didn't find all of my stuff when they got me last time. I've got a couple of pounds stashed away, but I'm so out of touch that I can't move it myself, I wouldn't know where to start. And I need some money. Soon."

"Come on, Roger," Fox groaned. "You can sell the stuff as easy as I can, you're just nervous 'cause you just got out." He looked at Morrit. "You *should* be nervous."

"I'll split the profits right down the middle with you."

Fox didn't say anything.

"I mean, half of the selling price. I ate the cost of this stuff years ago."

Fox shook his head. So much for big-time scores through Morrit. He didn't traffic in heroin in small amounts. The courts still viewed it as serious, and he could draw serious time for it. If he was going to deal, he'd deal in coke or marijuana; something no one really cared about. "Why don't you get your brother-in-law's crew to do it?"

"They won't touch it just now," said Morrit. "They got done for five marijuana grow operations lately and they want to lie low for a while." He shrugged. "They don't want to have pounds of horse lying around."

"Well," said Fox, "I can see you haven't lost your sense of humour."

"What else have you got going?" Morrit asked, eyeballing Fox.

He had hit a chord. Fox had nothing of substance going on at all. He would have to come up with something in the next while if he was going to resupply.

"Look, Danny, we've both seen bigger days." Morrit might as well have been reading Fox's thoughts. "You might see them again. I won't. I know who you are and where you've been and I respect you for it. I also trust you." He pointed a finger at Fox's thin chest. "Believe it when I say you're the only dope fiend I'd trust with this. Just a few scores." He waited. They both knew Fox would do it in the end.

Fox drained his beer and wiped his lips with the back of his scrawny hand. "What the hell," he said finally.

"Well, that's just great." Morrit was all smiles.

"You're not holding now, are you?" Fox asked. The stupidest place to have a lot of dope on you was a bar near skid road, even if it had just been renovated.

"No." Morrit shook his head. "I stashed some of it in a planter outside where I'm staying. The rest is safe."

"Okay. Good." Fox was thinking, planning, now that he was in. "It's Monday. The drug squad has Mondays and Tuesdays off. That's good. Okay." He was nodding absently. "Okay, look. I'm not going to hold more than I'd use." That way, if he got caught he could argue it was for his own use, and would likely avoid the more serious charge of possession for the purpose of trafficking. "I'll arrange the deals and I'll deliver, but you hold."

"Fair enough," Morrit agreed. "Where?"

"Where else?"

Morrit nodded. "Time?"

"I got nothin' going now," said Fox.

"Let's make it in an hour."

Fox looked at the stolen watch on his wrist.

"Okay. 8:15. Where'll you be?"

"Across the street, in the parking lot."

"Okay." Fox got up to leave. "And the shit. What is it?"

"Pure—eighty-eight percent or so." Morrit sounded proud. "Decked into points and grams."

"Okay," Fox nodded, "see you there."

• • •

"He's late," Corporal Lee said to his companion, a grubby-looking man sitting opposite him at a sticky table. They were drinking draft in the beer parlour of the Hotel Columbian.

The grubby man, Corporal Kahler, squinted at the pool tables in the corner of the bar, shaking his head slowly. "I'm not sure that he is," he said.

Kahler was watching a tall, long-haired shit-rat, sinking balls, taking money off people and laughing with them. An unusual combination. The hustler wore black leather pants, a black shirt and a worn black leather vest. The cowboy boots with their high heels and the tight black clothing made the man seem taller and skinnier than he really was—on reflection, he was about the sergeant's build. But his hair was dark brown, almost black, and long, tied back in an unkempt ponytail. His skin was darker than the sergeant's and instead of a straight, white-toothed smile, the hustler had crooked, stained front teeth. The eyes were wrong, too. Kahler couldn't tell exactly what colour the hustler's were, but they weren't the deep blue eyes he had seen on Cole earlier that day.

He got up and walked over to the long wooden bar where Constable Barker, the third member of the cover team, sat watching the game.

"Have you seen the Boy Wonder yet?" Barker asked as Kahler sat down next to him.

"I think I just may have."

Barker looked toward the door leading from the street.

"Uh uh." Kahler shook his head. "Look at the pool tables, just like he said. Look at the guy in the leather, skinning everybody and making them enjoy it. See anything familiar?"

"Well, I'll be damned," Barker said. "That would be an amazing makeup job, but you may be right."

The hustler, leaning over the marred green felt to sink the next ball, looked in their direction. And winked.

● ● ●

The Columbian was busy for a Monday night, which was good and bad. On the one hand it meant plenty of business, but there were a lot of faces Fox had never seen, which made him slightly nervous.

He had got to the bar just before 8:30 and sat down with a couple of other guys from the skids and a prostitute he knew. They were all drinking draft. Once the hooker found out he was dealing, he'd have to move tables. She'd be relentless, offering to trade everything he didn't want for a little scrape of the shit.

He decided to check out the men's bathroom for customers. He walked into the stinking room and surveyed it quickly, which was easy to do because all the stalls had had their doors kicked off. There was no one there.

He was just about to leave when a guy walked in who he'd seen before. Skinny and white, he had the marks of a junkie. "You got?" the guy asked.

Fox nodded.

"How much?" Unless this guy had just robbed someone,

he wouldn't be able to afford more than a point. Not a great start for Morrit's great comeback, he thought to himself.

"I could—I could do a gram." The junkie was shaking.

Just a mess, Fox thought. He never let himself get this desperate. "I can do you that. Three hundred." He looked at the guy. "You got that?"

"Uh huh," he nodded. "Right here." He bent down, dug into his loose, grimy sock and pulled out a small roll of bills.

Fox reached into a hole in the lining of his jacket pocket and grabbed a small paper packet. He watched the junkie count three hundred dollars, then took the money and passed over the dope.

"I leave first," Fox said.

The junkie wasn't going to argue.

Fox returned to his table and over the course of the next hour was joined briefly by a number of people. He sat close to them, shook their hands, passed them jackets or serviettes. Dealt the heroin in any way he could. Once in a while he went outside for a few minutes.

By 9:30 he had sold sixteen hundred dollars' worth. That was eight hundred to him. He sat back to wait for the next customer. The word was surely out; he didn't need to do the approaching.

While he waited, he watched the action at the pool tables. There had been a guy playing for most of the time Fox had been there, who'd been cleaning out almost everyone he played. Fox had seen him before but couldn't remember where. Certainly not from a bust—no alarm bells were going off inside his gut. He watched him now. The guy was a well-built son of a bitch; he looked lanky, but that was the clothes. His shoulders were wide and strong-looking. His teeth were shit. Crooked and brown; not the nice white of a police dental plan. His hair was long and messy. A biker, maybe.

Fox couldn't slot him, but he could see that the man knew

how to play pool. Every shot was clean and precise. There were times when his opponent didn't touch the ball once after losing it to him. Money was changing hands pretty well in one direction, but no one seemed sore about it. Fox thought about his eight hundred.

He picked up his beer and walked over to where the stranger was finishing wiping up the table with one of the bar's regulars. The guy pocketed the two twenties lying on the rim of the table and turned slightly away from Fox, as if not noticing him. Fox was forced to approach him.

"You still playing?" Fox asked.

Cole turned and looked at the small, wiry man speaking to him. He had the white pallor of a hype and short, scraggly, thin hair swiped over to one side. His lips were thin and there were several pale shiny scars at one corner and above the upper lip. A scrapper. He wore long sleeves but they couldn't cover the tracks scarring the veins on the backs of his hands. Cole noticed slash scars on the hands too—defence marks from a one-sided knife fight.

Cole was easily eight inches taller than Fox and had over fifty pounds on him, but sensed the other man's toughness immediately. This one didn't much prefer living over the alternative. Fox looked back at him evenly, eyes to eyes, and Cole knew instinctively that he was dealing with a killer: the eyes were a flat blue-grey, almost without colour, and the little man rarely blinked. The apparent physical advantage wouldn't mean a thing with this man.

Cole knew that he had seen him before. He tried to recall when and why they had met, and whether or not it would blow his cover now.

"Sure," he nodded. "I just thought I'd get myself a beer. Rack 'em up." He walked away from the table, thinking.

As he waited for his beer, he remembered: he had just

about ploughed into him leaving the hair salon that afternoon. Damn.

Cole reminded himself that since then he had dyed his face, added the dental prosthesis and the coloured contact lenses. It had been a brief encounter; the changes ought to be enough. He returned to the table.

"We'll shoot to see who breaks," the scarecrow said, unconsciously taking control.

Cole smiled to himself. He had been watching the man deal up a storm ever since he had arrived and had concluded that he was either supremely confident or really stupid. Judging from his approach to the game, it was confidence.

Cole had decided long before Fox came over that he was his target for the night. By making the target come to him, Cole planted the notion in the target's mind that he had found a safe new friend—who couldn't be a cop, since he had not initiated the friendship the way an undercover cop would. It usually worked like a charm.

Cole let Fox win the break.

Fox had spent years around pool halls, halfway houses and jails, and he had the skills to show for it: he sank five balls before Cole got his cue on the table. Cole played well but let Fox take the game. For the second game, Cole broke and Fox took the game for real.

"The best three out of five," Cole said. The competitive edge to his voice was real.

Fox laughed. "Okay. But let's up the ante." He peeled four hundred dollars from his roll and put it on the table.

Cole counted out four hundred from the cash in his vest pocket. "You're on."

They raised their glasses to each other and drank.

Fox started the third game, swearing at the patrons who had drifted over to watch the match and who stood in the way of his cue. Cole took the game. He then broke and aced Fox, never letting him get his stick on the green.

They were both enjoying themselves.

"This is the one that counts," Cole said to Fox, smiling. "Nervous?"

"Fuck you," Fox said good-naturedly. He racked up the balls and walked to the end of the table. Bending over, he leaned into his cue and sent the white ball spinning to the triangle of coloureds. He sank two solids. A few people actually clapped. Fox sank three more before turning the table over to Cole.

Cole had pretty well decided that losing and ingratiating himself to this man, maybe making him feel sorry for him, would work. He sank a striped ball and then mis-hit, sinking the white ball. He walked around the table and pulled out the one striped ball he had sunk.

As he watched Fox eye the table, he decided that having Fox lose would actually be better. He would have less money, so would be more motivated to deal, and he would want to get what he would perceive as his money back. As well, as long as his ego didn't get stepped on, hanging out with winners was always preferable to hanging with losers. Cole willed him to miss.

Fox sank a ball expertly. There was one solid ball left on the table. Cole watched the table as the white ball rolled to a stop. He almost smiled: Fox was completely boxed in by striped balls.

Fox cued up and missed.

"I knew there was an advantage to not having any balls down," Cole said cheerily.

Fox ordered them a couple of beer.

Cole assessed the table and then began to move. He sank six striped balls in less than two minutes. The seventh ball slowed him down a bit: he had to eye the right angle to bank it into the side pocket.

They were even.

Bending over the table to eye the lines, Cole looked at Fox, who was watching him. Fox nodded subtly. Cole looked back at the angle and agreed. He winked at Fox. He then pulled back on the cue, tapping the white ball gently. It rolled across the scruffy surface and gently bumped into the last striped ball. The green and white ball rolled over and over and over toward the hole in the side of the table and teetered at its edge before dropping over.

Cole looked up. Fox was smiling.

The eight ball was lined up directly behind the white ball, in front of a pocket. You couldn't miss. Cole took the shot.

He straightened up and walked over to Fox. They shook hands.

"Jackson Allan," said Cole.

"Good playing, Jackson," the scrawny man said. "Danny Fox."

Cole nodded. He reached over and scooped the eight hundred dollars off the table.

"Can I buy you a drink, Danny?" Cole asked, pocketing the money.

"Why not? You got all my damn money."

They sat down and the waitress appeared immediately. They'd get good service with those kinds of winnings. Cole ordered two double whiskeys, then lit a cigarette and offered the pack to Fox.

"No thanks." Fox waved them away. "Those things'll kill you."

Cole smiled inwardly, thinking of the tracks covering the backs of Fox's hands. He shrugged and tossed the pack onto the table in front of him.

"So where you from, Jackson? I don't think I've seen you round here before."

"Originally Toronto." Cole dropped the second *t* like a native. "Lately I've spent most of my time in California and Whitehorse. It just felt like it was time to get out of both. Vancouver looked like a place with opportunity."

"It's got that, all right," said Fox.

"What about you?"

"I been around these parts for over twenty years." Fox smiled humourlessly at the whiskey in his glass. "Not enough of what I need in Nanton, Alberta."

Cole was about to respond when Fox leaned back in his chair and, looking in the direction of the door, said, "Oh, Keee-rist." He had forgotten about Morrit, waiting outside with his stash for more sales. Cole swivelled in his seat to watch as a portly man in his mid-sixties walked toward them. The guy looked slightly pissed off. He also looked familiar.

"What the hell are you *doing?*" he demanded, ignoring Cole.

"Jeez, Roger, things got happening. Take a load off and let Jackson here buy you a beer." Fox was laughing, but there was nothing Morrit could do—Fox had his money. He sat down hard. A waitress brought a third whiskey.

Fox leaned toward Cole. "Jackson, Roger. Roger, Jackson."

Cole's show at being impressed was not a hundred percent act. Shaking the older man's hand, he said, "Roger Morrit?" He let a trace of awe slip into his voice.

No wonder the man looked familiar—his picture had been all over the papers in the early eighties, as a reputed mob connection. He had owned a strip club in town, renowned for providing whatever you wanted. Cole recalled that Morrit had finally gone down on a heroin pinch about ten years earlier, when he had been known as one of the biggest suppliers in the city.

Morrit leaned back in his chair, liking Cole more than he had at first. "Yeah, that's me." He took a slug of his drink.

"Man," said Cole, "you were a legend." He was thinking fast. Morrit must be a parolee, in violation just by being in the Columbian. He was with Fox, who'd been trafficking like a fiend to people who sure looked like heroin addicts. Cole bet that Morrit was the outside supplier Fox had been going to meet whenever a deal went down. If Cole was right, this situation had implications beyond a mickey mouse training exercise.

"Where do you know me from?" Morrit asked, cautious.

"The papers, man," Cole said, shaking his head. "Even back east we heard about you. My old man ran the odd errand for Sam Patrona, and he talked about you and your balls out here."

Fox and Morrit looked at each other briefly.

"How long you been in Vancouver?" Morrit asked.

"Just a few days," Cole said. "I was saying to Danny that I pretty well live in Whitehorse, with lots of time in California."

"What did you come to the coast for?" Fox asked.

Cole was ready for him. "I'm looking for a supplier that doesn't involve international borders." He had said everything and nothing. They would either bite, or they wouldn't.

"Huh," said Morrit.

"Tell me about Whitehorse, I never been," Danny said.

He and Morrit were working well together, giving nothing up but pumping their new friend for details that could be confirmed later. Cole had been to Whitehorse several times. He knew the layout of the town and the biker bars and criminal hangouts, and was counting on Fox and Morrit never having been there.

"Well, it's fucking cold in the winter and fucking buggy in the summer," he said, "but other than that, it gets into your blood and you don't have much of a choice but to live there. Good bars. Good girls. Lots of work." He paused. "Lots of people selling and buying things." He let the words sink in.

Fox ran the reference checks. "I got an old friend up there, part of a biker club . . . Can't remember its name."

"I know it," Cole nodded. "The Icemen. I think they're connected to the Warriors."

The other two men nodded. He was right on both points.

"What is it that you sell up there?" Fox asked.

"What do you think?"

"Look." The humour was gone from Fox's eyes. "If we cut the crap, we might be able to do a little business that would make the money you took off me tonight look like chump change."

Morrit scraped his chair back and pushed himself out of it. "Thanks for the drink, gentlemen. I have to excuse myself for this conversation." He walked back out of the bar.

Cole was sure Morrit wouldn't go far. If Fox was going to offer a heroin deal, Morrit was the supplier. Cole waited for Fox to speak.

"Do you move any 'down' up there? There's got to be a market," Fox said.

"Sure, there's a market. Though I pretty well stick to blow."

"There's way more money to be made in the other," Fox said. "And I got lots of it, for cheap."

"Is it any good?" Cole asked, sounding reluctantly interested.

"It's pure shit," Fox said.

Cole watched him carefully. Fox was the only heroin addict he'd seen who could talk about the stuff without frothing at the mouth.

"And no border," Fox said, smiling thinly. "I can guarantee you the police haven't a clue this stuff's around. You buy in bulk, you deck it up yourself into cute little packets and you sell it at a killer profit."

Fox had no intention of running the risks again for Morrit that he'd run tonight. But if he could middle a deal for a bulk sale, he could pocket a hefty profit for one transaction. That did interest him.

"Yeah, maybe," Cole said slowly. He would have to get authorization from the superintendent. And he'd have to get the buy money together. But it could happen—he'd just need time. "You got a sample of the stuff?"

Fox was delighted. "I just happen to." He reached for Cole's cigarettes and slid a small white fold of paper into the pack.

Cole picked up the cigarettes and casually slipped them into his shirt pocket. He stood up. "I'll be back in a minute," he said, walking toward the men's room. He had noticed that one of the men from the class, one of the cover men, had gone in that direction upon seeing Fox slip the deck into the cigarettes. Good instincts.

Cole walked into the dank room. The trainee, wearing dirty black jeans, plaid shirt and grimy John Deere ball cap, stood at the urinal. Cole glanced into the stalls. The men were alone.

"What's your name?" he asked quietly.

"Kahler."

"Okay, Kahler." Cole pulled the cigarettes out of his pocket, took out the small packet of heroin and laid the cigarette pack on a pool of scum on the sink. He then placed the deck on the pack and unfolded the paper. The white powder looked good.

"Do you know who the guy I'm sitting with is?"

Kahler shook his head.

"Or the old guy who was sitting with us briefly?" Cole pulled a small glass vial about an inch long from his vest breast pocket. He eyed the liquid in it and, holding the vial vertical, snapped off the top.

"No, sir," said Kahler.

"Well, it was bloody Roger Morrit. One of the biggest drug kings in this province's history. By my count, he must've just been released, which means he's on parole, which means he's in trouble just talking with my new friend, Danny Fox." Cole paused to lick the end of a paper clip he had removed from his shirt pocket. He dipped the wet end into the white powder, pulled it out with grains of product clinging to it, and dipped it into the solution in the vial. He covered the end with his thumb and shook it.

He turned and looked at Kahler. "Get a copy of the tape from tonight." Everything he had said or been told since he entered the Columbian had been recorded by the device he had taped to his chest and transmitted to a van parked across the street. "Get it to Superintendent Lawson. Tell him I need a hundred thousand dollars by tomorrow morning, cash. And I'll have Morrit back in the joint, with Fox in the cell beside him." He paused. "Tell Lawson that delays will kill it. These guys want money, but they don't know me. Got it?"

Kahler nodded.

Cole looked at the vial in his hand. The liquid was almost black. Fox had been right: it was pure shit.

"Okay," Cole said to Kahler. "Turn left and go out the exit down the hall. Get into the surveillance van and make them leave. Do not get in and get out: that's a sure sign there's surveillance going on. The trainees'll just have to do without the rest of the tape-recorded lesson if you travel out of range. My order."

Cole walked out of the room, dropping the vial into an

overflowing garbage can by the door. He returned to the table and sat down smiling.

"It looks good," he said. "Darker purple and it've been black."

Fox nodded, familiar with the Marquis field test. Anyone buying or selling in bulk used it to assess the purity of coke or heroin.

"So." Fox got right down to business. "How much d'you figure you can handle up north?"

"If you've got a unit, I could handle it."

"Can do," Fox said, almost absently, surveying the room and picking at a scab on his left hand. "When?" he asked Cole, without looking at him. He was watching two of the female trainees, who were too young and fit-looking for the hotel's crowd. Fox looked back at Cole, squinting. His gut feel hadn't really kicked in, but he knew that if he had any misgivings, now was the time to walk.

Cole could sense that Fox was edgy. Why not? It was a big deal, happening awfully fast, with a stranger.

"I could do it in the morning," he answered. Speed was essential for the cover story to fit. If he really was a dealer from up country, he'd have access to lots of cash, fast. But if he was a cop, he'd need approval, which would mean bureaucratic delay. Fox had played the game long enough to know the difference.

"Okay," Fox said, blowing out air, "9:30, on the bench outside the Pre-Trial Centre." There'd be lots of people walking in and out—lawyers, cops. He liked it. No one would ever believe that anyone would deal right there.

Cole saw the irony in it and smiled wryly at Fox. "The stuff will be as good as what I saw tonight?" he asked.

"Exactly the same. Tonight's was a sample," Fox said, getting up to go. "Bring a hundred and we'll do business." They nodded to each other and he walked out of the bar.

Cole stayed on for several minutes to finish his drink and then left, ignoring the familiar faces staring at him as he walked out.

The evening was still warm. As he watched for a cab, he breathed in the June air deeply. He hated the cigarettes but they were a good prop. A cab arrived before any of the trainees could come out and speak with him, and blow his cover if Fox or Morrit was smart enough to be watching. Cole got in and gave directions to a local hotel where he would register under the name of Jackson Allan. Just in case.

As the cab pulled away, Danny Fox pushed himself out of the shadowed alcove across from the Hotel Columbian and started walking toward Morrit's hotel. Allan hadn't been met by anyone and hadn't got into a private car. Both were good signs.

Fox's step was lighter than usual in anticipation of the fifty grand he would make tomorrow.

• • •

Cole sat on the edge of the bed in his hotel room, holding the telephone receiver and waiting while the phone rang in Superintendent Lawson's home at 2:15 in the morning.

Lawson's wife answered after four rings.

"Hi, Dory. Sorry to've wakened you. Is George there?"

"Jackson," she groaned, "only you could get George out of here at this time of night. But to answer your question, no, he's not here. He's at headquarters, putting together some rush paperwork to authorize some wild man's request for a hundred thousand dollars."

Cole smiled. "Is he on pager?"

"Aren't you all?" she asked sarcastically.

"Goodnight, Dory. And thanks."

"Good luck at whatever it is you're doing, Jackson," she

yawned. "Find yourself a woman and drop by sometime soon."

They both knew that was unlikely.

Cole hung up, then punched in the pager number and listened to the mechanical voice giving instructions.

"Room 308. Holiday Inn, Broadway." He hung up and leaned back on the bed to wait.

The phone rang within minutes. It was Lawson.

"You got yourself a big one first time you put your line in the water, didn't you, Jack? And you aren't even supposed to be fishing."

Cole knew that the suspension could pose problems, but it was simply a hurdle Lawson would have to find a way to get over: Morrit was too big to pass by.

"Life can be interesting, sir," he said unhelpfully.

"Can't it?" the superintendent said. "I liked your man Kahler, he was very professional. And persuasive. He seems to think that we should pursue your plan."

"Then in addition to being professional, he's smart," Cole responded. They were both enjoying themselves at the formal preamble because they both knew that in the end, what should happen would.

"When exactly do you need the money, Jack?"

"I'm meeting my contact at 9:30 tomorrow," Cole replied. "He's bringing a unit. And George, I tested it. It's close to pure."

"Shit," said Lawson. "You sure haven't given us much time, have you?"

"You know what I think? I think this is vintage stuff—that our friend put it down somewhere before he did his stint."

"Interesting times, those were. I wouldn't put it past him."

George Lawson had been a sizzling corporal in the early eighties, and Morrit was at the top of his list of people to do. But Morrit and Fox could recognize him, so despite his interest, he would have to stay far, far away from the operation. Including the cash drop.

"Okay, Jackson. You'll get your money. I'll have Kahler bring it by your room tomorrow morning. Will 8:30 give you enough time?"

"Plenty. Thanks, George."

"I'd love to be there."

"I know you would."

Lawson had been a superb field man. There was silence on the line for a moment.

"Good night, sir," Cole said gently.

"Good luck."

They rang off.

Cole sat on the bench outside the inner-city jail called the Pre-Trial Centre. Connected to the provincial courthouse by hallways and tunnels, the building was the holding centre for people accused of crimes who hadn't made bail. Cole wore jeans, boots and a worn long-sleeved shirt. He'd been careful not to wear a T-shirt, even though the day was already warm, fearing he might trigger a memory in Fox's mind of their meeting on the street the day before.

He leaned back against the bench, enjoying the sun, and squinted at his watch. 9:29.

Pretty soon or never.

Fox turned the corner, carrying a white plastic shopping bag with a brown paper bag inside it. He looked like he'd made it to the market early. Except that he didn't look like the type to be out running errands in daylight.

Cole ignored Fox as he approached. The money lay next to Cole on the bench, in a beat-up packsack.

Fox sat down beside the packsack, ignoring Cole. He put his bag on his lap, rummaged around and pulled out an orange. He then placed the bag on top of the packsack and leaned forward, face down, to peel the orange between his knees.

"You got it all?" he asked.

He's smart, Cole thought to himself. He coughed a few times, managing to say "Yeah, it's all there," while he covered his mouth. "You too?"

It was bad manners to count, but okay to confirm verbally.

Fox said "Yeah" to the pavement and popped the last section of orange into his mouth.

No one watching the two men sharing the bench would have guessed that either had spoken.

Fox reached over to the middle of the bench, pulled the pack toward him and lifted it onto his left shoulder as he stood up. He walked back in the direction he'd come from.

Cole stayed on the bench with the heroin. His job was over for now.

The trainee cover men had been replaced by pros, except for Kahler. Cole had insisted that he be allowed to participate in the operation, given his instincts and guts the night before. Sitting in the sunshine, Cole hoped they wouldn't screw up. If they didn't, and if Cole was right, Fox would lead them straight to his supplier for the divvying up of the money.

His pager went off less than ten minutes later. He retrieved the message with his cell phone.

"We got them," said Kahler's voice, excited. "At the Star." The hotel was about four blocks away, and it was notorious for criminal activity. Cole called Kahler's cell number.

"Yeah," the corporal answered on the first ring.

"Cole."

"Yes, sir. Well, things could be cooking here, because the

old man wants to talk to you." He paused. "*Before* he's booked in."

Morrit's request was significant. Once he was booked and lodged in cells, word would spread like wildfire in the criminal community that he'd been done again. If charges got dropped, people would think he'd made a deal, somewhere on something, with the police. But if he was never charged, there'd be no reason for anyone to think that he had sacrificed someone in his world to the authorities.

Cole was silent for a moment. If they didn't charge Morrit, they couldn't charge Fox. It would be completely obvious that something was up. On the other hand, if Morrit gave them something good, they could stand missing a pinch on Fox. He'd be back in the system on something, sooner rather than later. Plus they had the evidence: observations, fingerprints, heroin, and Fox and Morrit holding the money. If they couldn't work something out, they'd find the two cons again and charge them.

Cole had made up his mind.

"Split them up," he said. "Take them in separate cars and release Fox after taking an imaginary call saying the dope tested as glucose." He paused. Fox would think he'd been duped by Morrit into dealing off crap for heroin—something that could get Fox killed once the buyer figured it out, while allowing Morrit to resell his stock. "That'll explain our change of heart and minimize the chances of these two cooking up the same scheme next week."

"If Grandpa sees next week, with Fox being fed that story." Kahler was astute.

Cole chuckled. "I'd imagine Grandpa will be going for a holiday, if he really has anything significant to deal."

He instructed Kahler to bring Morrit, along with two of the other cover men, to his hotel room in thirty minutes. He paged Lawson and invited him to the meeting. Then he picked up the bag of heroin and walked slowly toward a catering truck where an RCMP officer sat in civilian clothes, eating a sandwich.

"Let's go to my hotel," he said, getting into the passenger seat.

They were there in ten minutes. Cole got out of the van with the heroin and headed for his room. He sat on the couch in the small sitting area and began to make detailed notes of the morning's events. If they ever did go to trial on the case, he knew that he would be examined and cross-examined on what he wrote right now.

Fifteen minutes later Lawson arrived. Cole filled him in.

The superintendent was excited. He had had Morrit in his sights several times over the years, but the old man's cunning and organization had made him virtually untouchable. Lawson had been away on medical leave when Morrit finally went down on the heroin bust. But he was here now.

There was a knock on the door. Cole opened it, admitting Kahler, Morrit and two plainclothes Mounties. When Morrit saw George Lawson he froze mid-step.

"I should have been surprised if you weren't here, Sergeant."

"Superintendent now, Roger," Lawson replied.

"And who's he?" Morrit pointed to Cole.

"Sergeant Cole," Lawson replied, "Roger Morrit. Roger, Cole. Roger, I'm no longer operational, so I'm not going to get involved in handling you. I'll just say this: what you've got had better be fucking great, because we've got you by the short and curlies." He turned to Cole. "I'll leave your cover team with you and get the paperwork going with the witness protection boys."

"What I've got to give you, I'm not testifying about," Morrit interrupted. "I'll give you the information but I'm not taking the stand. If I do, I'll never have any peace. I'd be better doing my time on this beef."

"Mr. Morrit." Cole spoke for the first time since they'd entered the room. His voice was low and cold. "You seem to be under the misapprehension that you have some control over your situation." He glanced at the heroin and then back at Morrit. "If we decide that you'll testify, you'll testify."

Morrit hated him.

"I'll see you later," said Lawson. He took the cover men outside with him to guard the hallway. Cole could look after himself.

Cole nodded, turning his attention to Morrit. "Sit down."

Morrit sat.

"What have you got that's important enough to us to keep you a free man, given your present circumstances?"

Morrit knew it had to be good. Information about someone the police really wanted to catch. Someone bigger than he was, doing something bigger than dealing a pound and a half of pure heroin seventeen days after being released from prison on parole. But if the criminals he was thinking about ever found out that he had ratted on them, he would be a dead man, sooner or later. And then there was his daughter and her kids . . .

He pulled at his shirt collar, breathing in gasps as though there weren't enough air in the room.

Cole watched him closely. "Roger, do you want a drink?" he asked, in a gentler voice.

The older man nodded. "Yeah, that wouldn't hurt."

Cole unlocked the mini-bar and selected two small bottles of whiskey. He peeled the paper off a couple of plastic glasses on the bar and poured the liquor into them, then handed one of them to Morrit.

Morrit made half of it disappear in one pull. "Jesus, you

know," he said, "I got four grandkids. I ain't even seen three of them. They were born while I was inside."

Cole didn't say anything. He'd seen the process before. Morrit had to convince himself that what he was about to do, contrary to his lifelong values, wasn't really so bad. He was about to turn into a rat. Morrit sighed deeply and finished his drink.

"I'd imagine the Warriors would go a ways to satisfying you guys?" he asked. The Satan's Warriors was a biker gang, established in Seattle in the early 1980s when the North American cocaine trade had started to boom. Their membership had grown and they had diversified their business: after a few years they ran any kind of drug available, and were heavily into hookers, games and extortion. The club had branches throughout the northwest, including four in British Columbia.

Morrit almost regretted that he'd spent two days the previous week at the East Side branch's clubhouse, getting reacquainted and updated by old friends. He'd even made "mass," the weekly meeting, on Thursday night, wearing a wig, a hat and thick glasses. If he hadn't been there, he wouldn't have anything fresh to deal with. This stuff could keep him out of the joint just to end up with a bullet in his head. He sighed again.

"Okay, let's do it," he said finally, his voice quiet.

Cole pulled out his notebook. "Okay."

Morrit looked up at the ceiling, then closed his eyes as if wishing he were anywhere but there. "The East Siders've joined up with a branch in the valley. The Langley section." Langley, a suburb of Vancouver, was an old farming community an hour out of the city which had become a bedroom suburb of sorts. "They're putting together the biggest meth lab in the country. It's at the setup stage: they're planning on exporting the meth around the country and into Washington and Oregon. Starting in two weeks or so."

"How do you know this?" Cole asked, mildly interested. As far as he was concerned, this was the warmup act. He wasn't stupid or green, so he wasn't taking this as satisfaction for letting Morrit walk on the heroin bust. Cole hoped Morrit was smart enough to have figured that out.

"I stayed with Paul Lucci for a couple of days when I first got out," Morrit went on. Lucci was the president of the city's East Side branch, a well-respected arm of the Satan's Warriors. "I made it to mass last Thursday and stayed around for a couple of drinks afterwards. Lucci and some fat guy—I think he's the president of Langley—were talking about it. They've got some hotshot chemist coming up from the States to show them the state-of-the-art production methods." He paused, tipping drops of whiskey onto his tongue from the empty glass. "They've already got precursors stored up in some barn somewheres."

Cole went to the bar and pulled out two more bottles. This time he emptied both into Morrit's glass.

"Where is this barn?" he asked.

"I don't know," Morrit replied. "That's the truth. Somewhere in Langley, that's for sure. Lucci talked about it being in some barn on some farmer's field that the Langley club's just bought. The fat guy said the name but I didn't know there'd be a quiz, so I didn't pay particular attention."

"Well, that's very interesting," Cole said. "Probably not enough to get a search warrant, but interesting."

He made a few notes and then put the notebook back on the table. It was Morrit's move.

"What do you want?" Morrit's voice was squeaky with panic. "Meth labs are a big deal, the new problem. You could stop millions of hits from making it to the street."

"Give me a body," Cole said quietly, looking at Morrit with his steel-blue eyes. "Prevent a killing or solve one.

That'll get you a walk on today's activities. Anything less, and you die in jail an old man."

Morrit had figured it would be like this. Still, he had hoped. He let out a long sigh. The next few minutes would be like time spent filling out his own death warrant.

"Okay," he said. He leaned toward Cole and lowered his voice. "Do you remember the death of that waitress at the bar in Burnaby, just east of Vancouver? Mano Tag got charged with it. I think it was manslaughter, maybe murder in the second." He rubbed his eyes hard, as if trying to erase what he'd seen. "He back-handed her and she fell and hit her head on the floor and was dead when she got to the hospital."

Cole did remember the case. The waitress had been a single mother, no criminal connections, just trying to make a living. Tag had been charged with murdering her. His connection to bikers had been great fodder for the local press and there had been heat on all bikers as a result.

A dozen witnesses had given statements to the police and could testify to what had happened. Three had been crucial. In the course of pre-trial procedure, the witnesses' statements were disclosed to the accused, complete with their names. By the time the trial date arrived, nine of the witnesses had amnesia and the three key witnesses had disappeared. They had never been found.

"What about it?" Cole asked cautiously.

"I can give you the missing witnesses," Morrit said. "Would that be enough?"

"Can you give us someone to say what happened?"

"I can give you the name of an unhinged cat who was involved in the transport of the three. I'm pretty sure that with a little pressure he'll give the whole thing up." Morrit leaned back in the chair and sighed. "To hear him tell it, there's at least one Lucci bullet in one of the bodies."

Cole was writing. "I need the source of your information. How do you know about this?"

"Do you know who I am? I been around these guys all my life. My little sister's married into them. They think I'm one of them, just without the patch on my back. I've heard about it a hundred times in clubhouse bullshitting, including from one of the guys who gave the stiffs a ride. Mike Rigley. Mike Rigley told me about it after some drinks at the Number Five. He said he still dreams about it. They got to their destination around midnight and I guess there was a full moon. The way Rigley tells it, once the ropes were off, the wind kept pulling the tarp off the stiffs. He said it was like they were watching him and his friend there. I think the other guy's name was Tom, or Tony or something."

"All three are dead?"

"As doornails. Laid out in some mine near Hedley."

"Hedley?" Cole asked, with some surprise. Hedley was a small mining town, mostly gone fallow, a hundred miles inland from Vancouver.

"Yeah, they didn't want them to be found, and there was so much heat they couldn't run the risk of being stopped with the stiffs on the way to dumping them into the ocean, so they went in the other direction. Rigley grew up near Hedley and knew about this empty mine shaft." Morrit got up and went to the mini-bar to refresh his drink. His confidence was returning. "It seemed like a hell of a lot of effort to me, but I guess they didn't want any hiker to find a fresh hole or any fisherman to pull in a corpse." He poured gin into his glass. "Anyhow, it seems to've worked." He shrugged, and drank.

"Where is the shaft, exactly?" Cole needed details for the warrant.

"To hear him tell it, it's just before town. You cross abandoned farm property just before the Welcome to Hedley sign, eastbound. It's about two miles out, toward the hills."

Cole leaned back, thinking. There had been a lot of public pressure on the police to solve the three disappearances and there were three nice families living with the hell of uncertainty. If this panned out, it was good information.

"Okay, Roger," he said slowly. "We'll go take a look at this mine of yours. If it's as you say, you've bought yourself a Stay Out of Jail card—assuming you give us a videotaped statement of what you just said." He looked at Morrit hard. "Because without that kind of leverage against Rigley, we haven't got shit."

"I can't give you a *statement* statement," Morrit whined. "You'll have your bodies. They'll kill me."

"So enter the program. Spend time with your family, out of custody, and then disappear once the statement's released. It's more than you'd have if you went down on this heroin thing right now." He stood up. "The thing to remember, Roger, is that you don't have too many bloody options. Now stay here with your chaperones until Superintendent Lawson can get something formal organized. It's your choice whether or not you enter the Source/Witness Protection Program after the trial, assuming there is a trial. But for what it's worth, I don't think a change of name and location would hurt your chances at longevity."

The older man was twitchy, thinking about it. "I disappear, and they get the statement . . . I got a daughter and grandkids. I don't want them to be made examples of if anyone puts two and two together," he said.

They almost never went after family members, but Cole didn't bother to say so. There was always a first time.

Morrit finished his drink and wiped his mouth. "I did the right thing, right?" he asked, almost pleading.

Cole didn't like the swings in mood. "You did the only thing you could have done," he said. "I may see you again, I may not. So I'll say goodbye."

As he closed the door, he thought he heard the older man crying.

Outside the room, Cole spoke to Kahler and the two other police officers. "I want two of you inside with him for the next while. Keep an eye on him, he's a little unsteady right now. Talk about his grandkids, hockey, anything that's *not* crime-related. Whoever stays outside, keep an eye open. I doubt anyone knows what's going on yet, but you just never know. Superintendent Lawson will send instructions on what's to happen next."

The three men nodded.

"Okay, I'll see you later." Cole walked toward the elevator.

He drove from the hotel's underground parking lot straight to the RCMP headquarters for British Columbia, parked in a visitor's stall outside the building and stepped down from the truck into the midday sunshine. It was the first time he'd been outside since the heroin takedown, and it was hot for mid-June. Easily eighty, and no breeze.

He signed in with the commissionaires at the entrance, stepped into the elevator with familiar ease and pressed 3. The doors opened onto a hall of plush red carpet and blue walls lined with framed photos of superintendents, past and present. Cole turned left and walked toward the inner sanctum of power, where operations and careers were approved and terminated.

Lawson's secretary sat at her post outside her boss's closed door. "Hey, Jackson," she said, smiling at Cole as he approached. "He's unavailable, generally speaking, but I bet you're going to tell me that he'll see you."

Cole smiled and winked. "That's right."

She pushed a button on her phone and said, "Sergeant Cole to see you, sir."

They both heard Lawson's gruff voice. "Send him in."

She nodded her head in the direction of the office. "Nice hair," she said, as Cole reached for the door handle.

He smiled at her again and then walked into the office, all business.

Lawson's office was one of the largest in the building. His desk and two tired red leather chairs occupied the left side of the room. The desk was huge and almost entirely covered with neat stacks of paper. In the superintendent's mind, half the desk was "in," half of it was "out." The rest of the office functioned as a meeting area, with a large oval table of highly polished mahogany circled by eight chairs. The far wall was made entirely of glass, allowing a panoramic view of the North Shore mountains across the inlet, on the far north side of the city.

George Lawson sat at his desk in crisp uniform shirt and black uniform pants with the traditional yellow stripe, eating a sandwich, a file open in front of him. "So, how did it go?"

"Pretty well. He doesn't like the idea of giving a formal recorded statement against the boys, but I think he understands that it's that or the pen until they carry him out in a box. He's given a location for the three missing witnesses in the Tag case. He's got a name, too. An admission by a guy named Rigley. And he says we'll find traceable bullets in whatever's left of the bodies." He paused, looking at the still magnolia trees in the garden beyond the glass. "It looks pretty good," he said. "Plus, as a little prenegotiating tester, he gave up some information on a meth lab that the East Side branch and Langley are putting together. For distribution and export."

"What do you see as our next move?" the superintendent asked.

"Well, sir, I think I should page Kahler and reinforce that nothing that's occurred in the last twenty-four hours is for the consumption of anyone, including the other trainees.

After that I think I'd better do up a report, and then go up to Hedley and see whether or not there's a mine where Morrit says there is. If there is, the best way to ensure the evidence gets admitted at trial is to get a search warrant before we actually go on the property."

The superintendent was nodding in agreement.

"Then we go in and do the search. If the witnesses are there, we've got a case and Morrit's got a deal. If they're not, Morrit's in jail so fast he won't know what happened."

"I think that's good strategy," Lawson said. "You can choose who you take, but I think you'd better take another member with you to check out the mine. Do it so you're not particularly noticed checking it. We don't want the bodies lost—assuming they're there now—after all this time. And Jackson." Cole looked up. Lawson almost never called him by his first name. "Whoever you take will have to swear out the warrant. Given the suspension, I think the less your name appears on paper, the better."

"Not being able to do the paperwork on this one isn't going to break my heart," Cole smiled.

"Fine," the superintendent said, looking back at the file on his desk. "Oh, by the way, you haven't forgotten about the one duty you're actually authorized to perform, have you?"

"No, sir. I'll be at the course tonight with bells on, trying to explain what happened last night without giving anything away." He paused and added wryly, "Nothing like lying to people to instill trust and a sense of team spirit."

He waved to the superintendent, already reading again at his desk, and took his leave.

They were back in the city just before 7:00. Not bad. And it had been an interesting day.

Cole had picked up Nicki Lauer, an undercover operator, at a suburban RCMP detachment at 7:30 that morning. With her overnight bag beside his in the trunk of the rented Miata, they headed for the interior of the province, Lauer driving as Cole slept. He had got to bed just before 4:00, after an evening of supervising fledgling operators and cover men doing low-end drug buys.

When they got to Hedley they checked in at the Colonial Inn, a heritage bed and breakfast, all lovey-eyed and cooing. A short time later they went out for a run together, through the small town and up into the hills, apparently serious athletes training. As they ran they speculated on where the mouth of the mine might be. They found it a couple of miles out of town, down a road that led nowhere but to an abandoned farmhouse, silvered with time.

They ran down the narrow dirt road past the farmhouse until they came to a cattle crossing and a metal fence with barbed wire on top. More barbed wire corralled the property. A sign read NO TRESPASSERS—GUARD DOG. DO NOT ENTER. Beyond the fence was scrub sage and a rocky hill rising out of the dusty ground. A black hole gaped in the side of the hill and rotten timbers leaned at odd angles across the mouth of the mine.

"Friendly," Lauer observed.

"This has to be it," Cole said. "These signs are relatively new, and there's nothing up in those hills but rattlesnakes and a mine that sure doesn't look operational to me."

"It's kind of creepy out here, isn't it?"

He knew what she meant. Even in the bright sunshine, the dilapidated farmhouse with its broken, faceless windows and leaning porch, combined with the almost unnatural stillness of the tall grass, made it seem as though the place had been abandoned by living creatures. Then there was the prospect of three skeletons in that yawning hole in the side of the hill a quarter mile away.

"Yes," Cole agreed, "it's got a certain Gothic ambience."

She laughed, as he had intended.

"We've seen what we needed to," he said. "Let's get back to the hotel and get cleaned up. We can grab a meal there and get out of here." He was already jogging back in the direction of the farmhouse and town.

● ● ●

Within three-quarters of an hour they were showered and dressed in triathlon T-shirts and jeans, and seated in the Colonial Inn café, apparently happily ordering a late lunch. Mid-coffee their voices started to rise and Lauer finally left the table in tears. She could be heard slamming the door to their room upstairs. Cole stayed at the table for few minutes and then sheepishly followed her. Moments later she was leaning against the passenger door of their car, arms crossed and packed bag at her feet. He was down shortly, standing at the front desk with his bag, apologizing profusely and assuring the manager that they would be back another time. The manager wasn't so certain, but didn't say anything since the guy hadn't asked for his money back.

After dropping Lauer off, Cole returned the rental car and picked up his Land Rover. By then it was 7:15. He had fifteen minutes to get to the hotel room where the trainees were meeting for briefings before their outings. He could just make it if he forgot about food entirely.

He decided to go straight there. Tonight would be fun. Instead of doing dope buys as undercover operators and cover men, all of the trainees would be going on a scavenger hunt of sorts. They would be leaving the hotel room with nothing and returning the next morning at 9:00 for the tallying up.

You got a certain number of points for every cigarette bummed. You got points for money begged or conned and you got points for getting your meals bought or food given. On some courses, some operators had even had hotel rooms rented for them by philanthropic passersby—a few of whom weren't even looking for sexual favours in return.

Tonight Cole's job was really to act as den mother, strolling the streets to keep an eye on his "street people." He decided to work until one o'clock and then go home and sleep for a few hours, pager on and close by.

He parked the Land Rover in the guest underground lot and ran the stairs to the hotel lobby. He still had a few minutes to kill so he walked through the automatic doors out into the evening air to stretch his legs. It had been a long day in a small car.

But the air was hot and dense and smelled of car exhaust. Unstirred for days now. He walked back into the lobby, preferring the air-conditioned sterility to the oppressiveness of outside. He ran the eight flights of fire stairs to the trainees' floor and knocked on the door of room 826.

A motley-looking long-haired specimen admitted him into the room. "Sir, nice to see you." Since watching Cole in the Columbian on Monday night, Corporal Barker, who prided himself on never kissing anyone's ass because of rank, was awed into using formal titles with Cole.

"Attractive as ever, Corporal," Cole grinned.

The room was crowded with the thirty trainees, all as grubby and hopeless-looking as they could get. It was also buzzing with energy—everyone was high with anticipation of the impending competition, for while it was juvenile in a way, it wasn't a bad marker of the credibility of your undercover approach.

As Cole passed over the threshold and into the room, the chatter stopped. Everyone stared at him in rapt attention.

"Good evening, ladies and gentlemen," he said. There was a ripple of laughter: the three days' growth on most of the men's faces and the temporary tattoos around biceps and throats made the formalities incongruous.

"Tonight is a good illustration of one of the key propositions I put to you when we all first met, so many sunrises ago. Tonight is about fun and it is about tangible results. As far as I'm concerned, that's what undercover work is all about. Never mind that no one's going to jail because of your efforts tonight, you'll be better tomorrow night because of what you do for the next few hours. You have to suspend your pride, your inhibitions; you have to go after whatever it is you want. Because if you don't, the person sitting under a blanket half a block down the street from you will. And in the undercover game, that is the difference between winners and losers."

Heads were nodding.

"We're also going to implement an aspect of the other matter I referred to, and that is safety. You're not going to have a cover team, *per se*, watching your activities. There'll only be me doing a stroll-by once in a while. For that reason I want each of you to take a partner and split a block between you, so that if one runs into a problem the other can be back-up. You're not going to be dealing with people engaging in crime, so chances are you won't encounter anything you can't handle yourself. But if you do, have someone close."

He looked around the room.

"Finally," he said, "we'll wrap this thing up at 3:00. By then most of the bars are closed and foot traffic is minimal. The tallying up will commence at 3:30 at my place." He gave an address on the north side of False Creek, less than a mile from where they'd be hustling but in some ways a million miles away. If his neighbours saw this riffraff drifting along the cobblestone lanes of the exclusive waterfront property, he'd have some explaining to do. "There will be food and spirits, for those interested," he went on. "And the winner, of course, gets to buy the beer after the wrap-up session Friday."

There was a ripple of approval.

"Good luck, then," he said. "See you on the street."

People began to filter out of the room, headed toward the five-block target radius, in the city's downtown theatre and bar area.

Cole walked his beat for three hours without incident, watching the trainees hustle moviegoers, sightseers, other street people—anything that moved. Finally he returned to the hotel to pick up his truck and then drove to his home. He parked in the secure underground and took the parkade elevator up to the marble lobby. Using a strip-coded security card, he took a second elevator to the suites and pressed 2.

The elevator opened onto a covered tiled patio overlooking the gardened plaza below and the ocean beyond it. He walked to the only door on the floor and admitted himself into the suite.

It suited his needs perfectly, with two bedrooms and a den, and a wraparound view of Mount Baker and the Pacific Ocean.

He moved past the first bedroom on his right, decorated in bright yellow with hockey stars' pictures everywhere—Michael's room—and continued toward the kitchen. With one glance at the dining room he confirmed that the woman he had hired to look after organizing the party tonight had done her magic. There were calla lilies in a large vase in the centre of the table, surrounded by serving plates and glasses. The fridge was stocked with sandwiches, fruit plates, smoked salmon slabs and sushi trays, along with beer and wine.

Cole walked through the living room to the master bedroom, with its sliding glass doors leading onto a private balcony overlooking the sea. He opened the doors and walked out onto it now, looking for the freshness of the ocean breezes. The same stillness that he had noted earlier that day suffocated the midnight air. He leaned out over the railing and looked up at the sky. Not many stars were visible. The smog was settling in over the city, blocking the true sky, and there was no sign of the usual cleansing winds.

He crossed back into the bedroom, pulling his shirt over his head and tossing it in the direction of the laundry. He continued through the walk-in closet to the ensuite bathroom and turned on a steaming shower. He stripped, removed the thong from his hair and stepped under the water. After a long hot soak he killed the hot water and blasted himself with shards of cold until his skin prickled red. He then turned the shower off, towelled down hard and went to task on his hair, fighting with the tangles and settling on a long braid for sleep.

Finished, he hung up the towel, walked to his bed and slipped between the sheets. Three hours.

Thursday, June 11, 1998

Cole bade goodbye to the last guest at just past 9:00 in the morning. It had been a good party—good food, good people and lots of laughs. Cole had enjoyed watching the acquaintances become friends, and he was sure that a few of the people there would keep in touch, even if they were eventually transferred to postings in different provinces.

An attractive blonde trainee from Montreal had won, having collected three packs of cigarettes and over a hundred dollars in handouts. Twice she had had dinner bought for her at a nearby diner, and four times she had been given take-out coffee. She claimed to have had several offers of a free place to sleep but she had declined the kindness; she also said that if she hadn't had to pee so often from all the coffee, she'd have made more money and got more cigarettes.

She had offered to help Cole clean up after the party but he had declined and helped her into a cab with one of the other female trainees. He then returned upstairs to survey the chaos. He wrote a note to his housekeeper, telling her to take the leftovers if she wanted and to pack up all the catering dishes ready for pickup.

Meanwhile he had agreed to meet Nicki Lauer at 10:00 to outline the grounds for a search warrant for the mine. At noon he was to meet Don at the dojo for a workout. By the time he returned home for some much-needed rest, the place would be spotless. He stuck the note on the fridge and left.

•　•　•

Nicki had done a pretty good job on the description of the site of the mine and the observations they had made. At Cole's suggestion she had requested a title search of the farmhouse property and the mine, and she had hit pay dirt: the farmhouse near the mine site had actually been owned by someone with the last name of Rigley for sixty years. That detail lent credence to Morrit's version of events, and credence to the story of the guy who had told him how the whole thing went down.

Lauer and Cole worked carefully on phrasing the paragraphs containing hearsay, and double hearsay, until the document not only set out reasons to believe the mine contained evidence of murder, it made you want to trot out and take a look yourself.

"Good job," Cole said, passing the document back to her.

"I'm not sure how much credit I can take for it, Sergeant Cole," she smiled. She still had a hard time calling him by his first name, although he had insisted that she do so from the moment she got into the roadster the day before. She simply didn't feel his peer. "But thanks. And thanks for thinking of me for this file—it's fascinating." She paused; then, alluding to his suspension, added, "I'm sorry you won't be there . . . If we find anything, it'll be because of you."

"If you find anything, it likely won't be anything I haven't seen a variation of before." He reflected momentarily on what he knew of the file. "For the sake of the witnesses' families I hope there is some truth to Morrit's story. Not knowing just what happened to your child or partner must be hell on earth."

Lauer looked across the desk at the man who had spoken these words, tinged with a touch of sadness. His tanned, raw-boned face and clear blue eyes and his fit, taut body made him appear younger than the experience in his voice revealed. She had heard stories of where he had been and what he had done, and she guessed right that he had seen his share of death and senseless violence, all committed in the name of politics or rage or sex or profit. For that passing moment, she wanted to ignore his rank and stature and ask him out for lunch, stretching out their time together. But she resisted the impulse. She had heard those stories too: he didn't date, so far as anyone on the job knew.

"Well," he said, "it's been a pleasure." He seemed to shake off the shadow that had settled on him moments before. "Let me know how the search goes."

She felt as though he had been reading her thoughts.

"Yes, I sure will." She tried his first name. "Jackson. Thanks again."

Cole was ten minutes late getting to the dojo. When he walked past the main room he saw Edwards, already robed, stretching. He tossed him a quick apology as he passed the door on his way to the locker room, and then hurried to get changed.

They sparred for fifty minutes, a tough, fast, high-kicking bout. Edwards was having a good day and was more of a match for Cole than usual. They showered and changed, then walked out into the parking lot together.

"I've got to say," Edwards said, "for my only friend who could make the cover of *GQ* on a regular basis, you're looking like shit, old man. And you were a touch slow in there."

"Only a true friend could make that kind of touching observation," Cole said, grinning. "If the truth be known, I'm about thirty hours short on sleep, as a result of this undercover course I've been baby-sitting and a couple of little twists that have come up." He searched his pocket for his keys. "Being suspended turns out to be more work than I'd imagined."

He unlocked the driver's door of the Land Rover and tossed his kit bag onto the passenger side, grateful he'd parked in the shade. It was another bloody hot day.

"How is that thing going?" Edwards asked.

"I'll know the results of the internal any day now. If I'm cleared internally, there's almost no chance that a Crown attorney will approve a criminal charge against me for the shooting. We have that higher standard of being prepared to eat our own," he said cheerfully, "whereas they require admissible evidence before they go after you."

"Well," said Edwards, "be sure to get your beauty sleep tonight. You're on for dinner tomorrow night at eight. Liz is making reservations somewhere downtown. I'll page you with the location."

"I can't wait," said Cole grimly, swinging into the truck.

He drove home and let himself into a sparkling apartment. All evidence of the early morning's activities had vanished.

He looked at the clock: 2:10. He had just over five hours.

Don was right. He did look exhausted, because he was. He hated to turn his back on a day like this—the ocean glistening in the sunshine, kayakers paddling bare-chested past the balcony. He'd have loved to join them, but he needed sleep.

In the master bedroom he closed the wooden slats on the

louvered window shutters, darkening the room. He then stripped to his shorts and lay on the bed, imagining the hands of a clock sweeping its face: 2:15 to 5:45. He slept for three and a half hours.

When he awoke, Cole had just enough time to dress in running clothes, tie back his hair and run the Stanley Park seawall before it was time to clean up for the last of the 7:30 meetings with the trainees. He let himself out and into the early evening blast furnace.

He was back in forty-six minutes, sweat pouring down his body. He showered and changed quickly and made a sandwich to eat while he drove to the trainees' hotel.

Tonight would be the usual undercover approach with an assigned cover man. Drug dealers were once again the target, because there were lots of them and the dealers were relatively receptive to strangers. The trainees would have to get lots of small-time field experience, dealing with people like the low-level drug traffickers, before they were assigned to take on anyone involved in high-end organized crime or a heavy beef, like murder. After tonight's undercover drug buys, everyone would do their notes and hand them in to Cole, who would review them before their next meeting at 11:00 the following morning.

At that meeting there would be general discussion of the night before—perceived weaknesses and strengths—and then Cole would use the notes to point out exemplary work and work needing improvement. No one except the notewriter would know whose work was being critiqued.

Then the course was formally over. Pass/fail assessments would be relayed through each trainee's supervising officer about three weeks after they returned to their regular duty. From what Cole had seen, only two of the candidates were not suitable for the undercover program. They were too egotistical and independent. The program required a very keen sense of teamwork. For that reason alone, he would axe them.

As he walked into the hotel lobby his pager went off. The call was from Superintendent Lawson, at his home phone number. It had to be something big. Lawson had rarely paged Cole personally. And he never called from home. Cole walked directly to the pay phones near the reception desk and punched in the superintendent's number.

Lawson picked up the phone before the first ring had finished. "Jackson?"

"Yeah, George. What's up?"

"Are you on a hard line?"

"Yes, sir."

"Well, Jackson, it seems Mr. Morrit won't be giving any formal statements against the club or anyone else. It seems our friend hanged himself with a nylon cord sometime last night. His sister called it in an hour ago, said she went over to his place with a casserole and there he was, three feet off the ground and dangling."

"Does it look like a good suicide?"

"We've got the boys from Serious Crime there now, but as far as anyone can tell he did this one himself."

Neither man spoke their shared thought. They had put Morrit under impossible pressure: dying old in prison or dying on the run, labelled a rat by everyone you've ever had anything to do with.

"Charming," Cole said, almost to himself. "Have you heard from Constable Lauer?"

"She's in position, with the signed warrant. A couple of our guys from the Hedley and Osoyoos detachments will go with her, as well as Corporal Townsend from our Identification section, in case there is anything up there."

"Well, if there is," Cole said, "without Morrit, we are starting at ground zero as far as proving what happened."

"Yeah," Lawson agreed. "It's just great news all around. Anyhow, I thought you should hear about it fast. You might want to tell your Corporal Kahler, as well, rather than having him read about it in tomorrow's paper."

"I'd already thought of that, sir. Thanks," Cole said. "And thanks for letting me know."

"Okay. Goodnight."

"Goodnight, sir."

It wasn't a goddamn good night at all.

• • •

The rest of the night's work went without a hitch. Together the class netted twenty-three grams of cocaine and four grams of speedballs, a mixture of coke and heroin. They met back at the main hotel room at 11:15, as agreed, to mark and tag their drug exhibits and do their notes. Cole leaned against a wall, observing the techniques of marking, saying little; they had learned well over the past three weeks.

When the last people had completed their notes, and cans of beer were appearing from the trainees' own hotel rooms, Cole asked for their attention. He got it.

"I have a bit of bad news that I'd prefer you hear from someone in the outfit rather than read it in tomorrow's newspaper. The fellow we pinched for the unit of heroin, Roger Morrit, was found dead tonight." He waited for the gasps and chatter to subside. "An apparent suicide."

He wondered how far to go with it. Few people in the room knew that they had tried to get Morrit to become a police informer. Given the views Morrit's family, friends and associates had on rats, Cole decided to keep it to himself, and prevent a low turnout at Morrit's funeral.

Looking at Kahler, who knew as much as he did, he said evenly, "Okay. That's it."

Kahler nodded almost imperceptibly. He was smart.

"See you tomorrow at eleven."

Cole left them to their beer and laughter and speculation, carrying a briefcase full of their notes to be reviewed for the last part of the course.

Friday, June 12, 1998

The wind finally arrived that afternoon. It came blowing in hot over the Pacific, boiling clouds in its path, and it moved down the sides of the mountains toward the inlet, poaching pine and cedar scent in its warmth. It came recoiling from the valley flats, dry. All three winds irreconcilable in the presence of the other two.

The inhabitants of the vortex were already noticing it by the time Rick Parker got in his car and turned on the ignition. Vancouver's "eye in the sky" helicopter radio traffic reporter was yammering on about the strong winds and impending rain. Parker slid a CD into the car stereo to cut off the predictable warning about traffic conditions deteriorating once the rain hit. No shit, he thought to himself. You could feel the weather change the minute you stepped outside.

The boats across from the brokerage house were yarding on their moorings, their riggings ringing, crazy. Even the water in the inner harbour of False Creek was grey and dangerous-looking.

Parker drove the two blocks to the deli, parked his black Mercedes illegally and jogged across the street and through the deli's tiny patio. In beige linen pants, webbed shoes and open-neck black silk shirt, he knew he looked good. Forty-two, a little grey in the dark curls, pretty fit, with eyes he liked to hear "sparkled." He entered the shop, enjoying its faux Tuscany walls and the ever-present Puccini in the background. The girl behind the counter was new, long hair and long legs, with a ring through her left nostril. The nose ring ruled her out completely for Parker. He ordered ripe olives and fresh, fragrant bread, antipasto and lots of cheeses. A good bottle of wine and he'd get laid tonight for sure.

Leaving the deli, he gave the girl one last look, shaking his head mentally. He walked back out into the wind and across the street to his car.

The new girl behind the counter watched him leave. She was certain he was the man in the Polaroid snapshot she had been given. As the Gucci sole of his left shoe stepped from the deli's mat to the patio brick, she picked up the phone.

• • •

Danny Fox lived in Vancouver's skid road, with Chinatown to the south, the city's business core to the west, the waterfront along the inlet to the north, and a low-end residential area to the east. For most Vancouverites there was no reason to visit his neighbourhood, and every reason to avoid it.

The aorta of the area was the 100 block of East Hastings Street, running east-west between Main Street and Carrall, a corridor known to the police as one of the most dangerous strips in the country with its hypes, murderers, knifers and thieves.

One block north of Hastings, Main Street crossed Cordova Street. Most residents of the 100 block of Hastings spent some time in the Main and Cordova area, either voluntarily or at the invitation of the state. The building on the southeast corner of Main and Cordova housed the homicide and drug detectives of the Vancouver Police Department. The northeast block was taken up by the provincial courthouse and Vancouver Pre-Trial Centre.

Across Main Street, opposite the courthouse, in mid-block, sandwiched between a youth project storefront and the Native courtworkers' office, stood the Auckland Rooming House. It was a remarkable building: eye-catching in any neighbourhood, implausible in this one. The front of it was painted cobalt blue. On the left and right sides of the front door, from street level to rafters, were two-foot-square ceramic tiles out of which jutted Buddhas and gargoyles and monsters' faces. The stony blue figures stared impassively, eyeing the city's most tragic figures, most evil demons, cops, lawyers and tourists, with exactly the same expression.

The door to the Auckland was always open in daylight, allowing a view from the street of a landing and a steep set of stairs yawning into shadows. Four windows were set in the blue brick face of the second floor. Sometimes men's shirts could be seen hanging in the windows, drying.

This afternoon the wind blew unchecked across Burrard Inlet. It tumbled south, straight down Main Street. Moving heat, not cooling breezes.

In the second window from the left, on the second floor of the Auckland, the wind whipped a blue plaid shirt hanging from the latch. The metal hanger played a tattoo against the windowpane and the still-wet shirttail slapped a blue smiling gargoyle relentlessly.

In the room next door, to the left, not visible from the street, Danny Fox sat in shadow. Heating white powder on a spoon with a lighter, he was celebrating his forty-first birth-day with a ritual he performed three times a day. Over those forty-one years, Fox had killed seven people. Most for money, but a couple because after you have a certain reputation you inevitably find yourself in situations that require you to do it again. He had beaten to death the asshole who'd come at him with a shank when he was unarmed.

Sitting on the room's only chair at the table by the window, watching the powder begin to melt, Fox considered adding to it and killing one last time. In the end, he let the contents be.

He had been sticking a rig in his arm, his hand, his neck, for twenty-six years now. The first time had been amazing: a rush of good feeling. Peace and invincibility. He'd been fif-teen years old, living in a rooming house near the railway tracks in Edmonton, and on that cold, clear day he knew that if he lay down on those tracks and a big old freight train came down the line and ran over him and shunted back twice, he could stand up, brush himself off and be none the worse for wear. He felt g-r-e-a-t. Better than anytime ever before in his life, all the pains and self-consciousness washed away by a lit-tle clear liquid and thin silver needle.

For the next ten years or so he tried to regain the sensa-tions of that day, but the needle never quite took him back there. He tried mixing the junk with cocaine or speed, but they didn't really take. So he jammed more "down" in his arm daily than most addicts could take in three, just to keep him functioning normally and stop him from getting sick. He had become a wizard in getting the stuff. He had to be.

When he was young he had worried about doing time, for one reason: supply. Cold turkey was the only thing in this world that scared him. But from his first sentence at age eighteen, experience had taught him that in prison you never have to worry about supply, especially if you draw more than two years, federal time. Wives, girlfriends, visitors, everyone packed. And the guards didn't exactly investigate or control it. Why would they? A con stoned on heroin is a sleepy, placid, easy-to-handle con.

After that first sentence, Fox was never scared of jail again. But he was thinking about it now.

That business with Morrit didn't jive. Fox couldn't buy the explanation that Roger had given him a pound and a half of fluff to sell to that cop. It just wasn't Roger's style—he liked to live. And he knew Danny well enough to know that he wouldn't live if Danny had delivered shit to a real buyer.

And now this suicide thing. Something wasn't right.

Having poured the melted liquid into the syringe, Fox reached across the peeling lino table, undid the window latch and pushed the window open. He wanted to feel some of the storm.

It was wild out. He watched people hurry out of the court-house across the street. Court would have shut down an hour ago and it was Friday, a day for early endings and drinks. Fox jammed the needle in his skinny arm and pushed the plunger. The skills of the finest anaesthetist.

Leaning back in the chair to wait, he noticed the sounds above the wind for the first time: tapping on glass, like some-one was rapping on a window with a spoon, over and over again, to get someone's attention. And a repeated slapping sound. Not a good beating, just slaps, slaps. Across a face, somewhere in the Auckland? He wandered in his head; they didn't usually let whores in.

Slap, slap. It wasn't him this time.

He drifted in the dim room. He hadn't taken enough to do the job. He'd wake up again. His pointed, grey-stubbled chin collapsed down onto his thin chest and he was gone for a few hours.

• • •

Lauren Grey stepped through the open French doors out onto the deck and made for the canvas deck chairs blown onto their sides. As she folded them and stacked them under the eaves, it crossed her mind that Martin would have heeded the radio's wind warning this morning, and done this before he left for work.

If Martin were here.

Everything she thought about was in that context; she couldn't help herself. She reached up several times and finally grabbed all of the wind chimes, which had been crashing into each other and into the side of the house crazily. Storm warning. She hoped the power wouldn't go out.

Across the inlet, low clouds clung to the cliffs of Point Grey. It was raining there already.

If Martin were here, he'd be coming home momentarily, just past five on a Friday. They'd mix iced martinis and perhaps sit under the eaves and watch the wicked waves and approaching storm and disgorge their day to each other. They would have steak and salad near the rain and make love before or after.

She wiped a tear away, cursing herself. Martin was not coming home and she knew it. Ever. He was, almost two years ago, but he did not make it. The police said it was liquor.

She never believed it.

He would not be coming home to her ever again.

Home to the house they had designed together, the house hanging onto the cliffs of the west side of the North Shore. Slate-floored, cream-walled, airy and cozy at once, with room for a family of six.

And now, instead of a family of six, or a couple of two with enough love for forever, she occupied it alone, as if it were an apartment for one in the larger shell of a house. She still used their bedroom and ensuite: to abandon this space seemed more painful than staying in it.

She used the kitchen and the den off it, leading onto the oceanfront deck. But she shunned Martin's study and the rooms of their dream children. She was sure the neighbours thought she was mad. Perhaps she was.

She unbuttoned her cotton dress and let it drop to the wooden deck. Standing tall, she let the fingers of God or the devil or whoever's wind it was today, whip her hair and stroke the streaming tears. She stepped out of the dress and moved to the deck gate, to the steps leading to the rocky beach, to the mad ocean and relief. Two gulls played on the invisible striations of wind, screaming at each other.

She felt so desperately lonely and dark inside. Digging her nails into her palms so that there was physical pain, she watched the white birds and waited for the mood to pass. Finally she picked up her dress and walked back into the house to find one of Martin's oversized sweaters to put on. A sweater lightly sprayed with Obsession cologne by the house-keeper on Mondays, as instructed by Mrs. Grey.

● ● ●

The canopy of cedar and hemlock branches danced in the chaos eighty feet over the forest floor, showering the ground with boughs and needles. It was still daylight outside, but the old growth shut out the grey sky almost completely. Inside the forest it was nearly dark. While the treetops rustled noisily above, the lower forest was eerily still: no birds, no chipmunks, just wind and conflict far above, and dropping debris.

Three men walked through this forest, tromping on the dry, fragrant floor. Two had been friends since childhood. The third had been a mortal enemy of them both. Alliances change.

Three hundred yards into the forest, the leader of the

group directed the other two off the wide path into dense underbrush of salal and sword fern. The ground sloped down.

Dovee went first. He was twenty-five years old, well muscled, and he carried himself erect even now. He wore his hair short, with a close-cropped beard, pointed, like Lucifer's. His clothes were casually expensive: black shirt, Versace jeans, cowboy boots that gave him no traction on the needle-slippery ravine he was descending into. As he skidded down the slope he tried to keep his shoulders back, wondering fleetingly whether he'd shit himself.

Oskar, blond, soft and beefy, came next. He had avoided Dovee's eyes continuously since he had persuaded him to enter his car less than an hour ago. He too dressed only in designer denim and leather, but he had exchanged his boots for running shoes, which he would discard shortly. He had known about the walk.

The third man, who had given Oskar the choice of roles, walked behind the other men—always. One never could predict regrets or changes of heart. Which is why he had ordered that no one speak after they picked up Dovee at the marina. No communication, no imploring, no weakening, no deals.

He wore the baggy sweat pants of weightlifters and a loose-necked sweatshirt that exposed the cords in his monstrous shoulder muscles. His eyes were surrounded by smile lines, and the lips below his well-trimmed moustache were pleasantly full. He carried an athletic bag in his left hand and a fully automatic 9 mm Smith and Wesson in his right. He planned on being in the gym within the hour.

When they had reached the bottom of the ravine, he directed Oskar and Dovee ten yards away from the stream to a small clearing in the brush. He placed the gym bag on a boulder, unzipped it and removed a length of wire with his left hand. His eyes seemed to focus on both men simultaneously, the 9 mm casually present.

For the first time, Oskar noticed that the gun handler wore thin, nearly transparent surgical gloves. He himself had not thought to bring any. Sloppy. Understandable in light of the strain, but inexcusably sloppy.

The gunman passed the wire to Oskar and spoke for the first time since leaving the marina. "Kneel down at the base of that tree," he said to Dovee. His voice was quiet and calm.

Dovee walked to an ancient cedar. He knelt at the base of its trunk, facing the other two men, knees bent but the rest of his body erect and high. He tried not to blink. As he watched Oskar approach, wire in hand, he thought of moments in their past that should have been premonitions of this betrayal: the soft, whining child, tattling on other kids and lying as necessary to increase his own reward or someone else's punishment. Many years ago, in their neighbourhood, a bitch and three pups had made their home in a piece of old sewer pipe, and Oskar had thrown stone after stone at the pups. He had kept throwing stones, long after all the little girls had run home screaming, long after the bloody furry mass had ceased moving and mewling.

Later, for many years, Oskar's facility for deception had been a good thing for all of them. His ability to kill without remorse had been essential. Dovee had always been superstitious and had trusted no one outside the circle. But now, as Oskar moved behind him with the wire, he realized he had made a fatal error. They had known and played with each other and worked together for twenty-two years, but Oskar had never been part of the circle. His circle was closed and singular.

In the near-blinding light of hindsight, Dovee realized that contrary to appearances, even Oskar's brother had been excluded. That was why Oskar could drive by his bullet-ridden body without stopping. Dovee shuddered involuntarily as he felt the touch of Judas. The wire cut into his wrists.

No whispered apologies. No whys. They had seen many endings of life together. This one was just more personal for one of them.

Oskar walked to the man with the gloves and reached for the sawed-off shotgun. He matter-of-factly checked the load, cocked it and stood about twenty feet away from where Dovee knelt, hands tied behind his back. He raised the sight to his left eye, in search of another eye. Finding it, he pulled the trigger and his friend and cousin's head blew apart.

Oskar walked toward the corpse and retrieved the spent shell. One had more than done the job. He handed the empty gun to the man with the gloves and waited while he packed it back into the gym bag. The two men returned the way they had come, the forest silent after the echo of the shotgun blast.

It started to rain.

● ● ●

As the summer storm hit the coast full force, the city tucked itself in. Thunder crashed over the mountains and lightning cracked the sky.

In room 206 at the Auckland Rooming House, it wakened Fox, who had been sleeping at the window table. He leaned partway out the window to close it, looking down as he did. A flash illuminated a man's long-sleeved blue plaid shirt, splayed on the wet sidewalk below like an empty corpse. The slapping had stopped.

Fox closed the window and drew the thin ratty drapes together in an attempt to shut out the storm. He went to the metal frame bed and lay down on the smelly striped mattress, crooking his left arm across his nose so he could smell his own skin instead of the host of others who had lain there.

• • •

Six miles west, Parker was making his closing move. Thirty minutes before, he hadn't been sure that this was what he wanted: she wasn't nearly as good-looking up close as she'd appeared at the gym, and she was boring. But now it was pissing down rain outside.

The visitors' parking spots had been full when he'd arrived, so he'd had to park a couple of blocks away. Walking in this slop would wreck his shoes, definitely. He looked at her again and smiled. She smiled back. Well, he thought, there are worse ways of spending a night. And in the morning, with luck, the rain would have stopped.

• • •

She turned off all the lights in the beach house except one in the kitchen, which gave a bit of light in the bedroom if she kept the door ajar. She checked the alarm again and took a candle, matches, a flashlight and her cell phone into the bedroom and placed them on her side table beside her bed. She wondered if these adult security blankets would permit sleep.

The ocean crashed into the shore close by. The groaning of the wind-bent trees was drowned out only by the boom of thunder. Lauren slipped in between the cold cotton sheets and sank back against her pillows, closing her eyes and wondering which would come first, sleep or morning.

• • •

Cole arrived at the restaurant just before eight, rested and actually looking forward to the prospect of a social evening. Even if the blind date was a bust, Don and Liz were always good company.

It had been a good day. The wrap-up session of the under-cover course had gone so well that he had relented and gone with the class for a sandwich at a nearby pub. Compliments of Thursday night's scavenger hunt winner.

He had been on the way home, intent on a run, when his pager went off. He retrieved it on his cell phone and switched directions. Internal was requesting that he attend at headquarters at his earliest convenience. He had called John Simpson, who said he'd already been contacted and that Cole wouldn't be needing any legal advice that afternoon. Cole knew it was good news. He had walked into Internal's office ten minutes later and been formally advised that the internal investigation had cleared him of any wrongdoing in the shooting. In fact, they were considering using the fact-pattern in a training manual as an example of an appropriate use of firearms in an emergency. Cole had left their offices shaking his head.

Instead of going straight home, he had driven back to Gastown and walked to the salon, taking a chance someone would be there. Nathan had been, and was more than happy to give Cole a good straight-razor shave and to cut five inches off his locks.

Cole didn't know what his next job would be, but having spent the money and the time he didn't want to throw all the length away just to find out he needed it again. The ratty beard could be back in three days. He went home, ran, devoured the day's newspaper and dressed. By then it was 7:45 and time to go.

When he arrived at the restaurant they were already seated at a candlelit table for four outside on the covered deck. He walked across the tiles past the potted palms, eyeing the group. Don and Liz looked happy and relaxed, and the stranger sitting with them was a good-looking blonde woman in her mid-thirties. She wore a pale flowered dress that showed off a good figure and lightly freckled arms. As he approached the table, she looked up. She had a good smile.

Cole and Janine Wright got along just fine, with Don and Liz exaggerating the similarities and commonalties between the two until it was beyond embarrassing and Cole called a laughing halt to it. From then on the evening was great: superb food accompanied by good wine and lots of laughter. After the meal, the four sipped brandies and watched the growing storm from the patio. Cole dropped her off just after midnight, thanking her for a nice evening and saying he hoped they'd see each other again.

Part of him meant it. It had been a long time since he had enjoyed a woman's company as much. Still, he had been tempted to add the inescapable truth: it was unlikely. He was involved in something big at work.

As he pulled away from the curb, the first jagged lightning strike seared the sky.

● ● ●

Having finished his workout, Frank Wesley had returned home. He had emptied the gym bag, placed the shotgun in the back of his bedroom closet behind his suits and tossed the bag, nearly empty, on the closet floor. Then he had taken the Polaroid photograph from the pocket of his sweatshirt, placed it in a white envelope and put it on top of the chest of drawers in his bedroom. He would deal with it later. After that he had driven to his ex-wife's place to pick up the kids. There were times when he couldn't have said what date it was, but he always knew whether or not it was his weekend.

Now both kids were in his bed, afraid of the thunder and lightning. His six-year-old daughter slept peacefully on his left; she probably wouldn't move all night. His four-year-old son was a different story: at 12:30 he was still squirming and demanding more sips of water.

Wesley thought briefly about the body in the forest. The rain was good—water and then the return of heat would speed up the rotting. He would lie low for a while: no deals, no money, no violence. Just to make sure things stayed cool.

No phones, ever. He had read his own words, spoken while a reel-to-reel turned round and round eight miles away in the bowels of a police station, recording every pause and nuance. His conversation, along with the target's, had been transcribed and the prosecution lawyers had given it to the target's defence lawyers before trial. Wesley hadn't said enough to get charged that time. But you never knew where the risk lay.

So, no phones and no contact with anyone from the club dealing with Oskar. There was no need: Wesley had ensured that the club owned Oskar. He had murdered a colleague and had been witnessed doing it, and there was physical evidence. Wesley was confident that Oskar knew if he stepped out of line, the prosecutor's office would make a sweet deal with Wesley for testimony and for the murder weapon covered with Oskar's fingerprints.

Not to mention Wesley's employers. They would deal with Oskar and his coke source from now on. Wesley's role was over unless things went sideways. He didn't expect them to. Not many people had had the guts, or stupidity, to cross him and remain healthy. And Oskar, who had had very few friends before this afternoon, now had one fewer.

Frank Wesley lay back between his children and fell peacefully to sleep.

• • •

Each crash of thunder was a gunshot blast. Over and over

and over again. Oskar was going crazy. It was God's retribution, like a cacophonic water torture. Boom, boom, boom, instead of drip, drip, drip. He'd taken to thinking about God lately, more than he ever had before.

His mother had kept a Bible in their home in Latvia, putting herself and the whole family at risk. She would read passages from the Old Testament about locusts and plagues and scare the shit out of Oskar and his brother, saying that God saw everything, punished everything evil. This, after they had stolen a biscuit or two out of the tin in the kitchen. He didn't want to think what her response would have been to his actions today.

He wanted comfort desperately. He craved relief—even momentary—from his situation. More and more lately, he'd thought of using a bit of his own product. Just to take the edge off. These last few months had been the first time since he started playing the game eight years ago that he had thought seriously about actually using the shit.

"Users are losers." Before things got so screwed up, that was one of the fundamental principles of their business. The philosophy helped minimize risks. The risk that one of them would be tempted to skim a bit off a kilo for personal use, or try cutting the product with glucose and hope no one noticed. Or the risk that one of them would become a dumb-fuck chatty Cathy paranoid, or an untouchable prima donna, believing that his actions or talk could never get any of them arrested, ripped off or killed.

But that was before. Before, Andris or Yuri would've beaten the shit out of him if they even suspected he was thinking like this. Now, neither of them was alive to beat him. But there were other concerns.

Oskar lay in the dark on the floor of the luxury hotel room, between the couch and the coffee table, where he had a good view of the whole room and especially the door, the only entrance to the room. Earlier he had taken the couch cushions into the bedroom and arranged them under the bedcovers with the pillows, satisfied that they looked sufficiently like a sleeping human form for his purposes.

He wore street clothes, but not the ones he had worn in the forest. Those he had sent to the hotel's dry cleaning service to have the powder residue removed. Not that it mattered much. They had him anyway. They had his prints on the murder weapon and they had a witness. The prints probably wouldn't last forever but the witness seemed fucking invincible. Everyone respected him, was scared shitless of him or thought he was just a nice guy.

There was no doubt the cops would cut Wesley a deal that would let him walk out the front door if he disclosed the circumstances of the murder, however heavily edited. Oskar would be left holding the bag and behind bars. He certainly couldn't go to the cops himself. He had no physical evidence against Wesley; his story would establish that he was a party to the murder, and every biker and wannabe would be trying to kill the man who had ratted out Frank Wesley.

He was fucked. And alone.

When Wesley had approached him earlier that day, with his ever-present 9-mil, he had offered him a choice: Oskar could either kill Dovee or be killed by Wesley right there. It hadn't been much of a decision.

It was clear to Oskar that the club wanted to weaken the competition he and Dovee had maintained since Yuri and Andris had died. But why leave either of them alive? There could be only one answer. The club wanted something, and Oskar's obvious asset was his coke connections down south.

He lay in the dark, hating Wesley and the fucking cowards who employed him. Not because they had forced him to kill Dovee, but because the fuckers had him.

He rolled into the fetal position, torso covered by his

leather jacket, listening to the storm, watching for the next shot of light on the far wall. He had very few options. With a silvery AK47 in his right hand, tucked between his curled-up knees, he shivered uncontrollably, waiting for the night to pass.

• • •

The rain had infiltrated the branches sheltering the forest floor. Filtered through the web of needles and barked spines, it fell more gently here than above the canopy. Below the path, by the ravine, it was very dark. The soft rain mixing with the thickened blood in the hair next to the gutted face could not be seen.

Morning light would reveal that Dovee lay on his back, partially sideways, as though he'd been thrown back by a blow. His knees were bent beneath him, and his hands were behind his back. His chin remained, the beard pointing up in futile defiance. The gore started where his lower lip had been and consumed the rest of the face up to mid-brow. His left eyeball, dislodged, hung by a bit of ocular tissue above the left ear.

In the deep black, the animal intervention began. Two coyotes and four rats. The insects of death had arrived too, and were at work on the demolition process started so effectively by human hands nine hours earlier. A two-inch slug crossed the inner hem of the right pant leg, then slowly worked its way onto, and up, the leg inside. Rain soaked the front of the black shirt.

The skies far above rumbled and flashed, but the shock of bright light was almost completely filtered out, leaving the left eyeball to stare blindly into inky darkness.

Saturday, June 13, 1998

The phone rang just as light was creeping into the eastern sky. As he reached for it, Cole looked at the clock: 5:03. It had to be work. Or England. Either way, unless it was an emergency—or Michael, who wasn't too good at converting time zones—it had better be good, given the hour. He was wide awake.

"Yes," he said crisply.

"Jackson, it's Jeff Thompson." Inspector Jeff Thompson was the right-hand man to Superintendent Lawson when it came to drug enforcement for the province. He had Cole's full attention. "Sorry if I've wakened you, but you're requested at a meeting this morning. 6:30, Superintendent Lawson's office. Can I tell him you'll be there?"

"Yes, of course."

"Good. See you then."

Cole went to the kitchen to put the kettle on, then headed for the shower. With a towel around his waist, he made a cup of coffee and took it back to the bathroom with him. There he finished dressing and pulled his hair into a long pony tail.

Thompson was a good officer but was uptight when it came to uniforms, appearance and protocol. Cole knew that Thompson viewed him as a necessary evil—an undisciplined maverick who just happened to get extreme results. The long hair would drive him nuts.

Dressed in fresh jeans and a starched white shirt, Cole was ready to go at 5:40. He took a fresh cup of coffee and a papaya and walked out onto the balcony to watch the rest of the sunrise. Last night's storm had blown all the clouds away and scrubbed the air clean. A gentle breeze ruffled the flags on the sailboats tied up at the dock below him. Regardless of the content of the meeting, he was glad for the wake-up call. It was too beautiful a morning to miss.

Cole arrived five minutes early at the Royal Canadian Mounted Police headquarters building for E Division—E Division being better known as the province of British Columbia. K Division was Alberta; F Division, Saskatchewan; M Division, the Yukon. The logic was clear to someone, no doubt. E Division HQ consumed two blocks in one of the city's most affluent neighbourhoods, amid manicured lawns and multimillion-dollar houses. For years there had been rumours that HQ would move from this gem of a setting to one of the outlying areas, where Mounties actually lived, not commuted to. It made sense in a way, but most of the hard drug crime—the importing, high-level trafficking and attendant murders—pretty much happened in the downtown area, about three miles from headquarters. So somebody was going to have to drive, sometime.

Cole liked the current location. It was close to the action for the job and it was close to his first choice of places to live, the waterfront.

He checked his watch: 6:26. He parked the truck in one of

the visitors' stalls close to the front doors, signed in with the commissionaire and walked through the silent lobby to the elevators. He reached the third floor at 6:28 and walked quickly to Lawson's office.

The door was open. At its threshold stood the impressive figure of the superintendent. As always he was dressed in full uniform, as though it were midday, midweek, and not an ungodly hour on a Saturday morning.

"Good of you to come on such short notice, Jackson," he said with a smile. "You're the last to arrive. Come in."

Cole entered Lawson's office. To his left, the huge oak desk with its brass reading lamp remained largely hidden under stacks of neatly piled paper. To his right, the highly polished meeting table was surrounded by six people and two empty chairs. Drapes covered the picture window completely.

The superintendent moved to the empty chair at the head of the table and gestured to Cole to take the other one.

"Sergeant Jackson Cole, I think you know everyone here."

Cole nodded, glancing around the table.

To his left sat Inspector Dave Webster, in charge of the Human Source Unit—"human source" being the police euphemism for a person who provides information. In court, such a person was referred to as a confidential informer and afforded a legal privilege which prevented his or her identity being disclosed. On the street, such a person was referred to as a rat, a fink or, if unlucky, a corpse.

One of Webster's jobs was to ensure that police "handlers" of informants kept accurate logs of meets and information. Another was to keep the informants alive, which involved working closely with the Source/Witness Protection Program and prosecuting attorneys. If Morrit had lived, he and Webster would have spent time together.

Next to Webster sat Sergeant Thomas McKeown, of the

Security Section. He was renowned across North America as one of the great lock men: so far, no locking device had eluded his expert mind or fingers. McKeown did some of his best work during surreptitious police entries to install listening devices pursuant to wiretap court orders. He went in first, picking locks undetectably, deprogramming alarms, disengaging counter-surveillance recording machines—always in time-limited circumstances and usually in the dark, with other officers covering for safety, their pulses racing and sweat flowing while the unflappable McKeown calmly did his thing like he was tying flies at his kitchen table.

Then came Sergeant Scott Wilson, the guru of wiretap, reputed to know as much about wiretap law as the prosecutors who obtained wiretap orders and then defended them in court. His legendary knowledge and pickiness for detail had been responsible for hundred-page affidavits that even the best defence attorney could not get kicked out of court. Six out of six of Wilson's last affidavits had been held by the courts to support the wiretap orders, which meant that in all six of Wilson's last investigations, the targets got to dress up, sit in a courtroom quiet as a church and listen to their own voices sewer them, their talk replete with the *fucks* and *cocksuckers* that now, as they sat there in their Sunday best, seemed so out of character.

Wire was intrusive. You became a fly on the wall in people's cars, offices, kitchens, bedrooms. Cole had no problem with the courts requiring the state to achieve near perfection in compliance with the statutory requirements before authorizing such an intrusion.

On the other hand, wire was extremely effective—sometimes the only investigative tool likely to produce the evidence you needed. That was why, in his view, if a wire was worth doing, it was worth doing right.

Across the table from Cole was Corporal Bobby Pearce, a

hotshot corporal who worked the Fraser Valley, an area east of Vancouver where villages and farm communities had grown into commuter towns too fast and were bursting at the seams with crime and other social problems. Pearce's jurisdiction was home to six correctional institutions, including a maximum security penitentiary, several men and women's medium security prisons, as well as farms and camps for sex offenders and scores of halfway houses for the rehabilitated. In his view it was an ideal place for a cop: rife with potential informants, and while most of the heroin and coke arrived at the airport or downtown at the harbour, a hell of a lot of it made its way to his area for distribution. Pearce was happy to let other people go after the masterminds and financiers of crime operations. He liked the street scene. He and Cole had shared information over the years, and if time had permitted they probably would have become friends. Pearce raised his left eyebrow in question as Cole sat down, and Cole responded with a smile and quick shake of his head.

The other man on the far side of the table was Staff Sergeant Peter Grant, a twenty-four-year veteran with a specialty in biker clubs. The Satan's Warriors, with their aggressive recruitment and multimillion-dollar profile, had been of particular interest to him since their arrival in the province. Clean shaven and dressed in corduroy pants and an expansive sports shirt, Grant looked like a harmless, out-of-shape office worker. Dressed in a black T-shirt, blue jeans and Daytons, with his frizzy greying hair grown long and two weeks' worth of beard, if there was a Harley in sight he looked like a menacing biker. Grant had played the outlaw biker role effectively twice, actually infiltrating two organized criminal bike clubs. But never the Warriors.

Years before, he had been the leading force in the specialized investigative unit targeting the Warriors. When the unit was disbanded two years later—whether because money or political will had run out, he never learned—he was ordered by his boss to oversee the destruction of the unit's files: cabinets and cabinets full of reports from informants, tips from neighbours and external agencies, surveillance records detailing the comings and goings of club members, club strikers, hangers-on and wannabes—all the careful paperwork on two years' worth of intense investigations.

Grant had concluded years before that undercover police infiltration of the club was impossible. A cop could grow old proving his allegiance and trustworthiness, first as a hanger-on allowed at parties but not in the clubhouse, eventually running joe jobs for the members. This might go on for years before you graduated to striker status, still not a member and not privy to club business, but entrusted with some involvement in its activities. That's when they really started to get stuff on you—running money for a small drug pickup or enforcing a club debt—and as they trusted you more, the stakes got higher. Grant didn't know of a single club member who hadn't participated in some form of gang sex assault as a striker before being admitted. And then, they had you. One refusal to play the game their way would blow your credibility sky high, and everyone knew a step out of line could result in a visit to your mama, your kid sister or your old lady. They had that kind of information.

This aspect of the club helped prevent club members from becoming police informers. It also complicated the creation of a believable cover story for an undercover cop, because everyone real has someone, somewhere, who's vulnerable.

Grant placed a high premium on the information he and his colleagues had gathered on the Warriors. Consequently, while not keen to disobey a direct order, he decided that the short-sighted stupidity of this one constituted the proverbial exception to the rule. He oversaw the destruction of seventeen moving cartons filled with various recycled office paper and labelled SECURITY: SECRET, then returned to his desk and prepared his destruction report.

On the day Grant moved back to RCMP headquarters from his office in the special off-site location, the government movers toted numerous moving boxes from his office, and also three locked filing cabinets, each drawer labelled with a different file name.

Having seen enough death to believe in it, Grant had told one person of his actions, just in case. It was his troopmate and friend, Sergeant Harry Rickson, who shared Grant's view of the destruction order and his belief that most officers seem to have their balls removed, along with a partial lobotomy, as a prerequisite to receiving their stripes.

That had been six years ago. Since then, while Grant had worked organized crime and gathered intelligence, regularly opening various cabinet drawers and adding to information on each of the four Satan's Warrior's branches in the province, Rickson had taken courses, and relocations, and had skyrocketed through the chain of command.

He now sat at the head of the table opposite Superintendent Lawson, a full-fledged superintendent in his own right. As far as Grant could tell, his old friend had managed to opt out of the surgery, even though he had scaled the ranks.

In his present position, Rickson held the purse strings for operations. His job was to find resources—money and personnel—where he believed in a project, and to axe such resources on files he viewed as futile or otherwise unworthy of the expense. He had less experience at the top level of command than Lawson did, but he had spent years on the street gathering evidence and years in the courts giving it, which had earned him widespread respect and credibility among both field police and his fellow officers.

Looking around the table, Cole guessed correctly that his

reputation had landed him at this sunrise meeting and would wreck his weekend. It wasn't his file, but judging from the players he could guess who the targets were. Things would have to be done right, I's dotted and T's crossed, because if charges were ever laid, you'd see the biggest, longest, most extravagant defence ever mounted in the province.

As Cole poured coffee into his cup, Lawson convened the meeting. "My apologies for the hour, gentlemen, but we appear to have an opportunity which I think you'll all agree is worth exploring." He paused, looking around the table at each of them. "We have recent information from two separate sources which may allow us to get wire into a Satan's Warriors clubhouse, for what I believe is the first time in Canada." He looked at Grant, who nodded.

"I have reviewed debriefing reports from Sergeant Cole and Corporal Pearce," Lawson continued, "and I believe that with some industry we will be able to get a court order. I'll get Jackson to outline the information he received last Tuesday about a methamphetamine lab while speaking with the late Roger Morrit." He nodded at Cole.

Cole thought back to his meeting with Morrit. The meth lab that Morrit had talked about had seemed like a throwaway detail to him—very difficult to detect without ongoing information. On the other hand, cooking up meth was the kind of offence for which a wiretap order could be given, and wire could give them exactly the type of ongoing information they needed. If they could ever get bugs installed.

All eyes in the room had turned to look at Cole. He dove in. "Roger Morrit, as many of you will recall, got caught with several units of heroin in the mid-eighties. He's connected to the bikers by marriage—his sister married Micky Scofield. Since the late sixties he has hung around with the club, although he never became a member. When he got busted there were rumours that it was the club's stuff that got seized.

At any rate, he's had opportunity to have information about the club's activities."

He took a sip of his coffee.

"Four days ago we pinched Morrit with another pound and a half of heroin and gave him a choice: co-operate or try jail again." Cole frowned at the table top. "Well, he was temporarily co-operative. He told me about a methamphetamine lab that he said the East Side boys are setting up with the Langley branch, with the assistance of some experts from the States. He said they were going to build the lab in a barn somewhere in Langley and that it would be larger and more sophisticated than anything we've ever seen and that the product was intended for the domestic market and for export.

"Morrit told me about something else, which will be confirmed or refuted shortly. That will go a long way to establishing his credibility, one way or the other." Reliability of informants was essential when trying to get a search warrant or wiretap court order based on what they've said.

"I can help in that regard," Superintendent Lawson said quietly. "Jackson, I'd intended on telling you after this meeting, but it fits in now. Constable Lauer called me late yesterday evening. Based on the information that Morrit had given to Jackson, Constable Lauer got a search warrant for a mine just south of Hedley. They found three bodies laid out in the mine. Two men, one woman. All three people had been shot through the head, execution style."

"Morrit said that we would find the three missing witnesses from the Tag trial in the mine," Cole said, filling in the blanks. "It sounds like we did."

"Morrit's information about the two branches' plans for a meth lab is evidence of a conspiracy to traffic in a restricted drug," Lawson said, using the word *traffic* in its legal sense, which included "produce or make." "We can get wire when someone is going to do that, but with the bikers, the practical problem is how to get the bugs into their premises. Corporal Pearce has the information to help us on that score."

All eyes turned to Bobby Pearce.

"I received information from a fellow in the security business," Pearce began. "A number of you may know him. He's extremely reliable." Cole was certain that Pearce was referring to an ex-Mountie who had entered the private sector for more excitement and multiples of his police salary. "This guy got information through his industry that the Warriors are interested in having a new location wired to the hilt—motion detectors, videos inside and outside the premises, along with the usual audio alarms. Apparently they've gone out of province for it, to some guy from California, who's coming up next week. So in light of this information I started to do some digging. It didn't take many full shovels to learn that the Langley Club has bought a place east of the town centre. It's a huge spread—five acres, on a slight hill. It's going to be the branch's new digs, away from observant neighbours and the local constabulary. We've had the place under spotty surveillance since Thursday. The previous owners are in the process of moving out."

Cole's thoughts were racing. "When does the branch take possession?"

"Monday noon."

All but the two superintendents looked at their watch: it was just after 7:20 in the morning, Saturday.

The wire man spoke their thoughts: "That gives us fifty-three hours to do everything."

"That's right, gentlemen," Lawson said, nodding. "Just over two days to do it all."

Except for the time pressure, it was beautiful. Installation after the place was occupied would be impossible, as it was with every clubhouse; but here, if the wiretap bugs could be authorized and installed this weekend, the police would be waiting for the bikers, instead of the other way around.

"Now," Lawson continued, "given the targets and their willingness to use unconventional tactics, if there's anyone who'd prefer not to be involved in this operation, I want to hear about it now. No hard feelings or recriminations. Some of you are family men."

He waited while the men in the room pondered those "unconventional tactics," such as videotaping and photographing police officers, and obtaining biographical data on cops who made the Warriors their targets. On one occasion two club members had visited the son of a particularly persistent investigator while the boy was in the hospital having his tonsils out. When the cop learned of the visit and saw the Tonka motorcycle they'd left as a gift, he became completely unglued. He'd been transferred to another part of the country shortly thereafter. Desk duty, by request.

The excitement in the room was palpable. No one made a move to leave.

"All right." Lawson's voice was hard. "If you're in, you're in. We have a lot to accomplish in the next couple of days.

"This will be the last meeting that will be held here until the wire is up and running. Until then I don't want any of you seen near a police station. Superintendent Rickson has arranged for a safe house for the operation. There's a computer, printer and scrambled secure fax machine at your disposal. As far as cell phones go, if you have to use them, the words you choose had better be the most innocuous words I've ever heard."

Everyone knew cell phone conversations were notoriously easy to pick up—by novice radio operators, scanners, baby monitors—but it didn't hurt to be reminded.

"Now, Jackson, it seems to me that you should be the one to swear the affidavit on this thing."

Cole nodded coolly. He had written wiretap affidavits before and knew that they involved a mind-numbing amount of work. But at the end of the day, you got to take the stand and spar with defence counsel, something he loved to do.

"I'd like you to work with Sergeant Wilson. I'm sure you know his reputation."

"A pleasure," said Cole, turning to the wire man. Wilson nodded.

Lawson then turned to Pearce. "Please gather your notebooks and meet with Sergeant Cole and Sergeant Wilson. I want every relevant detail of your information in that affidavit."

"Yes, sir," Pearce nodded.

The omission of minor details could be fatal: a good defence attorney could characterize an oversight as an attempt to mislead the judge who authorized the wiretap. If the argument succeeded, out went the wiretap evidence.

"I've arranged for a Justice Department lawyer to be available at one o'clock. You should have a good outline of the document by then."

Lawson turned to the security expert. "Tommy, you've seen the plans for this place, I understand."

Sergeant McKeown nodded.

"Okay. How long for the bug installers to do a top-notch job?"

McKeown had talked to Rathie, the sergeant in charge of wiretap installations for the province. "He said that if we get the go-ahead for rooms and phones, they can be in and out in under two hours. It's got to be done at night or we'll be spotted for sure. The only real opportunity I see is late Sunday night."

Cole had done the calculations and agreed. "We'll have

the paper in front of a judge by dinner time tomorrow night," he told Lawson.

The superintendent nodded and then spoke to the group. "The safe house is a suite at the Sutton Regency. Number 1412. I'd suggest Cole and Wilson go there now and get started. No secretarial help on this one boys, no extra mouths. The rest of you will have a slightly more leisurely start to the day. Go home and pack for the weekend and say your good-byes. You're out of town for at least three days on a job." He looked around the table at men he liked, respected and trusted. "And not one fucking word about this to anyone."

The superintendent reserved "fucking" for only the most serious emphasis. Clearly, even wives and girlfriends were not to be in the know about this one, under any circumstances.

"Pete," Lawson said to the Warriors expert, "I want you and your nonexistent files to high-tail it over to 1412." Rickson didn't meet Grant's sardonic gaze.

"Webster, you're on standby, to clear up any problems that might arise with Pearce's informant, capiche?"

"Capiche."

"Okay, gentlemen, let's get at it."

The meeting broke at 7:43.

• • •

Rick Parker awoke just before ten, uncertain of where he was. Once he figured it out, he just wanted to get out of there. He begged off with the morning meeting excuse and was gone within minutes.

He walked to his car through the city's West End, with its high-rise apartment blocks jammed into the downtown peninsula between the financial district and Stanley Park. The streets were pocked with deep puddles. He'd been right.

His shoes would have been ruined if he'd tried to get to the car last night.

He reached the Mercedes and circled it to ensure no one had damaged it, then started it up and drove through the deserted streets. The bit about the business meeting wasn't complete bullshit: he was, in fact, planning on going to the office, although not to meet anyone. He had started spending Saturday mornings there during his marriage, when the quiet office, a cup of coffee and the morning paper meant serenity. Since the bitch liked money at least as much as he did, she didn't object when he explained that he could double-bill because he was so effective in these quiet times. Later on, during the divorce, it all came out in her affidavits, which was a complete pain in the ass and no doubt contributed to the large award the judge gave her.

Parker drove into the secure underground parking lot. The elevator took him to street level and opened onto a streetfront plaza. He crossed to his two-storey Victorian-style office building and let himself in. After turning off the alarm he walked through the main floor, past the reception area and secretaries' stations, and climbed the stairs to the second floor, which was his office.

Upstairs, the wall overlooking the street was made up of windowed French doors leading onto a balcony. Inset in the west wall was a gas fireplace flanked by two deep green leather couches. Facing the fireplace, on the other side of the room, was Parker's desk, a huge oak masterpiece carved three hundred years earlier and worn black by time. On it sat a leather blotter, with his computer on the left and a stack of unread correspondence on the right.

The wall across from the French doors had two doors of its own. One led to a spacious bathroom with marble tiles, a jet tub and sauna. The other led to a small, windowless locked room containing secure filing cabinets and a few changes of clothing. It was to that room that Parker went now, whistling. Using the code that only he knew, he unlocked the door and turned on the light. He opened the closet and took out clean shorts, freshly laundered jeans and a black mock-turtleneck shirt. He left the room and rese-cured the door. In the bathroom he showered quickly and dressed in the clean clothes. He stuffed his dirty clothes in the hamper. His secretary would deal with them.

Parker then opened the mirrored cabinet. Versace or Boss? He selected a bottle of aftershave and slapped some on, his mind slipping to the young thing that might be on shift at the deli across the street.

As luck would have it, she was arriving at work just as he was about to cross the street to grab a coffee and pastry and head back to the office. That she wasn't alone didn't bother him a bit. He was feeling fit and tanned and strong, and while he was a bit older than her little friend, it was pretty clear to him who'd have the better-looking bank account. Unconsciously, he sucked in his stomach.

The guy dropping off Legs, as Parker thought of her, rode a chopper, a low-slung, extended Harley. He wore a skull cap, slit sunglasses and a goatee, all of which were slightly incongruous with his sweatshirt and long fleece shorts. A work connection crossed Parker's mind, but he discarded it. This guy wore no leather or insignia. He was probably just another idiot caught up in some misguided fashion trend.

The chopper was gone and Legs was behind the counter by the time he entered the deli. They remarked simultane-ously about last night's storm, Legs laughing flirtatiously at their collision of words. Leaving the deli with his coffee and croissant, Parker was certain that he had a chance with her.

• • •

In a waterfront park eight blocks away, a cellular phone rang. The chopper rider reached into his jean jacket pocket and flipped the phone open. "Yeah."

"It's me," said a high, tinny voice.

"Yeah, I know it's you. Who else do you know that's up at this hour? Just kiddin', sweetheart. How'd things go?"

"He left about a minute ago," Legs said, a little uncertainly. "He should be at his office any time. Mike, are you going to tell me what this is about?"

"Yeah, babe. It's about money. Lots of it, for you and me. Okay? I'll see you tonight."

"Okay. I love you."

He'd hung up.

• • •

Parker's private line was ringing as he re-entered his second-storey sanctum. For just a moment he missed a step. He looked at his watch. No markets were open at this hour on Saturday, not even the Nikkei.

He hurried to his desk, slopping coffee on the blotter. "Hello," he said.

He could hear traffic, but no one spoke.

"Hello," he repeated. Again there was no response.

"Fuck you." He hung up, slightly unnerved.

If it was a wrong number, why didn't they speak up? And if it wasn't, then who was it? Only a chosen few had his number. A few close friends and still fewer close business associates. He mopped up the coffee and sat down to enjoy his breakfast and review a recent gold prospectus. As he flipped to page four, the phone rang again. He picked it up on the third ring.

"Yes," he said.

No answer. Traffic and gulls. This was no mistake.

"Who is this?" He realized what a dumb-ass question it was as he asked it. He hung up.

Turning back to page four was useless; his concentration was shot. He was pretty sure he knew exactly who it was.

On the third call he let the phone ring and ring and ring, but the caller won in the end. Parker picked it up, a thin line of sweat on his upper lip. He waited for the caller to speak.

Two words: "How's Billy?"

Click. The line was dead.

Parker froze. Billy was his twelve-year-old son, living in Toronto with his mother, the Ice Queen, as he had for the last nine years. Parker never mentioned him to any of his clients. Especially these clients. For he was absolutely certain of the association of the caller, although he didn't recognize the voice.

How the fuck did they find out about his son? Christ, he *never* mentioned Billy to them. He'd known they were thorough, but why him? Why now? They couldn't possibly know that he wanted out, desperately. That was the only sin he could identify and he sure as shit hadn't mentioned it to Wesley.

He punched in an Ontario number and, sweating freely now, listened to the empty rings. Just as he was about to give up, his ex-wife's breathless voice said, "Hello."

"Hi, Jo."

"Oh God, it's you. Billy's not here right now."

"Well, believe it or not, it's not Billy that I phoned to talk to. How're things?"

"Things are fine, Rick." Her voice was flat. "I've got a million things to do this afternoon, so I've got to go."

"Fair enough." He didn't want to let her go. "Jo, is Billy doing okay?"

"Okay? Yes, he's fine."

"No strangers or anything have been around? Nothing odd?"

He heard familiar anger. "Oh for God's sake, what are you into now?"

"Nothing. Crime's on the rise out here, and I worry about you two."

"Rick, this is the first time you and I have said more than 'See you in court' in nine years. Cut the concern crap. What's up?"

An hour earlier he would have viewed her response as bitchy and hung up. Now, feeling responsible for risking her and Bill's safety, he was glad of her feistiness.

"Jo, why don't you and Billy go to Barbados for a month? On me. I've made a potful lately and I'd like you two to enjoy it."

"Great, Rick. Send a bigger cheque next month if you really want to help." She hung up, leaving him staring at the grey receiver.

It hit him then. After too much Scotch at his desk one evening the week before, he'd called his brother and had a long, rambling chat about life in general, including a description of how desperately he wanted out of a business arrangement he was in. He hadn't named names or organizations, but if you knew the players and heard the conversation, you'd know exactly what he was talking about and who he was talking about.

He looked again at the receiver in his hand.

The fuckers had tapped his phone.

• • •

Lauren Grey awoke early, having slept surprisingly well given her mood the night before. After her routine of situps, pushups and hurdle stretches, she ran for an hour in the neighbourhood. Up and down the hilly streets, enjoying the views of gardens and ocean. Freshly showered, dressed in a long cotton skirt and faded denim blouse and enjoying a rare feeling of well-being, she decided to go to the gallery for the morning, at least. She planned to inspect the latest shipment of paintings that had just come in from her buying trip in Quebec.

She drove with the top down, enjoying the air and the road's curves. She had always loved driving, and the black XJS Jag ragtop was her favourite gift from Martin, except for her wedding ring. As she drove over the Lions Gate bridge, connecting the North Shore with Stanley Park, she picked up the phone and pressed in the memory code for Rick's private line. For as long as she'd known him, he'd spent Saturday mornings in his office. Martin had said it had begun when he was married, as a means of avoiding time with his wife, then became a habit that continued even after the marriage had dissolved.

The line was busy the first time she tried it, and then it rang and rang and rang. She punched in the seven numbers manually; still no answer. Puzzled, she hung up. They had made plans to dine together that night but hadn't discussed the time or place. She decided to wait for him to call her.

She eased the car into her reserved slot in the under-ground parking lot, raised the roof, got out and locked the door. Out of habit, she kept her keys in her hand.

She didn't see him at first. He was standing in the shadows of one of the concrete pillars. When she did, she stifled a gasp. He was no more than twenty feet away from her, staring at her. He was short for a man, she guessed five-six, and skinny in the extreme. He wore dark pants and a blue plaid shirt several sizes too big for him.

She was aware of her purse, her gold chain and earrings and her sex, all at once. He stood off to her left, but between her and the underground opening. She considered running to her car, but didn't want to turn her back on him.

Danny Fox had watched her arrive with curiosity. He had seen her picture in the odd newspaper in the joint, mostly society columns about the local nearly rich and famous. That's where he had learned about her and her art gallery. Knowledge, he had heard it said, is opportunity. He had walked to the gallery after a breakfast of watery powdered eggs at the mission and he had drawn more than the occasional sideways glance, as he always did outside the skids. Fathers grabbed daydreaming kids out of his path. Not that he blamed them; he'd have done the same in their place. He knew that in their eyes he was a dangerous junkie. And in his case, what you saw was what you got.

Fox had been thinking hard while he walked and the more he thought about it, the more he was convinced that this was the route to go. He had spent hours on benches outside two different shopping malls, pretending to be passed out, watching Brinks guards come and go. The more he watched, the more he knew it would require at least three people: one to drive and one to help him deal with the guard and driver. Someone was likely to die.

He decided in the end that the only people he trusted enough were still doing time, and they would still be there, long after he'd died from withdrawal. He would have to move on things now. He needed to score soon and he wanted to make it a big one. Big enough that he could buy bulk— even a couple of units, and just put it away and live. He was smart with the stuff and confident that he could keep a stored supply and not abuse it. If he was wrong, then he'd just end up dead a little early.

He had done the math weeks ago, when he'd started thinking about resupply, long before Morrit had approached him. There were seven hundred grams in a unit and he used a third of a gram a day. That meant one unit would last about six years, if he kept true. Three units, bought now or over time, would last him more than twenty years. That would put him at age sixty-two. He doubted he'd care about seeing sixty-three.

At today's prices, three units would run about three hundred thousand, maybe a bit less. Even a Brinks job, split up, couldn't guarantee that. A contract killing definitely wouldn't do it. He'd have to do ten of them, and with that kind of repetition he'd get caught eventually.

And then he'd heard her name mentioned on a radio talk show at the mission a couple of weeks ago, something about an exhibit opening at the Quinn Gallery, and an idea had begun to grow. Far safer than a hit or a Brinks robbery, requiring no one's help and maybe not even illegal. Morrit's detailed information about the hit had been the clincher.

Fox had tried to remember as much as he could from the papers he had read in prison. Then, that morning, he had wandered around in front of the gallery for a few minutes, getting a good look at the art, the windows and doors, the security system and cameras. He didn't think he wanted his picture taken while talking to her. That was when a different approach had occurred to him and he'd gone looking for where she parked. He was just leaving, having seen her name on a Reserved plaque, when she drove in. He hadn't expected her to be the type to work weekends. But here she was. Obviously nervous.

One thing he didn't want was for her to be afraid of him. He searched for words in her language, hoping that that would make him seem less frightening. Not that he was ready to discuss anything with her yet; far from it. But he couldn't let this chance meeting pass.

Lauren was scared. But he hadn't moved since she had spotted him. Not a muscle. Oddly, he reminded her somehow of a deer trapped in headlights.

"Mrs. Martin Grey?"

The words shocked her. How would a street person know who she was? In spite of herself, she found herself nodding. As she did so, she recalled her parking spot, the Reserved sign with her name on it.

"Please don't be alarmed." His voice was low and hoarse, but he spoke carefully. "I mean you no harm. I'll leave now."

And with that he turned and walked out of the garage.

Lauren walked backwards until she felt herself bump into her car. Only then did she turn her back on the parkade entrance, pop the door lock and slip in behind the wheel, relocking the door. She was shaking.

Working in the gallery alone today was completely out of the question. She needed to be surrounded by a crowd of people, in sunlight. As she shifted into reverse, she looked at the garage wall ahead of her. The Reserved sign had her name printed on it, all right: Lauren Quinn. No reference to Martin Grey at all.

● ● ●

In the warming forest the face, so nicely opened up, was the perfect bed for larvae and maggots. The insects were attracted to the damp wounds and natural orifices, and the animals had helped. As noon approached, the flies and maggots thickened and the air putrefied.

● ● ●

Oskar had taken the chair from the writing desk into the hotel bathroom with him and leaned it against the door, under the handle. He tried it and it seemed to hold, but it was a movie move and no guarantee of anything except some warning if anyone tried to get in.

There was a gold-coloured platform for towels at the far end of the tub, about five and a half feet high. He removed all but one towel and placed the AK47 on it, fully clipped with silencer on and safety off.

He checked the lock on the door again and then stripped. He turned on the shower, ensuring the stream missed the towel rack. Only then did he step into the tub and close the curtain. Uncharacteristically, he didn't even glance at himself in the mirror.

In the daylight, freshly showered and dressed, he didn't feel half bad. Attaching his pager to his waistband, he discovered one new message. It hadn't taken them long to get down to business. On the other hand, they had him, and they certainly weren't in mourning. Why wait? Feeling more like himself than he had in the past forty-eight hours, he considered their instructions and realized that he wasn't afraid of a hit by them. Not at this stage, anyhow. Why kill the goose?

Not that he considered himself indispensable to them, not for a moment. He wasn't that stupid. But while they had other ventures, the city and interior of the province were relatively dry, and he had a connection who could supply a hundred kilos a week. A hundred kilos a week, if you're controlling distribution all the way down to the gram level, meant hundreds of thousands of dollars a week. Even the Warriors couldn't resist that.

If Oskar had one ace, it was that he didn't think his connection would deal with bikers. If he was wrong, it wouldn't take long to end up a dead middleman. He hoped he was right.

He was to meet some asshole in a nearby McDonald's parking lot at 2:00 that afternoon for "further instructions." That gave him more than two hours to come up with some way to avoid life as the club's pet monkey. He ordered room service and sat down to think.

• • •

By noon, Cole and Wilson had the first draft of the wiretap affidavit mapped out. It contained historic information from Staff Sergeant Grant about the Warriors' control over drug distribution in British Columbia, as well as their insulated practices. It set out the recent information received by Cole and Pearce and showed grounds to believe that wiretap would be the best—and maybe only—opportunity the police would have to get evidence of the offences. Fleshed out, Wilson thought it would fly.

At 1:00 there was a knock on the door of suite 1412. Welcoming an opportunity to stretch his long legs, Cole said, "I'll get it," and walked to the door to admit Felix Blackburn, the prosecuting attorney assigned to oversee the legal end of drafting the wiretap application and obtaining the wiretap order from a Supreme Court judge. An unpresupposing man in brown cords and a windbreaker, Blackburn was tall and lanky with a prominent Adam's apple belying his fifty years: he looked like an overripe gawky teenager gone grey.

"I just love what you've done to this place," he said, shaking Cole's hand and setting down his briefcase. The sitting room's serene pastel decor had been destroyed. Grant's filing cabinets had been dumped in front of the fireplace. Most of the hardback chairs had been removed from the dining area and lined up next to the sofa, the sofa not being long enough to accommodate the stacks of debriefings, reports and case law. Two computer terminals sat on the dining table and a printer had been set up on the teak sideboard. A revised draft was printing as Blackburn took off his jacket.

He and Wilson had worked together on four of the six wire affidavits Wilson had sworn, and in Wilson's view having him in on this file from the start had been a necessity. A smart perfectionist who knew this area of the law, Blackburn provided objectivity and precision after Wilson was immersed in the file. They were a good team. Blackburn knew Cole and Pearce as well, having encountered them in the courtroom during his years as a prosecutor.

Once the niceties were out of the way, Blackburn accepted a cup of coffee and a copy of the draft affidavit. It was already eighty-seven pages long. The room was silent, except for the hum of the printer. Cole watched Blackburn for a moment. The attorney had seated himself at the dining table, and was already reading the draft, pencil in one hand and cup raised halfway to his lips, lost in thought.

The printer finished the second draft. Cole took it and walked to a chair in the sitting room to review it one more time. Wilson and Pearce got their copies, and the printer and room fell silent as all four men flipped pages and noted corrections and suggestions.

• • •

Oskar arrived at the designated McDonald's parking lot and drove around it looking for cops and bikers. Cops were usually easier to pick off—they seemed to have a finite number of makes and models of cars, and always seemed to conduct surveillance in pairs. Bikers, on the other hand, had no financial restrictions and drove what they wanted. Oskar figured he would only know there were extra bikers watching if they wanted him to.

As far as he could tell, the lot was clean. Little leaguers poured out of minivans with their dads; families went in for a late Saturday lunch. None of these adults could be there for the meet—neither group would expose their kids to this.

Oskar parked in the corner of the lot farthest from the restaurant. There wasn't another car within a hundred feet of him. He got out and leaned against the driver's door of the four-door rental. He would return it or dump it first thing after this little get-together; the identification he'd used to rent it was fake, so not returning it wouldn't be a problem. In any other situation he wouldn't have given it a second thought. But right now, what he didn't need was any additional heat, of any kind, so this time he'd probably return it.

At 2:10 they arrived. Two guys in their early thirties in shorts and ball team T-shirts in a five-year-old Cavalier. No motorcycles, no leather or tattoos or chains. Nothing out of the ordinary except the bad goatee and glasses on the tall one. Oskar had never seen them before.

The taller of the two spoke. "Glad to see you left the Porsche at home."

In the years that he and the others had controlled the streets, Oskar had favoured black, torqued-up Porsche 911s. He merely nodded.

The tall man then reached into the car and pulled out a wrinkled T-shirt, identical to the ones that he and his companion wore. "Put it on," he said.

Oskar nodded in understanding. He took off his own shirt, unconsciously pulling in his stomach, and stood bare-chested in front of them. He turned to throw his shirt in the rental, in a move that let them see his back. No wire, back or front.

"So far, so good," the tall one said. He turned to his companion. "Take him over by the fence and get him to put these on." He tossed him a pair of grey fleece shorts. They were not taking chances. Oskar could be wired in his groin.

"I'm not wearing a wire," he said.

"I'm pretty sure you're not, but why take avoidable risks."

Oskar and the short flunky walked over to the fence farthest from the street, where overhanging branches afforded some privacy. Shorty, shielding Oskar with a towel, stood and watched while Oskar removed his cowboy boots, then his jeans, and put on the shorts. They reached mid-thigh and as he pulled on his boots, he knew he looked ridiculous.

The tall asshole laughed as he watched their approach. The three men would have looked, to a casual observer, like three friends getting ready for a ball game, one good ol' boy having forgotten his sneakers.

"Everything okay?" the tall man asked.

Shorty nodded.

"Okay, my man, the instructions are you go barefoot." He kicked a piece of broken glass toward Oskar, and he and the short man laughed.

Oskar took off his boots and socks and put them on the back floor of the rental. He looked at the two assholes. "Are we going somewhere?"

"Yep. Hop in, buddy." The tall man was clearly the leader.

Oskar locked the rental car and started to get into the back seat of the Cavalier, but the short man stopped him.

"You know, I think it'd be better if I sit in back and you sit up front."

It occurred to Oskar that the short man only appeared to be an idiot. He knew Oskar could kill both of them from the back seat. But where would that have got him?

The tall one drove the car out of the parking lot. "We may as well introduce ourselves," he said. "That's Roddy and I'm Mike. We're your ride for the day."

Oskar said nothing. While he was currently owned, through circumstance, by "the machine," these idiots were so far down the food chain that they didn't warrant respect on an individual basis. Their instructions only had to be followed because they were actually someone else's instructions. These guys were just wannabes.

They were almost certainly more apprehensive than Oskar was. For the time being, he had something the club wanted:

he was in no way indispensable, but he was of value. He sat back in the car and yawned his lack of concern, and waited to see what would happen next.

The one called Mike drove the car to the exit driveway and into the curb lane, heading east. About thirty feet from the first intersection after the restaurant, he slipped into the middle eastbound lane, then the left turning lane, and made an expert U-turn in a brief opening in the oncoming traffic. Heading west, back toward the city's core, he watched his rear-view mirror: no one could tail that manoeuvre without him seeing.

A couple of miles later he turned off the main thoroughfare and drove into one of the city's older residential neighbourhoods. Small stucco houses with gravel lanes behind them. With one car coming toward them and another two blocks behind, Mike turned into one of the lanes, drove halfway down the block and backed the car into an empty garage. He turned off the engine. No one spoke.

After five minutes had passed with no cars crossing their bow, Mike started the car and drove back down the lane the way they'd come. Satisfied that they weren't being followed, he began humming to the radio and beating the palms of his hands on the steering wheel, presumably in time to the beat of the music. Oskar hoped it would be a short afternoon.

Twenty minutes later they pulled into a strip mall and parked outside a Tim Hortons. Mike looked at his watch. "We're a bit early, anyone want anything?"

Roddy wanted a box of Tim bits and a coke. Oskar ignored them both. Mike left the car and went into the donut shop.

Roddy broke the silence. "So, I've been wondering to myself what they got on you, Mr. Big buck-stud, fuck-everybody renegade-turned-pussy. Yup, I've been thinking, it must be pretty good."

Oskar turned in his seat to fix his icy blue eyes on the chubby, yappy little man in the back. The look made Roddy wish he'd kept his mouth shut. Oskar spoke quietly. "Tell me you're not so stupid that you expect me to answer that, Roddee. If you knew, you would have to die. And your friends wouldn't give a fuck."

Roddy was saved from having to come up with a convincing response by Mike's return to the car.

After settling back in and giving Roddy his order, Mike looked at his watch again and said, "Now it's your turn." He jabbed a sticky finger at the pay phone outside the donut shop. "It should ring in a minute or two. It'll be for you."

As if on cue, the phone rang. Oskar stepped out of the car and walked over to it. "Yeah."

Turning, he leaned back against the phone booth and scanned the parking lot. He was sure they were watching him. He stuck his hand in the side pocket of the shorts and kicked at a rock with his toe. He hoped the fuckers got the idea that he didn't really give a shit about them or the situation he was in.

"Glad you made it." The male voice was cheerful. Oskar could hear traffic in the background. The caller was, without a doubt, at a different pay phone making the call. Pay phone to pay phone, there was no way to connect this conversation with anyone, without visual surveillance placing the speaker on the phone at the time of the call. Smart.

Oskar felt a small piece of paper in the pocket, folded in half. Without thinking he pulled it out and looked at it. A name and address were written on it, for somewhere in Yaletown, an old warehouse district of Vancouver that was being developed and gentrified at the speed of light. He stuck the paper back in and waited.

"You need to bring us a hundred next Thursday."

One hundred kilos, even at a good price—like fifteen thousand dollars in California—still meant $1.5 million US.

"Financing?" Oskar asked, without expectation.

"Get it fronted."

Oskar's California contacts were not going to like fronting him the better part of a million and a half dollars worth of cocaine, notwithstanding their history together.

"That's not likely," Oskar said evenly.

"Then neither is your breathing come Friday morning. Put it together. You'll be contacted about where to bring it sometime Wednesday. Keep your pager charged."

The caller hung up.

Fuck. A hundred kilos in five days.

He could probably arrange for delivery of the stuff, payment to be made after he sold it. But if he didn't pay his suppliers promptly, he would end up dead. Presumably the club would not want to turn the tap off right away. He was going to have to count on them covering his purchase cost once they sold the coke at almost double the price. If they didn't, it would be next to impossible to come up with the money to cover it. When he was running with Andris and Yuri he wouldn't have worried about it—they had all had substantial stashes and debts that they could enforce. Without the group backup, raising a million and a half would be tricky.

The only chance he had was if the club wanted an ongoing source of the drug. They knew how the business worked; if they failed to cover his costs, poof—he and the deals would be over. So it all depended on whether or not they wanted a one-shot deal.

Oskar walked back to the car and got in, almost not noticing Mike and Roddy. He was thinking. Five days to put together a hundred kilos for them and find an opportunity in the operation for him.

He felt different driving back to the restaurant parking lot, almost excited. Right now they held most of the cards and could play them the way they wanted, but he knew somewhere in the exchange today and those to come, if he was careful, there would be a chance for him to get an edge. And in getting that edge he'd find a way to fuck up Frank Wesley like he'd never been done before, and he'd find a way to get the club off his back.

He wondered how the name on the paper scrap fit in. He had never heard of Rick Parker.

Changing lanes, Mike glanced briefly at Oskar. He was smiling.

• • •

After reading the draft affidavit, Felix Blackburn had spent the afternoon grilling Cole about Morrit and Pearce's informants' reliability and information. Peter Grant's cabinets had been opened and reopened as the police officers and attorney worked to set out why conventional investigative techniques such as undercover and surveillance would not work against the Warriors. By six o'clock Blackburn, Cole and Wilson were pretty pleased with the product.

Having concluded that little more was required than proofing for typos, they agreed to break until morning for the final review. Blackburn had arranged through the on-call court registrar to meet with a Supreme Court judge at noon on Sunday to apply for the wiretap court order. If everything went according to plan, McKeown and his installation team would have their copy of the order well before dark the next day.

With nothing official to do until the next morning, Cole agreed to meet the others for dinner at a nearby sports bar after a trip home for a run and a change of clothes. The sun was still up and the day's heat lingered. He was looking forward to a long, relaxing run along the seawall before a well-deserved beer.

A block from his car he heard his name called and, turning, saw Janine Wright stepping out of a flower shop, her arms full of parcels. She was accompanied by a strikingly attractive woman: tall with large green eyes, high cheekbones and a wide mouth, and long wavy brown hair escaping from a wild pony tail. Her beauty was exotic and full-blown, as though nature had decided to not hold anything back. Wearing a washed-out shirt and long skirt, and holding a bouquet of cornflowers in one hand, she was sexy in her simplicity. Cole realized he was staring.

He recovered and smiled at them. "Hi, Janine, what a nice surprise," he said. "You look like you've had a busy day."

She laughed. "We've been on a spree, to cheer up Lauren after a lousy start to her day. Only I've ended up doing the spreeing and she's been kind enough to be my sherpa." She motioned for her friend to join them. "Lauren, this is Jackson."

The woman stepped forward and extended her hand. It was cool and soft, but the grip was firm. Cole found himself wanting to remember this touch.

"A pleasure, Sergeant," she said, holding his eyes with hers.

Janine must have told her about Cole, and about their date the night before. He felt slightly off balance. "Jackson, please," he said to her. Reluctantly he let go of her hand. Turning to Janine, he asked, "Can I help you with your bags?"

"Sure, Jackson, that would be great." Her enthusiasm was evident. "While we walk, Lauren can tell you about her morning."

The beautiful woman with the green eyes demurred in her

low, throaty voice. "Why don't you two go ahead. I'm meeting a friend for dinner in the neighbourhood, so I think I'll just wander around for a bit." Lauren kissed Janine on the cheek, waved briefly to Cole and turned and walked away.

Cole had seen a flash of gold as she waved. She wore a wedding ring. It occurred to him that it had been years since he cared enough about a woman to notice that detail.

Janine did most of the talking as they walked two blocks to her car. After helping her load her parcels into it, he said it was nice to see her again.

No mention of future dates.

• • •

The room was aglow from the setting sun, a huge fireball that had just begun dipping into the molten ocean when Rick Parker was seated at his favourite table. It was tucked in at the far end of the room, opposite the entrance. It commanded a spectacular view of the ocean, and of the entrance of the restaurant.

Tonight he felt like he needed a wall at his back.

He watched Lauren enter the room and rose as she approached. She was the only woman in his life who he did this for; it was an almost unconscious display of appreciation. Their relationship had evolved over the past two years to the point where she was also the only woman that he had been alternately desperate to sleep with and thankful that he hadn't. She was without a doubt the only woman with whom he was truly friends.

Reaching him, she took both of his hands in hers and kissed him on the cheek. "It's so good to see you, Rick."

Right now he felt like she was probably the only person in the world who felt that way.

"You look beautiful, as ever," he said. It was true. She had changed her mind and gone home after leaving Janine, just long enough to shower and change into a black linen sleeveless dress. Her only jewellery was drop pearl earrings, a gold bangle and her ring.

They both knew that they were the most unlikely pair to become friends and that the bridge between their differences had been Martin. They had both loved him and their casual friendship, which had grown out of Martin and Rick's business dealings, had become cemented and special in the wake of his death. After what he had viewed as a healthy amount of solitary grieving, Rick had become a relentless pest to Lauren, refusing her "no's" to various invitations; arriving at her home the day of Christmas Eve with a car full of presents to take to the children's hospital, urging her to return to her own painting, keeping at her to reopen the gallery, pulling as many respectable strings as he could to ensure that the reopening gala was an event.

She was grateful to him and knew exactly how he had helped her return to the living. He had acknowledged that making her his pet project had been therapy for him as well. In return he had received her gratitude and loyalty and committed friendship: a place to go for a home-cooked meal with no expectations or pressures. A source of advice without judgement.

Lauren was aware that there were aspects of Rick's personal and business life that she didn't need or want to know about. He had grown up on Montreal's east side, the son of Italian immigrant garment workers whose life was a constant struggle. At a young age Ricky Pascelli had rejected the idea that poverty and glory were somehow connected. He had changed his name to something strong and waspy, and started cultivating business skills and a fast mouth which got him in and out of trouble. By the time he arrived in Vancouver he had made more money selling substandard condo units in

Toronto than his parents had earned between them since landing in Canada forty-six years before.

With a bit of a cushion, Rick had decided to leave residential sales behind and go after a bigger score: commercial real estate. That's when he had met Martin, who had been looking for an investment and heard about a marketplace complex going up on the west side. It had been started by some new kid on the block who'd got himself into trouble with overfinancing, and it could be picked up for a song. Rick had been the new kid on the block.

Martin had liked him immediately, sensing a highly developed work ethic and a good imagination underneath the bullshit and bravado. After two hours explaining what life would be like if Martin invested and how it would be if he didn't, the bullshit and bravado were gone. That was twelve years ago.

While only five years apart in age, Martin and Rick were miles apart in experience and sophistication, but Rick was a fast learner and keen to grab whatever tutelage Martin would offer. He had followed Martin's lead and obtained his securities licence, and they had opened their brokerage house, offering financial planning and advice and brokerage services, and mixing chutzpah and balls with expertise and refinement. Martin's instincts had been right. They made a good team and they made a lot of money.

When Martin had died, Rick had tried to appeal to the type of client Martin had attracted, but a sufficient number of their clients left to have a noticeable impact on the business. Rick had moved from the offices he and Martin had shared in the business core, to the smaller but trendier spot in Yaletown. He worried to himself and to Lauren that he couldn't make it without Martin. She always tried to convince him to the contrary; he wasn't so sure.

Then, about eighteen months ago, shortly after the office

move, a new client showed up. His name was Frank Wesley and he arrived promptly, dressed conservatively in a navy suit and dark paisley tie, and carrying a briefcase. He looked strong; not overdone, but solid and muscular under the wool gabardine suit. His face was pleasant.

He said he was interested in investments for his personal corporation, a surprisingly lucrative rose-growing business in the Valley. After being hugely pleased with moderate results, Wesley had introduced Rick to a few of his friends who also wanted investments.

It hadn't taken long for the certified cheques to be replaced by bearer bonds and cash. Rick was pretty sure he knew what was going on, but some of it was sticking to him and no one was getting hurt and he didn't know the source of the money for certain.

Then, about a year ago, Wesley approached him with a proposal: reactivate his realtor's licence and act for some clients on commercial and residential purchases, for a healthy commission plus a finder's fee to the tune of fifteen percent.

No questions asked. Except the one today: "How's Billy?"

Fuck.

He looked at Lauren, who was apparently mesmerized by the sunset. He couldn't tell whether she was simply being polite while he'd been lost in thought.

"Sorry I'm such bad company," he said. "It's been a lousy day. I talked to Joanne this morning, which always throws me off."

She smiled, "How's Billy?"

Rick froze for a moment, from the echo of the morning's call. Recovering, he smiled, "Superb without my influence, apparently." He wanted to stay away from the topic of Billy tonight, to stay on safe subjects. He had no intention of telling her about today's phone calls, or about his own greed and lack of moral fibre. He leaned forward. "Tell me about your day."

"Well, it started off rather strangely. I went to the gallery this morning to get things organized for the Tremblay show and when I got out of my car in the underground a man approached me. I initially pegged him as a homeless person who'd slept in the garage overnight, but now I'm not so sure . . . He spoke very well and he knew my association to Martin. He called me Mrs. Martin Grey."

Rick arched an eyebrow. "What exactly did he say to you?"

"He told me not to be alarmed. Not 'scared' or 'freaked out,' but 'alarmed.' It didn't fit him. Anyway, I was completely unravelled."

"What did you do?"

"Got out of there as quickly as I could, called Janine and went window shopping and lunching in the sunshine downtown."

"Sensible," he nodded. They both laughed.

Turning serious again, Rick looked at her with concern. "But you're right, Lauren, that is a bit strange—the name thing. Although if he's only recently down on his luck, he may have seen you at charities or in the paper."

"I suppose," she said. "But it was dark in the parkade and I have to admit I was unnerved. Scared, I guess, but now it doesn't seem so sinister."

"Good," he smiled. "Speaking of sinister, let's have an order of the Mussels Diablo and one more drink before we look at the menu. It's been too long since we've done this, and I want to draw it out as long as I can."

She confirmed that he was, in fact, brilliant, and sat back in her chair to enjoy the evening with this swaggering, glib man who had showed her his heart and whom she held to be a friend.

• • •

Wesley liked the room.

He had driven by the place often enough but had never stopped in. Surveying the length of it, candlelit and jazzy, he decided he would like to come back for pleasure.

He had declined the hostess's offer of the last table and made his way to a seat at the bar, a long mahogany antique with bevelled glass and ornate detail, spanning the wall, reflecting bottles and the dying sunset. And, from where he now sat, table fifty-seven.

He wanted to be seen before he made his move. He believed that dread—anticipation gone sick—was often more effective than surprise in these types of situations.

Until the meth farm purchase was signed, sealed and delivered, the pressure had to be maintained. It had to be impressed upon Parker that pursuing the kind of thoughts he had slurred about on the phone the other night was simply not an option, that he was so far past the point of no return that it wasn't even worth considering. The call that he'd arranged about the kid was probably enough, but Wesley never believed in taking chances: as long as he was being paid to ensure Parker's co-operation, he'd ensure it.

The club had no problem with the concept. Fucking with someone's head was always good fun, and there was no way Parker could be allowed to go to the police for a chat. Too much was already invested.

Wesley hadn't been planning on working for the next little while, but he'd got a very brief, cryptic call from the president of the East Side branch first thing that morning. Paul Lucci had made it clear that he'd appreciate it if Wesley would cement Parker's co-operation by paying him a little visit. Wesley couldn't see a down side. It was totally unrelated to the stiff in the bushes. It wasn't illegal. And it needed doing.

So there he was. Earning the ten-thousand-dollar-a-month retainer that was paid, tax-free, into a numbered account in Switzerland.

Parker had been under the club's surveillance since he left his office early that afternoon. Lucci had called Wesley an hour ago with Parker's position for the evening. A striker for the club had followed him to a restaurant in the West End and had seen Parker seated at a table in the back, looking out into the restaurant, alone.

Sipping his Beck's, Wesley studied Parker. Even with the omnipresent bags under his eyes, Parker looked more relaxed and happy than Wesley had ever seen him. He was no longer alone. He and a lady were finishing off their martinis and having an animated discussion with a waiter.

All Wesley could see of the woman was a tanned, toned left arm and black dress strap as she reached up and handed her empty cocktail glass to the waiter. Sleek arm, pretty hand, gold ring. The word *elegant* crossed his mind. He dismissed the thought: the woman wasn't his target.

Wesley ordered another Beck's and asked the bartender where the men's room was. He glanced back at Parker, who had spotted Wesley's face in the bar mirror. Parker had frozen. Wesley raised his beer to Parker's image in the mirror and smiled.

• • •

"What is it?" Lauren asked.

"Not what. Who." Rick wanted to find a way of not lying to her, but was not going to be truthful about his distress at an apparently chance meeting with this "client."

"A client is sitting at the bar," he explained. "Over the last few months we've lost a fair amount of money through deals that I've recommended. He's got quite a temper. The last thing I want to do tonight is discuss business with him."

As he finished, Wesley was easing off his stool.

"Fuck. Here he comes." Rick never used the word *fuck* around Lauren.

Wesley was walking toward them, looking tall and well-built and legit. Straight at the two of them, smile on his face.

"Ricky, what a coincidence." Wesley grasped Rick's shoulder and squeezed it hard. The lie in the greeting wasn't lost on Rick.

"Frank, good to see you." Rick had no choice but to play along. "Lauren, this is Frank Wesley. Frank, this is Lauren Grey."

The woman extended her hand and studied him openly with large, warm green eyes. "A pleasure," she said, in a low voice.

It was Wesley's turn to be startled. She had changed over the last two years. Nothing big—same great figure, hair. But the eyes had new lines from what he remembered, and the creases when she smiled had deepened. He felt a sense of sadness emanating from her. He shook it off.

Lauren caught the stranger's lines with an artist's quick appraisal. He was dark and powerful-looking. He wore a cashmere blazer over a black crew-neck sweater over a wide-shouldered, muscular body. His face was good, too: strong jaw, tanned skin above a short beard. All in all, a handsome man. He would likely give Rick a run for his money with the ladies. Was that what Rick's discomfort was about, more than bad business deals? There was definitely something emotional between them.

"Lauren Grey," Wesley said. "Aren't you connected to the Quinn Gallery on Georgia Street?"

"Yes I am," she said. She couldn't help smiling back.

"I was reading about your upcoming Tremblay exhibit," he said, charming. "I'm hoping to come and see it."

"You know Tremblay?" He was her favourite Canadian artist, and she enjoyed discussing his work with others who shared the passion.

"Not well, but I know what I like," Wesley said, smiling at her.

Rick could barely contain himself. This asshole was sounding humble and charming with, of all people, Lauren. The only way to salvage the evening was to make Wesley disappear. As the waiter arrived with the mussels, his opportunity came. He opened his mouth to ask Wesley to excuse them.

"Won't you join us in a glass of wine and a mussel or two?" asked Lauren. Rick stared at her incredulously as she smiled at both men. "No business talk, just art and wine for the duration. How's that?"

Wesley was smiling broadly at Rick. He turned to Lauren. "Thank you, Mrs. Grey," he responded, "but I don't want to intrude. Perhaps I'll drop by the gallery sometime."

"Please do."

And with that, he left.

"He seems nice," she said to Rick, who appeared to be sulking.

"He's not."

"Why not?"

"Let's not spoil dinner, Lauren. Just take my word for it, he's a most unpleasant man, even if he has heard of Louis Tremblay."

"Rick!" she admonished him. "Don't be a perfect prick." She laughed. "All right. We'll leave it. Let's dive in."

She squeezed lemon on the mussels and popped one in her mouth. Rick followed suit. They were cold.

Nothing tasted good to him for the rest of the evening.

They finished the affidavit just before ten Sunday morning. It wasn't literary perfection, but they were satisfied that it disclosed reasonable grounds to believe that evidence of a drug conspiracy would be found if a wiretap court order were granted and bugs were put into the new clubhouse.

Felix Blackburn sat at the dining room table of suite 1412 and reviewed the final draft one last time. Cole and Wilson sipped coffee quietly and watched him read. A question from Blackburn would mean more changes, possibly more tracking down of information which, after a good night's sleep, he might deem necessary to make disclosure of the investigation complete. Questions always meant more delay.

As the minutes ticked by and the pages turned, Cole felt a growing optimism. He tried to caution himself, for they had shared similar moments the day before, and then the lawyer had thought of another area that they needed to cover, and two hours later they were still working on it.

Finally, at 10:36, Blackburn put the red pen down, turned the final page and, pinching the corners of his eyes under his glasses, said, "Well done. I think we've got a winner here." He handed the document to Cole. "Read it over and confirm you're ready to swear to it."

Cole reviewed the affidavit one last time, ensuring that everything in it was something he'd be prepared to testify to in court. "Yeah, Felix. It's all here and it's all true."

The lawyer signed as commissioner of oaths and dated the document. "Okay," he said, "let's find us a judge." He reached for the hotel phone.

Cole left the lawyer to his arrangements and began making his own. He checked his gun and placed the shoulder holster on, covering it with his jacket. He placed an extra magazine in his briefcase along with the affidavit. You never knew.

He checked himself in the mirror. Acceptable. Tired-looking and in desperate need of a shave, but given the circumstances, presentable enough for a Sunday morning.

He left the hotel with Blackburn and Wilson and walked the two blocks to the Supreme Court. The security guard let them into the foyer, but only the lawyer and Cole were permitted into the innards of the building. They walked down dim halls faintly lit by slatted windows, past hundreds of shelves of court files and empty clerks' desks, until they reached the back of the building. There the guard stopped at a bank of elevators. He placed his security strip through the electronic scanner and the elevator doors opened. They entered.

Judge Sooles was waiting for them in his chambers on the fourth floor. He was seated at his desk, reading, but from his dress it was clear that a golf course was somewhere in his plans for the day.

"Judge, good of you to come in," Blackburn greeted him. "Sorry to've pulled you away from your game."

The older man laughed. "It's what I get paid the big bucks for, Felix." He turned to Cole, extending his hand. "Nice to see you, Sergeant."

"And you, Judge," Cole said. They shook hands and sat down around the judge's desk.

Sooles had been on the bench for more than ten years and Cole had testified before him twice. Once in a straightforward drug case and once in a gruesome murder case where the victim was a seven-year-old girl. Cole had obtained confessions acting undercover in both cases. In the murder case, his detailed testimony of what the accused had told him had brought even the court clerk, a woman with over twenty years' experience, to tears. It had been a long, tough trial that had shown off Cole's operational and inner strength. The judge had remarked on his uncanny recollection of detail, his objectivity and his professionalism. After cross-examining Cole, the defence counsel had told the prosecuting attorney that he wished he'd never heard of Sergeant Jackson Cole.

In both cases Cole had found Judge Sooles to be fair and logical and not afraid to control his courtroom. Before being appointed to the bench, Sooles had been known as an extremely good lawyer, and now he was renowned as a great criminal judge. As far as Cole was concerned, Sooles was the perfect draw for this particular task. If he reviewed the affidavit and said the grounds for a wiretap weren't there, then they weren't. On the other hand, if he found that they were, almost any other judge reviewing his finding would undoubtedly arrive at the same conclusion. Either way was good.

But there was more than that: Cole was certain that Sooles would ensure there was absolutely no leak from his office about the wiretaps.

"Let's have a look at what you've got. I assume, Sergeant

Cole, that you're the affiant on this application, is that right?"

Cole nodded.

"Okay, and Felix, you, in a leap of optimism, have an order prepared for my signature, assuming you've met the requirements?"

"That's right," the lawyer confirmed.

"Okay," the judge said. "Let's have 'em."

Cole passed the affidavit to the judge and Blackburn passed the prepared order.

"What are we looking at," the judge asked. "Chinese heroin?"

"No." Cole shook his head. "It's a bit different. It's an investigation into a Satan's Warriors' methamphetamine lab operation."

The judge raised an eyebrow. "Okay, you had better leave me to it. You can wait in the waiting room out front, or I can page you when I'm done, assuming that you're on pager."

"I am," Cole confirmed, "but I'd just as soon wait nearby, if you don't mind."

"Not a bit. Here," he said, passing over what he'd been reading. "You can fight over this to stave off boredom."

Cole looked at the publication in the judge's hand. It was no great treatise on legal principles; it was the current edition of *People* magazine.

An hour and a half later, Judge Sooles appeared at the door of his chambers and beckoned them in.

"I'm satisfied that this application should be granted," he told them. "And that there's urgency here." He looked at Blackburn. "I've signed your draft order. I'll just make you a copy and then as usual the order and the affidavit will be sealed, at least until charges get going before a trial judge, if there is a trial."

He copied the order, gave Blackburn the copies, then

placed the original affidavit and order in an envelope, sealed it and initialled the flap. Sooles placed the envelope in a wall safe. "I'll take the packet to the court registry personally tomorrow morning, and see that it's filed properly in the safe downstairs."

As he returned to his desk there was a knock at the chambers door.

"Come," the judge bellowed.

The security guard entered.

"Here's your escort out of here, gentlemen," the judge said to Cole and Blackburn.

He rose and shook hands with both men. They thanked him for his time and followed the security guard through the quiet courthouse out into the brilliant sunshine. 1:27.

Cole punched Superintendent Lawson's pager number into his cellular phone. "Cole here. We got it, sir," he said cryptically, then ended the call.

"That message should get things rolling," Blackburn said dryly. Cole nodded. "Well, Jackson, I didn't leave anything in the hotel room, so I think I'll get back to my Sunday. Here's your copy of the order."

He handed Cole the five-page document. The order set out the exact terms of the authorized wiretapping: who could be tapped, where and how. The technical people would need a copy to work from during their installation, to ensure compliance. This particular order authorized the police to install "automatic" bugs on the telephone lines of the new clubhouse and in its kitchen, living room, den and basement. These bugs would intercept and record continuously all conversations. The order also authorized "manual" bugs in the bedrooms of the house, meaning that communications could only be intercepted and recorded when specified people, or targets, were identified as speaking in the rooms.

"Thanks, Felix," Cole said. "I'll let you know how things turn out."

Blackburn looked at him. "Be sure to do that."

As Cole crossed Hornby Street on his way back to the hotel, his cell phone rang.

"Jackson?"

"Yes."

"Got your message," said Lawson. "Good work. Get your stuff together and come back to the meeting room. Grant and Wilson can pack up the equipment. All drafts are to be burned by them personally once they return to the office today. Pass on my order, will you, and impress on Grant that I expect this one to be followed."

"Yes, sir." Cole picked up on Lawson's stern humour.

"How long will you be?"

Cole looked at his watch. "Three-quarters of an hour, give or take."

"See you then," Lawson said.

Just under an hour later, Cole knocked on the closed door of Lawson's office.

"Enter," said McKeown's strong voice.

He walked in. McKeown, Lawson and Pearce sat around the large meeting table. Cole joined them.

"We'll bring you up to speed on what we've put together since our meeting yesterday morning," Lawson said.

Cole nodded.

"The security boys are ready for an entry into the residence at 11:00 tonight," Lawson said, nodding unconsciously in McKeown's direction. "The monitor room's been set up, in anticipation of your getting the order. The monitors are ready to start intercepting once the bugs are in." He paused. "Anyone not directly involved in the entry or the monitor room has been assigned to cover. We've had the place under surveillance since our meeting yesterday. So far no one's shown up."

"How are we going to ensure there's no surprise visit by one of our 'friends'?" Cole asked.

"We're working on that," Pearce said.

"I haven't seen the place yet," said Cole, "but you said it was at the end of a cul-de-sac, up on a hill, right?"

Pearce nodded.

Cole was thinking out loud. "Anyone coming to visit the house will be driving there. I think that's a safe assumption. Car or motorcycle."

Pearce nodded again in agreement.

"In a cul-de-sac there's only one way of getting in," Cole continued, "so we need to find a way to block that entrance, to either prevent an approach to the house while our people are inside, or at least slow the approach down sufficiently to let our men get out undetected."

"I had thought of that, too," Pearce said. "I was thinking about something like road construction."

Cole shook his head. "There are two problems with that: one, we couldn't pull off a realistic construction site in the time frame we're dealing with. Two, the bikers have people in the municipal works office who could tell them whether or not the work is legitimate."

There was silence around the table.

Cole finally spoke. "Why don't we stage a motor vehicle accident right at the entrance of the cul-de-sac, and ensure that it blocks the entrance completely. Add an undercover operator to pose as an injured pedestrian, and we've got an ambulance and attending patrol cars. All kinds of vehicles to obstruct passage into that street. That way, if anyone unexpected shows up, the officers posing as drivers can radio the installers and warn them that the bad guys are approaching on foot. I would think that a walk from the cul-de-sac entrance to the house would take enough time for our people to clear out."

"Yeah." Pearce was smiling and nodding. "I think that would definitely work."

Lawson liked the idea. It was easy to orchestrate, believable and likely to be effective. "What were you thinking of for the accident?" he asked Cole.

"I haven't got it completely worked out, but two long vehicles, like an old station wagon and a big '70s Fleetwood or Lincoln would work. They'd be long enough that if it was a head-on accident they would block the street to other vehicles, and they should be relatively cheap to get, for those money-conscious lads among us."

The others liked it.

"Pearce," Lawson directed, "page Inspector Rickson and get some money, and you and Staff Sergeant Grant can go car shopping."

"Consider it done," Pearce said. His enthusiasm was obvious as he strode out of the room.

Lawson turned to Cole. "I want you inside when the installations are being made."

He didn't have to say that Cole was perfectly suited to the task of supervising the installation of wiretap bugs. He was steel-nerved and made for high-stress assignments, exhibiting uncanny judgement in situations that would be too much for most men. He instilled confidence in nervous types just through his confidence in himself. On top of that, he was a master at stealth, surveillance and countersurveillance. And finally, he wasn't afraid to kill when necessary.

"Inside" meant providing cover at the installation site. If things went awry and someone got to the house with the installers still inside, Cole was one of the police officers who would prevent any of the police team from being hurt.

"Once the installations are done, you or Pearce will run the monitor room," Lawson said, looking at him. "It's your wire, so you choose the role you play."

Cole had run the monitors once before. It entailed ensuring security in the room where the tape recorders were rolling, and security and continuity of the original tapes before, during and after their duplication. It required co-ordinating and supporting the "civilian" monitors who worked the tapes and recorders, noting down significant conversations and tape footages in logs to bring to the investigators' attention.

It was an important job and it required commitment and organization from the start of the operation to the end of it. Cole knew he could do a good job, but the thought of being confined to that role, while others were out in the field following up leads off the tapes, made the choice easy.

"I'd like to stay in the field, if you don't mind," he said.

Lawson smiled, not surprised. "I'd do the same," he acknowledged. "All right, setup time is 22:30 hours. Do you know the Langley Legion, near the fairground on King George Highway?"

Cole did. It was a nondescript building on the outskirts of Langley, and it would be empty—except for the die-hards, who would be more interested in what was going on in their bottle than in the parking lot. The lot, which was huge, doubled as parking space for the adjacent fairground; it would be dark and nearly empty at 10:30 at night. It was a good choice for a meet.

"Meet your ride there," the superintendent instructed him. "The fewer vehicles out, the better. You and the installers will go in together; Pearce will drop you off. Black clothing and gun. You know the drill. And here." He tossed Cole a pair of night-vision goggles.

Cole caught them and placed them in his briefcase. "Anything else?" he asked.

The superintendent became serious. "Yes. You'll be in charge out there. I'm going to co-ordinate things from here, but it's your job to get those installers in and get them out, safely."

"Yes, sir," Cole said, knowing that getting caught by the club could be fatal. "It'll go fine."

The schedule left Cole with a few hours of his own, so he took the elevator down to the second floor and walked through the maze of bullpens to his office. He had done his notes detailing the meet with Morrit Friday afternoon. He would start now to log everything that had happened since the phone call Saturday morning.

Three hours later, he finished. Throughout the documenting of his police life over the past thirty-odd hours, had come the unbidden recollection of the striking woman who was with Janine the day before. Cole had been too busy up to this point to let her effect on him sink in, but now, trying to recall every detail about her, he had to admit that she had had one.

Excellent, he thought to himself sarcastically. He couldn't recall having such a strong feeling about someone in ages, if ever—not on the first glance. He tried to remember if that was how he had felt initially about Kate; if it had been, the feeling had been so mutated through their marriage that he couldn't remember it now.

A strong feeling about a complete stranger who was a friend of a perfectly fine woman, who happened to be a good friend of his best friend's wife. And with whom he had gone to dinner. Excellent indeed. It would be nearly impossible even to make modest inquiries about her without looking like a complete cad.

In his mind he could still see her smiling and waving. She was beautiful. As he examined possible ways to learn more about her without hurting Janine, he recalled with a jolt a detail: a gold band flashing. She was married. That solves that, he said to himself.

He secured his notebook in the office safe, intending to leave well enough alone. But on an impulse, walking past his desk, he picked up the phone. He told himself that these days a ring didn't always mean what it used to.

"Hey Jacko, what's up?" Don Edwards asked when he heard Cole's voice.

"Not much," said Cole casually. "Well, that's not quite accurate, but if I told you, I'd have to make you eat a cyanide capsule." It was an old line, but they both had a laugh. "I'm actually calling about someone you may know. How well do you know Janine Wright's circle of friends?"

"Pretty well," Edwards answered. "She and Liz have known each other for years. I don't think she's a security risk, Sherlock, if you told her something you shouldn't have. She's great, isn't she?"

"Yeah, she's great," Cole answered. "We bumped into each other downtown yesterday."

"Good," his friend said.

"Well, you might not think that when you hear the rest," Cole said.

"Uh oh, what happened?"

"She was with a friend of hers, a woman." Cole began to describe what had happened.

Edwards cut him off. "You've got to be kidding," he said incredulously. "You're interested in your blind date's friend? Jesus, Jackson. You know, Liz has a theory that you can't get into relationships with potential any longer, that you're obsessed by your job and that you should get your head read. I'm starting to agree." He stopped to catch his breath. "What is this woman going to think if you call her up behind Janine's back, not to mention Janine's feelings? I think she liked you."

"Yeah, Don, I know all that, and thanks for the vote of confidence on my mental health. I wouldn't be phoning you and giving Liz more fodder on that topic if this woman with Janine hadn't . . . hadn't . . ." He stopped, searching for the right word. "Struck me. You know that rare, rare feeling, when you feel like you've met someone before, or were destined to meet them? Have you ever had that feeling, Don? Has Liz?"

He'd hit home. Don and Liz were a good couple; they worked well together and Jackson was fond of his friend's wife, but it seemed to him that the days of being sure that they were made for each other were long gone.

Neither man spoke for a moment.

"When was the last time I spoke about a woman like this?" Cole asked.

"Okay, okay," Edwards relented. "What's her name?"

"Lauren something. I don't think Janine mentioned her last name."

"Lauren," Edwards mused. "No bells. Can you describe her?"

"She's thirty-three to thirty-seven. Long dark hair, wavy; amazing eyes, kind of greyish-green. Classy, beautiful."

Don began laughing. "Wedding ring?" he asked.

"That's partly why I'm calling."

"Well, Jacko," Don said, clearly enjoying himself, "you may not set your sights often, but when you set 'em, you set 'em high. That's Lauren Grey. She's a widow. Independently wealthy, and independently independent. She runs the Quinn Gallery on Georgia Street. Oh, and Jack, there's one more thing you should know about her."

"What's that?" Cole wasn't sure he liked the delight in Edwards's voice.

"She doesn't date."

"Well, that's encouraging," Cole said dryly.

"It was a pleasure filling you in." Edwards sounded like he meant that. "Drop by for dinner soon. The kids miss you."

"Maybe I'll bring the undateable Widow Grey."

"You'd be a good match on that score."

They both laughed and hung up.

Cole looked at his watch. 5:40. On a Sunday. Most shops would have closed at five.

Even if she was interested, it was not fair. His time was completely unpredictable: one week he would be here, the next he would be gone. For months.

He grabbed the phone book, wondering why he was doing this. As he flipped through the pages he knew that the answer was simple: if he didn't, he'd wish he had. And that hadn't happened in a very long time.

He looked up the address for the Quinn Gallery and then phoned the florist he called whenever a friend's wife had a baby. The proprietress answered the phone.

"Hey, great, you're still open."

"Actually we're not," she replied. "I thought you were my ride calling to say why you were late."

"Hmm," said Cole. "This isn't Janet, by chance, is it?"

"Yes, who've I got?"

"It's Jackson Cole," he said. "The Mountie."

"Well, hello, officer. I suppose I could still be open for you."

He laughed. "That's just great, Janet. I appreciate it."

"Another baby?"

"No, actually, they're for a grownup this time."

"Aaah," she replied. "And what are you looking for?"

"Something amazing," he answered. "Lots of summer flowers. You're the creator, use your imagination, but lots of colour and scent." He thought of Lauren. He wanted the flowers to make her beautiful face light up.

Janet described a number of flowers, some of which Cole recognized the names of. "It will be spectacular," she said.

"That's what we want."

"And what should the note say?"

He hadn't thought it out that far. He wanted to get to know this woman, and didn't mind her knowing it. On the other hand, a bit of mystery wouldn't hurt, and it might give him some time to speak with Janine.

"Something simple," he replied. "How about, Lauren, it was a pleasure meeting you yesterday. I hope we meet again."

"Cupid struck at a first meeting?" The florist couldn't resist. She had never been able to figure out why this hunk always seemed unattached.

"Yes."

"Well, for what it's worth, I'd like it if I was getting it. It shows you like her but it's not mushy."

"Good enough. If she doesn't, maybe I'll just track you down," he said lightly.

"In my dreams, Jackson Cole, but it's a nice fantasy," she laughed. "Where do you want the flowers delivered?"

He gave her the gallery's address.

"Okay," she said. "I'll bill you."

"Excellent, Janet. Have a nice evening."

"You too."

They hung up. He was excited.

• • •

Cole arrived at the fairground parking lot at 10:25. He wore black pants, a black turtleneck sweater and black shoes. A black fanny pack held his extra clips and goggles. He felt for his gun and grabbed a wool balaclava as he got out of the truck. He would be tough to spot in the shadows.

The rest of Team One were already there. The three installers, Sergeant Rathie and Corporals Winter and MacDonald, had arrived together moments earlier in a Pathfinder truck, dressed like Cole and carrying their equipment.

Pearce arrived last. He wore casual civilian clothes. His job was to drop the team off near the site and pick them up at the same spot once they advised him by radio that the job was done.

Team Two was made up of four top-notch cover men who had been recruited for the night to make the entry, along with McKeown and one of his security men. They were already at the site, checking to ensure that it was unoccupied.

Cole joined the other Team One members in the Pathfinder. As Pearce drove the vehicle toward their destination, Cole used a cell phone to speak with Superintendent Lawson, who had assumed the role of operation commander. He was in telephone and cipher radio communication with all three teams and was aware of their respective progress.

"Cole here. How are things out at the site?" The need to be cryptic was extreme: cellular phone conversation could easily be picked up by scanners.

"All clear," replied Lawson. "Your ETA?"

"Ten minutes should do it," Cole replied.

"Fine, I'll advise the other two teams."

Team Three was composed of three middle-aged undercover operators. Two of them were parked a block away from the intersection near the cul-de-sac, in opposite directions, in big, old beat-up cars. The third operator was on foot, walking toward the intersection. He moonlighted on movie sets as a stunt man. Tonight he carried a small rubber sack concealed in his left hand and another one in his left front pants pocket. When punctured, they would release imitation blood.

Team Three's timing was going to have to be perfect for the head-on collision to occur in the exact spot desired, with its attendant pedestrian victim. The cars would start rolling toward each other once Lawson gave the word. The pedestrian would receive the signal through the radio transceiver hooked behind his ear.

Eight minutes later Cole's team passed the site. The driveway to the new clubhouse started at the end of a short street and wound up a long hill to the house. Most of the trees had been removed during the landscaping process five years ago, and as a result the house afforded an unobstructed view of the property and street. Conversely, anyone watching the house would easily spot someone approaching it from the front, even in the dim light of nighttime suburbia.

They continued past the cul-de-sac and drove a circular quarter mile to the entrance of a heavily treed municipal park. The park backed onto the rear of the property. Pearce pulled the truck into the parking lot and stopped in the corner farthest away from the lights. There, in the shadows, Cole and the three installers got out of the truck and made for the cover of the tall cedars.

None of the four men had been in the park before. Cole had studied a map and photos of the area taken by an operator earlier that day. Now, wearing the night vision goggles Lawson had given him, he led the way. He had calculated a path through the park to the edge of the target back yard. It was marked by a twelve-foot cedar fence that no doubt would be replaced by wire and electricity once the new owners took over.

The area had been checked out by Team Two, the security men and cover team that had preceded Cole's group thirty minutes earlier. No booby traps or countersurveillance devices had yet been installed by the club, or Cole would have heard.

They travelled quickly through the forest, stepping over fallen trees and through brush. At a near-run it took them almost ten minutes to reach the fence. They scaled it and surveyed the other side.

The house was still several hundred yards away. The first two-thirds of this distance was still forested, giving way to sloping lawn nearer the house. The security boys had assured Cole that that would be one of the club's first changes: open up the back view to prevent exactly this type of activity.

The wind picked up as they moved across the property, keeping in the cover of the trees. They moved in concert toward the darkened house.

When they reached the edge of the clearing, Cole whispered to the three men with him to remain there, in the dark shadows of the black trees. He ran the last hundred yards to the house. It looked deserted, but when he crossed the back porch and reached the kitchen door, it was unlocked. The security team was in.

He ran silently back down the porch steps and waved to the installers to follow. Three dark figures stepped immediately from the forest boughs into the clearing. They joined him at the back door.

Cole entered first, gun drawn, just in case. He scanned the kitchen quickly. McKeown was standing by the stove, clothed in black, gun also drawn. They nodded and Cole waved the installers in. There had been no talking since they had left the truck.

Now Rathie, in charge of the installation, took command.

Cole returned to the back porch, watching the area from which they'd come. He knew the other members of the security and countersurveillance team were doing the same thing about the property. Radio silence was to be broken only in case of an emergency.

He looked at his watch: 10:57. They were to leave exactly two and a half hours after the time of their entry. He set his watch alarm and stood, legs apart, back against the house, gun in hand.

The house was strangely silent for a building that had nine people in it. Nine intruders, silently and darkly entering and leaving rooms, performing tasks they had carried out on hundreds of similar nights.

The wind pushed clouds across the face of the moon, killing all outside light. Frogs chirped noisily from somewhere down the hill until the rain started. It began daintily, soft drops on the verandah roof, and then the sky opened up and it poured.

Cole was grateful it had waited until they were in: rain would have meant mud, and the possibility of mud being left behind, or having to be cleaned up. Risks and delays.

He checked his watch: 12:11. He was freezing. The house and grounds were so quiet that he felt like the only person there. He had often had this experience when on surveillances, the sensation of being oddly alone once the team dispersed.

At 12:35, Rathie, the chief installer, joined him on the porch.

"Everything okay?" Cole asked in a whisper.

"The installations that are in look good. MacDonald and Winter are wrapping up the last two bugs. I'll just do a quick check on the transmitters." His last task on the install job was to use his mini-receiver to ensure the transmitters hidden in the house were working. He looked at Cole's dark profile. "Okay to walk around the property?"

"You'd have to be God to see someone tonight," Cole replied, "but I'll cover you." Both men stepped off the porch and into the downpour.

As they approached the west side of the house, Cole's pager vibrated. He lifted the edge of his sweater: the pager's face glowed "911."

"Hold on, Pat," he hissed.

911. Emergency. It was the "go to radio" signal.

He pulled his hand-held free from his belt and turned it

on. They were using a scrambled frequency, but technology being what it is, no chances were to be taken—including direct references to the night's activities.

"Cole," he whispered.

It was Lawson's voice, tense. "Two feet have penetrated the perimeter. Clear out. Do you copy?"

"Loud and clear."

Cole was already moving. "Feet" was a code for pedestrians. The perimeter was the entrance of the cul-de-sac where the car accident had been staged to cover the team as it went in. Now, for some reason, two people were walking toward the clubhouse. Lawson's instructions were crystal clear. Regardless of the progress, all team members were to get out of the house immediately and get back to the trees, to the park for pickup.

"Trouble?" Rathie asked in a whisper.

"Yes, we've got company. Time to clear out. How did you do?"

"I'd like five more minutes to confirm the living room installation," Rathie whispered back, "but we've got definite coverage for the kitchen, family room, basement and two of the bedrooms."

"Good enough," Cole said tersely. "Wait by the back door. I'm going in to get the others."

He ran up the stairs to the verandah. Just as he was about to step onto the porch planking he remembered the rain. No muddy prints. He had to take valuable seconds to untie his shoes.

In his stocking feet he ran into the dark kitchen. Empty. He made for the living room. McKeown and the other security man were there. "Is there anyone else on this floor?" Cole asked.

McKeown nodded. "Winter is just finishing up the camera installation at the front."

"Okay," said Cole, "I'll deal with that. Meet us at the back door. Tom, go to the basement and let the guys there know it's time to evacuate, pronto."

Cole raced into the front hall where Winter sat on a three-foot stepladder, hunched over something. The wires from the hall light fixture dangled above him. Winter looked up as Cole entered the hall. "What's up?" he asked softly.

"We've got to get out of here. Company. Where's the light fixture?"

"Right here." Winter pointed to his lap. "I can't get the fucking lens to angle properly." It was Corporal Winter's task to install a video camera, to photograph visitors to the clubhouse. "Right now," he went on, "all we're gonna get is a bunch of navel shots."

"That's better than our getting shot," Cole said evenly. "Forget the install. Get the light back up and let's go."

Winter was moving. "How much time?"

"Not much," Cole replied.

He looked out the living room window at the sloping front lawn. Through the pouring rain he could make out two figures approaching the driveway. They would be at the front door in less than five minutes. If they reached the house before Winter finished, the first thing they would see when they opened the front door would be a lean cop dressed like a black ant standing on a ladder. And Cole's gun.

The project would be blown. Illicit club activity would stop until the bikers figured the cops had gotten bored and given up. They might even try a few civil suits against the Mounties for entering. Post-traumatic stress disorder as a result of bumping into Adam Ant at midnight.

Fuck.

Cole ran back to the front hall. Winter was now standing on the ladder, arms outstretched, holding up a glass and chrome dome. "How much longer?" Cole asked.

"I'm almost done. It'd be going faster if I wasn't sweating like a pig," Winter whispered. "It's an awkward angle, the screwdriver keeps slipping."

"We have no time," Cole said through gritted teeth. "They'll be here in a couple of minutes. I'm going to tell the others to go, and when I come back we leave."

Winter grunted. He had not once averted his glance from his task.

Cole ran through the house to the kitchen. Through the window he saw McKeown and the seven other men standing at the foot of the verandah stairs. He opened the door. "Move out," he ordered. "Winter and I will meet you at the pickup site. Move!"

He turned and ran back in. The adrenaline was turning to acid in his stomach. He crouched at the living room window. The two figures were less than fifty feet away. He could make them out now: a male, late teens, and a girl a bit younger, both soaked. No leather, no hogs. No club members. Likely not even wannabes. Still, they had eyes and mouths. What the hell were they doing here?

Then, ten paces closer to the house, the boy pulled the girl toward him and they kissed. The penny dropped.

Cole ran to Winter. "We've got to go. Now," he ordered. "They're a minute away."

Winter turned away from the ceiling and stepped down the three rungs of the ladder. He collapsed it noiselessly and placed a screwdriver and spool of wire into a small black backpack. "All set," he whispered.

Cole grabbed the ladder. They heard laughter just beyond the front door as they sprinted for the back of the house.

In the monitor room, at 00:42:07 hours, Installation Number Two, which was located in the front living area, transmitted the sound of the front door opening. Installation

Number Six, located in the kitchen, transmitted the sound of the back door being opened at 00:42:05 and shut and locked at 00:42:09.

Monday, June 15, 1998

S un filtered through the alder and cedar, dappling the shore of the little creek and the rock against which Miss Kitty Trimble leaned. She was happy to have a moment of repose: the walk into the forest with her grade threes had set off that terrible wheezing. She closed her eyes, enjoying the solitude and sounds of gently flowing water and excited children on their scavenger hunt.

She wasn't quite asleep when Jeffrey screamed.

Later, talking to the Vancouver City Police homicide detectives, she recalled that the scream seemed to stay in one place for a long while, and then it came "lickety split" toward her and their base camp. Eight-year-old Jeffrey broke into the clearing, hysterical.

Miss Trimble grabbed the sobbing boy by the shoulders and pulled him to her fleshy bosom. "What is it, sweetheart? Calm down, now." She was trying to remain calm herself. "Where are Matthew and Tyler? Are they all right?"

Jeffrey pulled himself together enough to nod and blink his wet, dark lashes. He swiped at his nose with the back of his hand and the snot clothesline snapped as Matthew and Tyler ran into the clearing. From what Miss Trimble could gather, the boys had seen something ugly and terrifying, something that smelled bad. They refused to show her the exact spot of their grisly find. They were so upset that she believed that something horrible did lie within the shadows of the leafy forest.

After settling them down somewhat, she blew her steel PE whistle four times—the emergency signal—to gather the group. The rest of the kids and the three helping mothers met at the bridge.

It sounded as though the boys had stumbled upon what the newspapers would call "human remains." However, knowing her charges' insatiable appetite for Power Rangers and mystery, Miss Trimble decided to check out the situation before troubling the authorities. She had no desire to be the laughingstock of the teaching staff by calling in the police over a coyote corpse.

She took charge.

"All right, Mrs. Walker, you have a cellular telephone with you, don't you? Very good. You stay here at the bridge with Matthew, Tyler and Jeffrey. All the rest of you," and she clapped her hands for attention, "you go back to the class-room with Mrs. Ma and Mrs. Chester. No straggling. All right, away you go. We'll be back soon."

She and Mrs. Walker sat the three boys down on the bot-tom step of the little footbridge. She pulled out a bag of candy dinosaurs and insects and, after taking a handful, passed them to Jeffrey to share around.

"Now, Jeffrey, what exactly did you see?" She was on her haunches, eye to eye with him.

The words tumbled out. "I saw a dead guy. I was looking

158

for a horsetail and heard the sound of water, so I went into the bush and found a spot and there was a bad smell and I saw this guy. His face is all yucked up slimy and flies are crawling all over it. He looks," Jeffrey was crying again, "he looks like a black monster."

Miss Trimble patted his hands comfortingly. "Could it have been pretend, Jeffrey?" she asked quietly.

"No."

"Could you show me where it is?"

"Nope." He shook his head, looking at the ground.

"Fair enough. Can you tell me how to get there?"

The little boy nodded.

"Okay," she said. She waited for Jeffrey to look at her. "Jeffrey, you know that calling the police is a serious thing to do, don't you?"

He nodded and swiped his nose again with the back of his small, dirty hand.

"Jeffrey, should I call the police because of what you saw?"

He looked straight at her and nodded earnestly.

Miss Trimble believed in her children and believed it was important that they know it. "Mrs. Walker, based on what Jeffrey has said, I think we should call the police. Perhaps I should just go take a look, so that we can tell them exactly where to find it. What do you think, Jeffrey?"

He nodded once more and described how to reach the spot: go past the cedar tree with the white fungus growing out of it, referred to in question number seventeen in the scavenger hunt, turn right almost immediately, down into a dry ravine and up onto the other side and toward the creek, into a clearing.

"All rightie." Miss Trimble brushed the crease in her canvas shorts nervously. "I'll be back shortly." And off she went.

She spotted the fungus in no time and hurtled through

fern and salal into the gulch and up the other side. She could hear the stream again. She careened out of the foliage and into the clearing at a run.

The stench made her halt. And then she saw it, and vomited all over her freshly pressed blouse and cotton shorts.

• • •

"What a fucking mess," Detective Bell said, almost absent-mindedly.

"You said it. She had dried puke in her nostrils, and what was that blue and green jelly shit on her shirt?" his partner asked.

"I wasn't talking about the civilian, I was talking about Mr. Carrion over there." After years of investigating homicides, Detective Bell had gotten good at guessing the gender of corpses that had played more than their fair role in the food chain, by looking at the scene evidence, if enough was available. He was even pretty good with transvestites and transsexuals, where the rotting clothes gave one message, the femur size another.

"Isn't this delightful," he continued. "We've got a rotten corpse, delay in crime discovery, a crime scene that's been disturbed by a kid, a teacher, a flatfoot—not to mention all of Bambi's friends and relatives. And to top it off, Mr. Carrion is not the victim of a jealous husband, he is a Somebody in the game."

Detective Patroni sighed. Bell was right, only Somebodies got hit like this. By another Somebody.

"Who do we know that's missing?" Patroni asked.

"I haven't heard a peep about anyone." Bell shook his head as he opened up the Crime Scene Kit.

"Me neither."

They had worked together on homicide for eleven years

and were plugged into the scene. If someone important was missing, they'd hear about it.

"Judging from the size of our friend here, he isn't Asian," Patroni observed.

Bell nodded in agreement and tossed his partner a roll of yellow tape with the words Police Line—Do Not Cross written repeatedly over its length. "Still fresh meat," he said. "Still house flies around. I'd give it four or five days."

The two detectives began to rope off a 160-square-foot section of the forest around the body. This area would be examined scrupulously, dirt sifted for clues discarded by the killer, soil samples taken for signs of larvae, everything inspected for indications of the time of death. Both men knew it was probably futile as they began the painstaking procedure required at a murder scene. The forensic entomologist would likely be able to pin down a reasonably accurate time of death, but much evidence would have been washed or eaten or carried away.

Bell voiced their thoughts. "Rain, animal intervention, people. Pro's. Fuck."

The body lay in the centre of the yellow ring, melting into the earth.

The left eye was gone now. The larvae laid by the blowflies had stopped feeding and wandered away from the body, into the clothes and into the soil, to find a safe place to pupate. They were the only living clues the detectives expected to find in this homicide investigation: the insects' stage of development would help the coroner establish a time of death. It was unlikely that anything else alive would be stupid enough to give up clues about this hit.

• • •

Danny Fox was exhausted. It had been a busy night, desperation being the mother of motivation. He'd ripped off a minivan from a theatre parking lot after watching a family of five disembark, the kids excitedly talking about the movie. He figured he had two hours, at the outside, before the van was reported stolen.

He'd headed for the suburbs south of the Vancouver city core, driving the speed limit.

8:55. The light was against him: because of daylight savings, it wouldn't be good and dark for another hour or so. Dusk would have to do. He visited three homes, each time parking the van in a covered carport, backing onto a laneway. He was fast and efficient and didn't really care about being confronted by anyone.

The first two houses were disappointing. Very little jewellery, just the usual electronic equipment, which was fenceable but low in resale value, and bulky. He'd tossed both places, taking little. At the third place, he hit pay dirt in the ice cube trays—a pair of good-sized diamond earrings and an emerald pendant. Gold chains and hoop earrings in the walk-in closet, along with what appeared at first glance to be a decent coin collection. A home alarm company would do business with these folk tomorrow, he thought, getting into the van.

10:10.

He considered returning the van to the cinema lot and decided against it. If the old man had just been dropping the rest of the family off, the van would already be hot. He drove down a lane a mile away from the third house, parked the van, locked it and left. Then he headed for the skids.

He traded one of the gold chains with Daisy, a transsexual prostitute with a penchant for glitter, for a gram of heroin and headed for his room. He'd get rid of the rest of the stuff properly tomorrow. The stones were probably worth a fair dollar. Then he'd resupply and begin the score in earnest.

He cranked a tenth of a gram into his arm, reread the note he'd written one last time, and staggered to the bed frame with its soiled mattress of stripes.

Tuesday, June 16, 1998

L auren let the Jag idle by the laurel hedge at the top of the driveway as she hopped out to grab the mail. She figured she just had time to shower and change before Janine picked her up. They had reservations at a new Italian place in Yaletown and tickets to a rare performance of Bette Midler at the Orpheum Theatre downtown.

She guided the car down the curve of the drive, beamed the garage door open and parked. She turned off and reset the alarm and walked into the kitchen, sifting through the mail: a catalogue from Sotheby's, an American Express bill, a postcard from a friend travelling in Italy and a postcard from Vancouver, showing the downtown skyline at sunset. A promo for what? she wondered, turning the card over. "To Mrs. Martin Grey." She didn't recognize the hand. The message was short, printed in block letters.

She sagged against the oak cupboards and slid down to sit on the tile floor.

DEAR MRS. GREY,
IF YOU ARE INTERESTED IN KNOWING
WHAT REALLY HAPPENED TO YOUR
HUSBAND, MEET ME. THE WHALE
STATUE AT THE AQUARIUM TOMORROW
AT 2:00. NO POLICE. YOU WILL KNOW
ME. I MEAN YOU NO HARM.

Lauren felt dizzy. It was surreal. She had had to accept the coroner's conclusion that Martin had been impaired when he had driven off that cliff, but she had never believed it. She knew Martin. He had been a social drinker and he never drank and drove. They both had too much to live for, and the price of a cab was meaningless when you considered that.

I MEAN YOU NO HARM. The little man in the underground had used the identical phrase.

She looked at the postcard again. What was it that wasn't right? And then she noticed: there was no stamp or postmark. He had hand-delivered it. He had been here. He knew where she worked and now he knew where she lived.

He might still be here. Watching her.

She looked around quickly. There were no windows he would be able to see her through right now. But if she stood up she'd be visible through the kitchen windows facing the ocean and side windows to the west. He might have seen her slide down, which might make him think she was weak.

She crawled across the kitchen floor to the knife drawer and pulled out a cleaver, sweating hard. As she closed the drawer, the phone rang. She jumped. The phone was on the counter, ten feet away. Human contact would be good. Reach the outside world and get help.

Unless it was him, maybe calling from one of the other phones in the house. She remembered a ghost story that she'd always hated as a kid, about a babysitter and a psycho who'd killed all the kids and then phoned the sitter from inside the house. She was paralyzed.

She watched the phone and the answering machine, crouched against the cabinet, clutching the cleaver, as she listened to her voice fill the kitchen: "Please leave your message after the tone . . . *beeeep.*"

Blood thundered in her ears. What would he say? Why was this happening?

"Lauren, it's Janine. Call me when you get this. I'm running late and think Japanese would be faster than Italian. Let me know if that appeals—"

Lauren lunged for the phone, knocking the cradle off the counter.

"Janine," she whispered.

"Lauren, what's wrong?"

"Janine, can you come over, right now? Shower here, borrow something to wear. Please?"

"Jesus, Lauren, you're scaring me. What's wrong?"

"Please come. Probably nothing. Use the front door, okay?"

"Okay. I'm on my way."

"Are you on your cell?" Lauren asked.

"Yes."

"Okay, don't hang up. If something happens and I stop talking, call 911 and don't come in."

"Lauren," Janine said, "maybe you should come out."

"I can't, Janine." Her voice fell to a hoarse whisper. "It's about Martin."

They agreed to look as casually normal as possible, just in case someone was watching, and they stayed on the line as Janine located her keys, got in her car and drove over. She announced her arrival by a cheery honk of her car horn, then got out of the car, still wearing her suit from a day of meetings. She waved to Lauren, who stood in the doorway in a pleated tennis skirt and sweater.

"Great legs!" Janine shouted. She regretted the words the moment they were out. What if this guy who might be watching was some sexual psycho? "Boy, could I use a drink."

They entered the marble tile foyer and closed the door. In the cool privacy, the two women hugged.

"What's going on?" Janine asked.

Lauren showed her the postcard.

"Very weird, and very creepy," Janine observed. "You're right. It was hand-delivered by someone." She paused. "'You will know me.' Who do you think it is?"

"Remember the guy in my parkade at the gallery?" Lauren asked.

Janine nodded.

"I'm convinced it's him. That's exactly what he said—'I mean you no harm'—when he saw me there."

"If he wanted to talk to you, then why not talk to you there?"

"I don't know," Lauren murmured. "He's going to an awful lot of trouble to get my attention. Maybe he didn't want to scare me off. Let's face it, not many women are going to hang around a dark parkade to discuss their dead husband with a strange man."

"But then why go there at all?" Janine persisted. "Why not do the postcard thing from the start? He could have left one there."

"I don't know."

"What are you going to do?"

Lauren poured a couple of ounces of Glen Livet into two crystal glasses, plunked ice into each and turned back to her friend.

"I'm going to meet him," she said simply. "You know that."

Of course Janine knew it. Lauren had never wholly believed the police's theory about Martin's death, and if some sicko was aware of that, they could twist her. After tortured dreams and long periods of dark depression, Lauren had been doing well for over a year.

"Let's think about this," Janine said. "What could he want? I'm sure if he were just Joe Honest Citizen who had something to tell, he'd have come forward long ago." She paused, sipping her drink. "You said the guy in the garage looked destitute, right?"

Lauren nodded.

"Then he probably wants money," Janine surmised. "Lauren, honey, the gallery's been in the paper because of the Tremblay show, you've been in it because of the fundraising, and Martin wasn't exactly an unknown. Don't set yourself up for something. Just let it go."

Feeling the Scotch burn the back of her throat, like it should, Lauren tilted her head back and closed her eyes, leaning against the counter. She had listened to every word her friend had said and knew that she was absolutely right.

"So," she said to Janine. "Will you come with me?"

Wednesday, June 17, 1998

They had missed the concert, electing to have another drink as Lauren packed an overnight bag. Sleeping in the house would be impossible, so she had accepted Janine's invitation to spend the night on the couch in her condo.

Still, she awoke exhausted. The night had been filled with dreams and awakenings: in one, she was at the gallery, approaching a patron whose back was to her. She could see his left hand as his fingers traced one of the jade sculptures. It was Martin's hand. She spoke his name in her sleep and he turned to her, but his face was the face of another—the face of the man she had met at the restaurant with Rick. She awoke, sickeningly disappointed. 2:47. Eventually she went back to sleep, slightly disturbed. Then she slipped into the world of the Aquarium, where she sat on a sunlit bench and waited and waited and waited. No one ever came. She heard a man laughing somewhere.

It was a long dream. 3:04.

At 6:12 she gave up and went quietly to Janine's kitchen to make coffee. It was pouring rain outside. So much for sunlit benches and dreams.

Eight hours to kill.

• • •

Fox awoke in the Auckland Rooming House about an hour after Lauren had awakened. He heard rain pounding on the street before he opened his eyes. Shit. He wondered if she'd show up in this weather.

He'd chosen the location of their meeting carefully. The Aquarium was the perfect spot—crowded, upbeat, full of tourists and families all over the place, right in the middle of Stanley Park to make her feel safe. And it was not unusual to see street people near the entrance, hoping for a handout, so he wouldn't stand out or be asked to leave. They could speak to each other without attracting too much attention.

This first real meeting was crucial: it was his only opportunity to sink the hook. If she didn't bite the first time, he'd have to give up on the idea. He didn't need an influential lady going to the police and laying a nuisance complaint against him. He was pretty sure there was nothing illegal in his plan, but being on parole makes you careful.

And now it was stinkin' raining.

He stood on the chair, pulled out the loose ceiling tile in the corner and grabbed his stash from the night before. He fixed and sat on the bed to think.

Around ten, he convinced himself that the rain had let up a bit and decided to go ahead with his plan. He placed the pants and shirt that he had washed the day before into a plastic bag, along with a disposable razor, a sliver of soap and a comb. He put on his shoes and socks and, wearing the T-shirt and shorts he had slept in, picked up the plastic bag and let himself out. He walked down the stairs and out past the gargoyles and monsters to the mission for breakfast and a free shower.

• • •

The bronze Haida sculpture of the killer whale jumped statically in its pool outside the entrance to the Aquarium. In the middle of the afternoon on a sunny June day the place would have been crawling with people. In today's deluge, it was deserted.

The lights in the gift shop were warm and inviting. Lauren was glad that Janine was in there now. Close enough to get help if necessary, but not so close as to be evident and spoil the meeting. Standing by the sculpture underneath an old golf umbrella, she checked her watch. 1:58. She shivered, more from dread and excitement than from the cold damp.

"Where's your girlfriend?"

Lauren jumped. The voice was low and husky and very close behind her. When she turned, she was face to face with the scrawny stranger from the parkade.

She almost said, "What girlfriend?" but something in his cold blue eyes changed her mind.

"Inside the gift shop," she replied evenly, "watching us."

He nodded. "I don't care that you brought backup." His voice had a singsong rhythm to it, laced with a hint of amusement when he referred to backup. "But don't ever make the mistake of thinking I'm stupid when you're dealing with me."

The eyes were almost white.

Lauren nodded, wondering how he'd known Janine had accompanied her. They had arrived in separate cars, parked at least ten spaces apart, and Janine had entered the

Aquarium area a good five minutes before Lauren got out of her car. Walking past Lauren's Jag, Janine had barely looked at her.

Fox guessed what Lauren was thinking, but decided to let this woman be a bit off-kilter, impress her with his knowledge of people's ways before getting down to the deal. The answer to her question was easy, for anyone who has spent hours and hours and hundreds of days watching people—especially people trying to communicate covertly. For example, in a prison. The girlfriend's swift glance and flick of her wrist toward Grey's car as she walked by it was a slam-dunk signal that they were together. Plus, they matched: mid-thirties, good-looking, well looked after.

From his concealed vantage point thirty feet away, Fox had known that the widow had brought someone with her. He didn't care. In her shoes, he'd have done the same. And the woman in the shop was no cop, he was sure of that.

He stood in the pouring rain outside the scope of Lauren's umbrella, all the careful folds he had pressed into his clean pants and shirt already washed away by the rain. The thin cotton pants clung to his skinny thighs and the blue plaid shirt hung on him. Rain collected in the brim of his cap and dripped onto his nose.

Lauren hadn't decided whether or not she was scared of him.

She had never seen eyes like his, almost lifeless. But nothing in his manner toward her, apart from his warning not to treat him like he was stupid, made her feel instinctively like running. Besides, the postcard said he knew something about Martin. If it was true, it was worth the risk.

She tried to regain some control of the situation. "I'm not sure that I'm going to *deal* with you at all," she said coolly.

"But you're here."

"Yes, I'm here."

"Did you connect the postcard with the parking lot?" He guessed that she had.

She nodded.

He watched her, wondering which question she'd ask first. Finally she spoke. "How did you know my husband?"

He looked at her with his dead eyes. "I didn't, lady. I didn't have the pleasure." Fox was a master at reading people and he knew that this lady would need kind words about her man if she was going to deal with him.

"Yet you say you have information about him."

"I got some information about him," the scarecrow man said. He took a breath. "It'll cost you three hundred grand."

"I see." She didn't see at all. "Who are you?"

"The name's Danny Fox. I'm a con, an ex-convict, and how I got the information about your husband was that I was in the joint at the right time and got approached by some people in relation to him."

Her face closed. "Mr. Fox," she said, turning away from him, "my husband would *never*"—she spat out the last word—"be involved in anything illegal. Goodbye."

As she began to cross the wet stone plaza toward the Aquarium, Fox said, in a voice as flat as his eyes, "You're right, he wouldn't. That's why they killed him."

• • •

Inside the souvenir shop, Janine watched with relief as Lauren turned away from the creepy little man and begin walking toward her. Lauren's jaw was set and her eyes hard; the creep had obviously made her extremely angry.

Good, Janine thought. That would be the end of that. She hoped Café de Medici would still be serving lunch at 2:30. She was starving.

She bent down to gather her rain jacket and umbrella from

173

the shop floor. When she looked up seconds later, Lauren was walking back toward the stranger.

• • •

Fox had planned a less direct delivery, but he'd had no choice. This was not a second-chance deal; he was certain that if she walked away today, she'd call the police if he ever tried to contact her again.

She opened her mouth as if to speak, but said nothing. The umbrella had slipped from her grasp and now rocked gently upside down, gathering raindrops. The rain hitting her face was already melting her mascara down her cheeks.

"I'm sorry," he said quietly, "but it's true."

"I believe you." Her voice was a husky whisper. "You'll have to tell me a lot more, but you have my attention, Mr. Fox."

The three-hundred-thousand-dollar price tag was a meaningless detail now, if the information could be confirmed. Lauren could simply have Rick liquidate part of her portfolio. He would be keen to know the truth about Martin, too. For while he had accepted the police findings, he too knew Martin well, and knew how unlikely it was that he would drink and drive.

Lauren felt her heartbeat quicken and her caution dissipate. This scruffy stranger had spoken words she had thought but had never dared say out loud. She had voiced her concerns about police incompetence in accident scene investigation, but late at night, alone in the darkened house, she couldn't help wondering whether someone had somehow caused the "accident," on purpose.

Watching her, Fox knew he had her. Selling was always the same: dope, jewellery, a hit. Once your buyer knew you had the real thing, they were yours, even if they didn't love your price. The time was right to talk money.

Three hundred thousand dollars. He ran the calculations again: if he could keep it to three points of smack a day, this money would last him nearly twenty years. If he was smart, he could move to a town in the interior of the province, somewhere like Lytton or Osoyoos, get away from the fuckin' rain and live for a song and keep his habit happy.

He felt sure to the bone that this score was going to happen. The lady was smart: she had already smelled a rat when it came to her old man's death. He was smart, too, and had the truth. That would be worth something to her.

They looked at each other, standing in the pouring rain, both of them aware that their relationship had changed. She looked younger to him than she had when he'd first seen her, younger and more vulnerable.

"Do you want to grab a coffee?" He pointed at the kiosk a couple of hundred yards away. "I wouldn't mind a hot cup to hold while we . . . chat." He hit a sardonic note with the last word and smiled, exposing cracked, stained teeth.

The park was deserted and Lauren knew Janine would freak if she moved from the designated spot, but if this man wanted to hurt her, he could have done so easily enough in the parkade. She nodded and they walked to the concession stand.

Coffees cupped in their hands, they stood beneath the eaves of an empty animal cage. Fox was shivering. Wet, skinny and shaking, he looked like a junkie straight out of the movies.

"Are you an addict?" she asked, eyes searching his face over the brim of her styrofoam cup.

He laughed a good laugh. "I sure as hell am, lady."

"Heroin?"

"Is there anything else? Have been for over half my life. If we do business, almost all of your money'll go into my arm. Not making excuses for myself or nothing, but to supply a hay burner of a habit like mine takes a fair bit of cash, and I haven't been shy about making mine on the other side of the law. I've robbed and broken bones for money, and if times were tough enough and the target was right, I've even killed a couple of people."

Lauren got that dizzy, surreal feeling again. Looking at this small, thin man she couldn't believe he was capable of such things—except when she looked at his eyes.

"Are you with the Mafia or something?" she stammered.

"No, I'm not with nothing, I'm on my own. But the organized guys, the gangs and stuff, know about me and if there's a situation too hot for one of theirs to do, they call me."

"And someone came to you in this," she reached for the right word, "capacity about Martin?"

"They did."

"Who?"

"I'm not gonna tell you that yet. No games, now. I'm gonna tell you some stuff and maybe you can check some of it out. Then we'll talk about the money and then I'll come through with the rest, and I'll trust you to come through with the cash."

"What are you going to tell me now?" she asked, almost frightened to be finally hearing the truth.

"I'll tell you the approach and how I hear the hit went down." It was way more than he'd planned on telling her at their first meeting, but she was ready.

Lauren's coffee was cold. She drank it anyway, never taking her eyes off him.

"I was in Kent," he began. Lauren knew that Kent was a maximum security penitentiary about forty miles east of Vancouver. "Closing in on the end of a fiver I was doing. This would've been three winters ago now. I had a visitor. How he

176

got through the visitors' check at the front desk, I'll never know. Anyways, he's a Warrior." He paused. "Satan's Warrior. Not wearing colours or anything—sports shirt and slacks—looking the yuppie all the way. So we have a visit and it turns out he and his buddies are looking for a hit on a businessman who wasn't playing their way. I guess the guy had refused to wash their money." He looked at her. "You know, move it through legit deals so you can't tell it's come from drugs or whoring or wherever.

"Anyways, the target is a guy I've read about. Not that the Warriors gave me the name, but I figured it out. I read all the papers in the joint—the *Vancouver Sun*, the *Globe*; my lawyer used to bring me in the Sunday *New York Times* once in a while. So I'd read all about this big shot Martin Grey and his business partner Parker. And I'd read about you—your art charity stuff. The deal didn't have the right feel to it, it wasn't like your old man was a player. In fact it was pretty clear he wasn't a player. A hit like that's pretty different from taking money from one shit rat to kill another shit rat, if you'll pardon the expression."

She nodded. "Did this person say anything else?"

"It had to look like an accident. They didn't want any heavy police investigation on this guy, 'cause they didn't want nothing coming back to the club. Not ever. Anyways, I said thanks but no thanks, I'm out in three months and on parole. What do I want to be whackin' some rich family guy and facing life when I've barely breathed fresh air yet?" He stopped and drank the dregs of his coffee.

"And so?" she prompted him.

"And so, I was at the mission about four months later eating what they call breakfast and came across a newspaper a couple of days old. The accident was in it. I knew right then that the club had found somebody to do it. If I wasn't such an old con, I'd probably be worried about them knowing that I know, but all the evidence is dead and buried and who'd believe me and who'd believe that I'd ever go to the cops? I'm a lot of things, but I'm not a rat and they know it.

"So I'm having a beer with a buddy who's just got out of the joint and who's pretty connected to the club. We're catching up. This guy and I go back years. I told this guy I saw where they got someone to do the hit and I asked him if he knew about it. Turns out they'd got someone else, like I figured."

Fox wasn't sure how much more he was going to tell her today. He didn't want to give too much up for nothing. On the other hand, he had to give out enough for her to believe the information he had was worth big money. He noticed that she had turned white and had placed one hand against the filthy glass of the cage, as if for support.

"Go on," she said. It was a whisper.

"Okay, well . . ." He was unsure of what to say next. For some reason he didn't feel like mentioning the money right then. On the other hand, he wasn't naming names until they had the numbers hammered out and he had some of the cash.

"Have you ever heard of a Russian hangover?" He was damn sure she hadn't.

"No."

"It's a way of killing someone without it looking like they've been murdered. What you do is you get your victim loosened up, usually with booze that he's drinking. Then you force high-octane alcohol into him—fifty-one proof booze and two strong men'll do it for an average male. I heard it said that the true Russian way is to pour so much down the guy's throat that he dies from alcohol poisoning. But enough for a pass-out and then a car ride to a cliffy area and a gentle push, and puuufff"—he motioned with his hand—"you've got a DWI fatality.

"The lab'll do blood samples and the coroner'll explain

the cause of death, which'll be drowning or crushing or whatever, and no one will look at the inside of the throat for bruising, and the flesh'll rot quickly and by the time it occurs to anyone that a forced visit with Silent Sam might've played a role, it's way too late. Footprints and car tire tracks at the scene are washed away and the body's long rotted."

"And this is what happened to Martin?"

It was his turn to nod.

"Could you be more specific?" Many of the details of Martin's last night must be contained in the police or coroner's report. She was sure she could get copies of both and compare their contents with Fox's story. But there was another reason she wanted him to continue. She felt certain that somehow she would know the truth if she heard it.

"All I know is from the guy—sort of out of interest as to how it was done, as opposed to how I might've done it," Fox said. "Apparently your husband went out for dinner with some business types or somebody at some Italian joint downtown."

She blinked. It had been Il Verde, one of their favourites, with two major clients from Seattle.

"There were two guys involved," Fox continued. "They conned the valet into leaving them his jacket and to vamoose for a while for a few lines of coke. When your husband and his buddies came out of the restaurant, the hit men posing as the valet guys got their car first, then your husband's. Only when your husband went to drive away, Buddy dropped the jacket and hopped in beside him with a very impressive .357. I guess your husband thought it was a robbery. Anyways, they drove across the bridge to the North Shore and put in down at some park or somewhere. Buddy gets your husband to pop the trunk and boom—out jumps his friend, with the whiskey. I guess your husband put up quite a fight, but they got him liquored in the end anyway."

Lauren could almost see it: Martin in an ink-black park, tall trees, no one near to help, fighting for his life, wondering what was going on. She bet he had figured it out. She felt her eyes grow hot.

Still, Fox had not said anything that couldn't be made up, with a few known facts thrown in for authenticity.

"Go on," she said.

"After a while they put him in the passenger seat and Buddy drove to the place they'd decided on for the accident. The other guy followed in a car they'd stashed in the park ahead of time. The rest you can probably guess at. They moved your husband into the driver's side and punctured the gas tank. Then they lit the car on fire and helped it roll off the cliff." He stopped speaking for a moment and looked away. "I'm sorry, lady, but your husband didn't have a chance."

She had believed for so long that something like this was the true cause of Martin's death. She just had never visualized it before. Neither of them spoke for a few minutes.

"Anything else?" She dreaded more detail, but had to ask.

"Just that he kept saying something, over and over." For some reason Fox remembered this detail, and now he recognized that it could be important. "He kept saying your name—Lauren, he said, over and over, and another name. Brandon, or something." He didn't tell her that the detail had been interesting to Morrit because he had wondered whether Martin had swung both ways, sexually.

"Braydon," she said, matter-of-factly. "It was Braydon." How odd it was that at times it was easier to speak to people you didn't know about difficult things. "We had a baby boy die, just before he was born. We named him Braydon."

"I'm sorry," he said in his singsong voice. "I didn't know."

"I know that," she said softly.

It had been a long time since Lauren had allowed herself to dwell on the night of Martin's death. Recalling it now, in light of what Fox had said, she felt surprisingly strong and surprisingly angry. She believed Fox, and she believed he knew the names of the people who had killed Martin. If he or anyone else knew the truth, she'd give up everything she had to learn it.

"Why three hundred thousand?" she asked.

"I've got it worked out that if I do things right, that amount will keep me going for as long as I want," he answered easily.

"And then you'll just quit?"

"In a manner of speaking," he replied.

"Ah." She understood what he meant: it had crossed her mind too. It does, when you feel you have nothing to lose. In some ways, she thought, she and this scarecrow of a man had more in common than it would seem. "Are you sure you know who killed Martin?" she asked.

"One guy, really. The other guy was just a flunky." He nodded solemnly. "Yeah. I'm sure."

They were silent for a long time.

"What if I'm not sure I believe you?" Lauren asked.

Fox thought for a moment, pretty certain he knew what she was doing. He smiled briefly, acknowledging the effort. "Okay, lady, one more thing. The guy telling me this stuff, his brother-in-law's name is Micky Scofield. Run that name past your husband's old partner. I bet he knew about the club approaching your old man. Would that be enough?"

She nodded. When she spoke again, her voice sounded detached and cold. "How about a hundred and fifty for the name of Martin's murderer?"

"That's only half of what I need, lady." Fox shook his head, while thinking that if she wouldn't go up, one-fifty was a hell of a lot better than a kick in the ass for so little work.

She stared out into the dark afternoon. "I know it's only half, but a hundred and fifty thousand dollars is a lot of money." She stopped, wondering how far to trust this stranger. For the first time in seven years she wished she had a cigarette. She had to trust him; there was no one else. "And I think there may be a way for you to earn the other half." She looked at him directly, eyes to eyes, and they both knew what she was thinking.

"Two hundred to start." He drew in a breath. "And then we'll talk." Fuck. There wasn't going to be anything illegal about this deal. Sure.

Without hesitation she extended her right hand. "All right. I'll confirm that name, Scofield, with Rick, and we'll have a deal."

He had never shaken hands with a woman before.

"How do I reach you?" she asked.

"I'll call you."

"All right." She gave him her cell number. "I'll try to speak to Rick tonight. Could you call me when you get up tomorrow?"

"Sure," he said. "Sometime after nine."

"Fine," she nodded. "Thanks."

He nodded and moved away into the rain and into the depths of the park. She watched him go, feeling a peculiar warmth toward him. He was the only person she knew who shared her views on Martin's death. She finally pushed herself away from the glass and walked back toward the Aquarium.

Janine had left the shelter of the gift shop and was standing near where Lauren had dropped her umbrella, which was now folded up and neatly tucked under her friend's arm. She realized that when she and Danny had moved to the kiosk and nearby cage, Janine had been forced to leave the shop in order to keep Lauren in sight. Now she was shivering and soaking wet from the gusts of wind that drove the rain sideways at times.

"You're wonderful," Lauren said.

"And you're nuts!" Janine's voice was almost hysterical. "Lauren, what are you doing talking to that guy? He looks like a criminal."

"Yes, I know," Lauren agreed. "He *is* a criminal."

She had already decided not to tell Janine everything Fox had said. Her friend would think she was being conned and try to talk her out of dealing with him, and Lauren didn't have time for that. She wanted to speak with Rick right away, to ask him about Scofield and to find out if he had known about the Satan's Warriors putting pressure on Martin. And, if he had known, why he hadn't told her.

She also had to talk to him about the money.

It was just after 2:30. Rick would probably still be in the office. She could instruct him to liquidate two hundred thousand dollars' worth of stocks on the TSE or the NYSE and have the money on the West Coast before Danny Fox ever thought about getting up tomorrow.

Lauren felt like all of her senses were heightened; she felt fast and decisive. She knew Fox had told her the truth.

She declined Janine's invitation for lunch, claiming cold and fatigue. The two women got into their cars and, one after the other, drove out of the park along the winding, cedar-lined road.

Within moments, both of them were on their cell phones. Lauren called Rick's office. Busy. She decided she would go speak with him in person before going home.

Janine watched in her rear-view mirror as Lauren carried on past the North Shore turnoff where Janine was travelling. Lauren was not going home for a hot bath and nap, which did not surprise Janine. She had already figured out that Lauren was way over her head in something that she didn't want Janine to know about.

As she drove toward the bridge, she fished through her

purse and found the card that Liz had given her. It bore the insignia of the RCMP and a horse and rider, the name Sergeant Jackson Cole, and a phone number. She punched in the digits. It rang five times before a recording device picked up the call.

She felt both relieved and disappointed that she wouldn't be speaking with Jackson in person. She hadn't missed the way he had looked at Lauren, but he was still the sexiest man she had met in a long time, and speaking with him would have at least presented a possibility . . .

If she was right and he was interested in Lauren, all it meant was that he'd waste his time for a while and then they'd both be alone.

"Hi. It's Janine," she said to the recorder. "I hope this doesn't sound ridiculous, but I have a favour to ask and you're the only cop I know." She wondered if she should have said "police officer." "My friend Lauren, who you met on Saturday, is being bothered by a creep. A real criminal type. I think he's trying to blackmail her by saying he has information about her husband's death a couple of years ago. Anyway, I was wondering if you could speak to her. I think she's in way over her head. Sorry to ramble. Here's her number." She left it. "Thanks. Hope to see you soon."

She hung up. Well, she might see him again.

• • •

Lauren parked her car half a block down the street from Rick's office. She ran through the rain with her jacket over her head, skipping puddles, to the covered entrance. The brokerage house looked closed, the lights off downstairs and the staff obviously gone.

She checked her watch: 3:02. The market would have

stopped trading an hour and a half ago, but there would still be lots to do. Why would Rick shut things down early?

She tried the door. It was locked. She let herself in with the key Rick had given her when he had first opened up shop. She locked the door behind her. The foyer and secretaries' areas were gloomy. She could hear Rick's voice upstairs and was about to bound up the steps when she heard a second voice, speaking to Rick harshly. The words were indistinguishable.

She walked up the stairs quietly, wondering who could be so angry at Rick. She hadn't heard of any huge drops in the market lately and Rick was a good investor for his clients, and smooth. Even if he had done something you didn't like, it was hard to get angry at him.

As she approached the landing, she decided that she would breeze in with a quick knock on the door, and try to diffuse the mood. With luck, the client would improve his manners and whatever it was could be resolved quickly, civilly, and he would leave. Driving over, she had realized that she was ravenous. Once they ditched the client, she would grab Rick and take him out for a hearty, uninterrupted lunch. They had a lot to talk about.

She reached the third to last stair and looked into the office, and she froze. Rick was directly opposite her, his back right against the wall. But he wasn't looking at her. His eyes were rivetted on the face of the man who was holding him against the wall by the throat. Lauren recognized him immediately: it was the back of the man in her dream. The man at the restaurant Saturday night. He was screaming at Rick and shaking him hard against the wall.

Lauren scanned the rest of the office. Rick and the animal attacking him were the only ones there. On the desk were several piles of inch-thick bundles of money, bills held together by elastic bands.

She wanted to do something, but she was terrified. She stood there for several seconds, frozen in shock and indecision. Then she heard a noise and realized that someone was in Rick's ensuite bathroom. If she stayed where she was, she'd be discovered.

The smartest thing was to run down the stairs and get out, but she couldn't just leave Rick here, alone. She looked around frantically. On the landing in front of her, to the right of the door, was an Oriental ceramic pot with a palm in it. On the left was a huge eighteenth-century armoire.

She ran up the last steps, pulled open the door to the wardrobe, crawled in and pulled the door nearly shut behind her.

She could hear Rick's voice, low and pleading. Then the response, loud and brutal: "Why the fuck should we, you stupid fuck? Do you think we're gonna let you just walk away from this?" It was the voice of the man who was choking Rick, the good-looking charmer at the restaurant. "You stop when I say you stop, and not a motherfuckin' second sooner. You wanta go to the cops, go to the cops."

Lauren could hear the wall shaking. She pictured Rick being thrown against it.

"What the fuck are they gonna do when your kid's dead and I was in Hawaii when it happened? Huh, smart guy? So what you do, asshole, is you take this fuckin' money and you clean it so it sparkles and you convert it into something that I can liquidate within three months. Are you going to have a problem with that?"

"No." Rick's voice was thin and weak. "No problem."

The monster, as she now thought of him, spoke to someone else in a light, conversational tone. "Okay, Mike, I think our friend here's got the message. Let's go."

She heard their footsteps pass out of the carpeted office onto the wooden landing. Through the crack in the door of the armoire she saw the monster, and behind him a tall man of medium build wearing blue jeans and a black T-shirt. He had a small, pointed beard and wore narrow sunglasses, even in the dimness of the office landing. He was smiling.

The monster spoke again, close and low this time. "We better look after that loose end across the street in the next day or two."

"Mike" grunted in response.

Lauren sank back in her hiding place, wondering what loose end they were talking about. When she heard the downstairs door close, she realized that she had been holding her breath since they'd walked out of Rick's office.

She could hear Rick crying.

She didn't know what to do. Danny Fox had said that Martin was killed by someone connected to the Satan's Warriors for not laundering their money. Two years later, here was Martin's partner, surrounded by cash, being threatened if he didn't continue to do what Martin had refused to do.

Lauren was freezing.

No wonder Rick never talked to her about the Satan's Warriors pressuring Martin. Poor Rick. The whole time she had been plaguing him with theories of how Martin might've died, he must have known that he was working for his friend's murderers.

And to threaten Billy! They'd have Rick's assistance forever.

Lauren was furious, with a hatred she had never felt before, a hatred that almost felt good in its intensity. She thought she knew exactly who Fox would identify as Martin's killers for his two hundred thousand dollars. She was convinced that she had just seen them walk past her.

It would be the other hundred thousand dollars that

would be well spent. She settled down on the hard, narrow boards to wait for Rick to leave.

Thursday, June 18, 1998

L ess than a mile away from the Aquarium, at the only Westin in town, Oskar tipped the bellhop who placed the two tan leather suitcases on the bed. He had registered as Keith Wagner. Fake ID was never a problem.

It was a shitty day out. Not inconsistent with closed drapes. He closed them. He put the Do Not Disturb sign on the door, bolted it shut and returned to the suitcases. His watch read almost 10:20.

He had watched the mules load the stuff into the suitcases in Seattle. He'd then taken off, leaving them to cross the border. They were the brothers of Donna, the broad he was fucking, and seemed to think that somehow the sugar-daddy train extended to relatives. It was easy enough to keep them all happy, and someone's family loyalty—even if it wasn't his—was better than nothing. But greed was the real cement.

He unlocked the first suitcase. Someone would be here in about forty minutes; he had lots of time.

They had ordered a hundred kilos. There were two other suitcases in the car in the parking lot. He had ordered an extra five kilos and defrayed the cost across the board. It would only cost the club a twentieth more per kilo to pay for his freebies.

Since the order had been placed, Oskar had worked out a plan. It involved fucking Frank Wesley and getting the hell out of Dodge. He just wished he could fuck the Warriors in the process.

He put on medi-gloves and lifted a brick out of the suitcase. It was a solid hard rectangle, about eight inches by five by two, wrapped in paper covered with the Coca Cola insignia. He hefted it in his right hand. It felt like a kilo.

He carried it into the bathroom, put a towel on the counter and placed the brick on it. Using a razor blade he cut a small *V* in the wrapper and pulled the tongue, exposing the coke.

"Shit," he said aloud.

It was shit. It was yellow, and when he flicked it with the blade, it crumbled. No one would pay anything for this because it would burn the shit out of your nose. Somewhere in Colombia, someone had fucked up with the recipe and put way too much ether into the mix. The club was not gonna be happy about this.

On the other hand, how could he have checked when the supplier was standing there? They'd dealt together too many times for Oskar to question the product in front of him. It would insult him, probably to the point of not dealing with him again. And where the fuck would the bikers be then?

He didn't think the boys would kill him. He had a reputation for putting out good product, and the club knew it from competing with him. Getting stuck with garbage happened once in a while in the business. There were no refunds and that would definitely be his problem, not theirs. He'd just have to buy a little time to rectify things.

He checked another brick. Yellow shit.

The next one was beautiful: white and hard, crystalline when he flaked it off. He checked every key. Out of the fifty he had in the room, twenty-one were crap and twenty-nine were magic. He checked his five "freebie" kilos. They were pure.

Oskar considered his options. He could give the club five more good kilos, or he could keep the good stuff even though his plan didn't require quality.

There was a knock on the door. He looked at his watch. 11:00 on the nose. He decided to leave things as they were: a little supply for sale, if it took longer to leave than he anticipated, wouldn't be bad news. He stashed his five bricks in the cupboard under the sink, closed the bathroom door and walked toward the room door, asking in a sleepy voice, "Who is it?"

"Friends of Frank's."

He opened the door and admitted the two men in their late twenties, beefy but well dressed in dark sports coats and slacks. They looked amazingly straight.

The door had barely closed when one of them asked, "Where is it?" This was not a social call.

"Half of it's on the bed," Oskar answered. "Some of it's great. Twenty-one are shit, out of what I've checked. The rest of it's in the trunk of a rental car in the lot downstairs. I didn't see any point in bringing all of it up here. Now I do. All of it will have to be checked."

"What do you mean, some of it's shit?" said the younger man, mimicking Oskar's eastern European accent.

"I mean nearly half of them have been burned. They're gyp rock." He would have liked to garrot the asshole.

"Why?" said the older one, voice low and quiet. "Didn't you check on that before you bought it?"

Oskar would have ignored him, but he didn't feel like being taken from the hotel room at gunpoint, to a deserted spot to have the piss whipped out of him. "The person who sent you will understand," he said slowly, as if speaking to idiots. "You don't buy this many kilos that way, when you're dealing with guys you've done business with before. Face, respect, you hear of that? I'll explain the situation to my guy and the next stuff'll be sweet, without a problem. I'll eat the bad stuff and work it out with my supplier. It won't affect you, except you get twenty-one less keys than you thought."

And I get twenty-one more, he thought, as he gave the younger man the trunk key to the rental car. The flunky was back in less than ten minutes with the other two suitcases. Oskar checked the last fifty kilos of cocaine while the other two men looked on; six kilos were garbage.

"Tell your boss that I'll add twenty-seven keys to the next order," he said.

The tall man nodded and the two strangers left with three of Oskar's suitcases filled with cocaine. The twenty-seven lousy kilos lay on the bed near the last empty suitcase.

While it was useless to users, it would still analyze as cocaine in a lab, and if he was busted right now he would be in possession of cocaine for the purpose of trafficking. An indictable offence. Twenty-seven kilos. Thirty-two, counting the freebies.

It was perfect.

He retrieved the five kilos from the bathroom, arranged all the bricks in the suitcase and placed it in the bedroom closet. He then called Donna's cell number. He told her that he had just finished up business and wanted to celebrate.

She was there in less than half an hour, pressing her hard high tits into him and grinding her crotch into his. She was gorgeous. Thick blonde hair, big smile and dynamite figure, and a full-blown coke addict. Her suspicious nature, which came from using the drug, drove him crazy at times but he could always supply her, which kept her hooked on him and useful.

He pushed her away. "I know you want some blow, baby."

"I'll blow you," she giggled. With long, silver-nailed fingertips she rubbed her nipples through the thin fabric of her blouse, making them stand hard.

"Yeah. Sounds good." His voice was flat. "We've just got one call to make and then we'll party."

"Another one? Aaaah," she whined. "Can't it wait?"

She was moving very close to him. He could feel her desperation.

"We'll make it quick." His voice was stone. "And then you can fuck me."

She wilted. She sat down on the edge of the bed, nearly in tears, and looked up at him with china doll eyes. "What do I say this time?"

He had it all figured out. "Tell them you've called before. Give them your identification number, then say you were with him today and he told you that he's going to receive at least ten kilos of coke soon. Can you remember that?"

She nodded.

"Tell them you'll call back if you learn anything more."

"Okay," she said quietly.

He dialled the police department's Crime Stoppers Tips phone number and handed her the phone. He then took a vial from his vest pocket along with a mirror and blade. He poured some of the powder onto the glass and began chopping. She watched him intently as she spoke into the telephone. She performed perfectly and hung up.

"Yum, yum!" She was delighted. He passed her a fifty-dollar bill rolled into a tube and she attacked the lines. Within seconds she was ecstatic.

Oskar didn't feel like he had time to spend in the hotel room, but he needed allegiances. He let her use a little more of the powder to sprinkle on his cock. He liked the lingering sensation as his skin absorbed the drug and as she devoured it. He decided to let her binge.

• • •

They had been waiting for Fox when he returned to his room after meeting Lauren in the park Wednesday afternoon. He hadn't seen either of them before, but they were good, did things by the book. They'd got a warrant before they'd entered his room. Arrested him with reasons and rights when he walked in. The only problem was, they had the wrong man.

It seemed that they had heard that before.

A rat had fingered Fox as the stickup man in a gas station robbery that had happened the night before. Of course he had no alibi. He had been shooting up in his room alone and planning this afternoon's events, which he didn't bother to relate to them.

Everything was fucked up. His lawyer was out of town until the end of the week, and promised by long distance to come down to the lockup and take care of the bail hearing, but not until first thing Friday morning. After that they wouldn't let him make any more calls, not that he could have called Lauren without someone listening or tracing the call. He was fucked.

Thursday morning, 9:00 came and went and he could do nothing. This could blow the whole thing. She could come to her senses and decide that she was dealing with a complete flake. He felt like twisting someone's neck off.

By 2:30 he was zonked on stuff a visitor had brought in for one of the other guys.

• • •

Oskar checked out at five, paying cash but asking for a receipt. He declined the leotard-wearing Yeoman's offer of help with his suitcase and walked to the rental car alone.

Despite the fact that he owed the club twenty-seven kilos, pronto, he was feeling pretty good. The screwup had turned into an opportunity; his plan was speeded up by weeks. He placed the suitcase in the trunk of the rented Chevrolet and caught himself whistling.

He'd sent Donna on her way half an hour earlier, with a large flap of coke and a pat on the ass. He said he'd call her. For the rest of the day he would stash this coke and then get on with travel arrangements.

Thirty-two kilos would fetch federal time, easy. He would add his five to the twenty-seven because he wouldn't be needing its revenue; he wouldn't be around long enough. He figured that he had a week—ten days at the most—to replace the lousy coke with good stuff. After that he'd have leg-breaking visitors. If he did things right, the apple cart would be so overturned that the club wouldn't be worrying about their cocaine.

He decided not to spend any time organizing the next shipment. If he was around when it was due, he would probably be dead. It was time to concentrate on getting out of here.

Getting behind the wheel of the car, he thought again about stashing the cocaine. When he had first worked out his plan, he figured on hiding a few kilos at a time so it wouldn't be a problem stashing the stuff in the woods somewhere. But packing thirty-odd kilos into the bushes unnoticed, whether it was one trip in the suitcases or back and forth a bunch of times, wasn't going to work.

The new compressed time frame and bonanza of crappy coke had thrown his plans off. He needed to adapt smartly. Use the changes to his advantage.

He found himself driving east, out of downtown and toward the Trans-Canada Highway, leading to the outlying suburbs. Toward where Wesley lived. He drove conservatively: three or four miles over the speed limit in the slow lane, using his turn signals when he changed lanes. There was no way he wanted a traffic stop with enough coke to fill a police exhibit locker.

As he drove, he thought. Moving this load close to its ultimate destination was smart. Moving it once only, right to that destination at the outset, was even smarter. A plan was developing.

He had cased Wesley's house several times in the dark and had had Donna drive up the driveway and knock on the door when no one was home. Donna reported that she could see no surveillance cameras at the door or on the eaves. Oskar had seen an alarm company's stickers on the doors and most of the windows, but nothing apparently out of the ordinary for a residence. It was a rambling rancher; tricycles and toys were strewn about a large backyard, with fruit trees and a playhouse. A big laurel hedge ran along the back of the lot, which backed onto a lane. This would be his entry.

But he was getting ahead of himself. He had a few things to do first. He looked at his watch. 5:40.

He spotted a Wal-Mart and headed for it, then parked in an open-air lot with lots of people around. While he didn't want the police, he also didn't want the car or its contents ripped off. He locked the door and walked to the store, whistling. He looked relaxed and calm.

In the bedding section he picked up a pair of dark green pillowcases. In the hardware department he selected a good solid shovel, coveralls, work gloves, duct tape and a box of garbage bags. He passed through women's wear and grabbed a pair of nylons, and his last stop was at sporting goods, where he chose a gaff hook with a sixteen-inch solid wood handle. Smiling, he made his purchases and left the store.

He set his pace so that nearby fellow shoppers had moved on by the time he reached the car. He put the shovel and the bag containing the garbage bags, work gloves, duct tape and gaff hook, into the trunk and closed it. He got in the car and placed the Wal-Mart bag with the rest of his purchases on the passenger seat beside him. He was hungry.

He saw a Denny's across the lot and headed for it, but decided against it when he saw two marked police cars in front. He settled for a McDonald's drive-thru. Once loaded up with food, he returned to the highway and drove to a nearby rest and picnic area. While eating, he considered what he knew about his target.

He knew the house: its location and exterior layout. He knew the vehicles: a green Chevy Suburban and a beat-up yellow GM pickup. Wesley had two kids—daughters, Oskar believed—who lived with an ex-wife. No complications there. Hooked to the club, but not a member. No legit job requiring regular hours. Lots of time at the gym.

Oskar decided to start there.

He didn't have this part planned exactly, and was relying on luck a little more than he'd like, but what the fuck could he do? He had to find the prick before he could make things happen.

After his meal he got out of the car and put his garbage in a can, casually assessing the other visitors to the rest area. There weren't many: the drizzle made it a lousy day for a picnic. It was mostly families, stopping to use the bathrooms and returning to the highway quickly. There shouldn't be a problem, he thought.

He took the Wal-Mart bag from the front seat and headed for the men's washroom. It was empty, but he used a stall to put the coveralls on over his jeans and T-shirt. They were baggy and long enough that they felt okay. He decided he didn't look too odd. He tore the cello wrap from the pillow-cases and put one inside the other, then pulled them over his head, Klan style, and looked up toward the bathroom light.

He couldn't see a thing. He put the pillowcases back into the Wal-Mart bag.

Next he took the nylons out of their packaging and stuffed them in the right side pocket of his coveralls. He tossed the wrappings and tags from the pillowcases, nylons and coveralls into the garbage on his way to the car. No one gave him a second look. So far, so good.

He took the duct tape and gaff from the trunk and added them to the bag with the pillowcases and nylons. He closed the trunk and got in behind the wheel of the car with the bag beside him. He hoped he'd need it.

Carefully observing the speed limit, Oskar drove for ten minutes before passing by Wesley's home. He spotted the old yellow pickup parked at the side of the garage. There was no sign of the Suburban. Good, he thought. He didn't want to start this at Wesley's home.

He headed for the gym, five minutes away.

Muscles Unlimited took up almost half a city block, attracting all types. The parking lot was huge. Oskar spotted Wesley's truck mid-lot. Seeing no one around, he drove to it and hopped out of his car. He walked to the Suburban and touched the hood. Cool. Given the proximity of the house to the gym, that could mean anything.

Oskar could feel himself getting pumped up: he was getting a plan. The key was improvisation with no stupid mistakes. And speed.

He parked his car four spaces away from the Suburban, opened his glove compartment and took out a device resembling a TV remote control. He walked toward the truck casually, pressing a series of numbers. Bingo. The door lock released. There was still no one close enough to worry about.

Oskar returned to his car and grabbed the Wal-Mart bag. From the trunk he retrieved a pair of latex gloves he had stashed in the wheel well, then put them on and shouldered one of the leather suitcases. He locked the trunk and looked around. A couple had parked ten cars down and were getting their gym bags out of their trunk. They all exchanged brief smiles and then the couple were on their way into the gym. Oskar figured he looked like a working guy going to the gym. Still, the fewer people who saw him, the better.

He walked confidently to the passenger side of the Suburban, farthest from the gym. He opened the door and climbed in. The height of the vehicle gave him a pretty good view of the surrounding lot: unless another utility vehicle or van parked nearby, he'd have lots of time to see Wesley approaching.

He tossed the suitcase onto the back bench seat, passenger side, and closed and locked the door. He moved into the back seat, next to the suitcase, directly behind the driver's seat. There he laid the pillowcases, one inside the other, over the back rest of the back seat. Next he began tearing off pieces of duct tape two and a half feet long. He stuck the top of each strip to the top of the back seat, with the rest of each strip dangling into the rear storage space. The gaff hook lay near his feet.

He was excited. Now that he was putting his plan into action, the familiar adrenaline that came from risk and impending violence was flowing. He wished he had water. He kept an eye on the gym and glanced in the other directions occasionally. People of all different shapes and sizes came and went.

He had waited almost an hour when he saw Wesley walking toward the Suburban. He carried the same gym bag as he had on the afternoon in the forest, only Oskar was betting it didn't have anything more dangerous than a weight belt in it. He wondered briefly where the gun was. It wouldn't matter soon.

Oskar reached into the pocket of the overalls, brought out

the nylons and pulled them over his head, flattening his nose and lips grotesquely against the translucent elastic. He crouched perfectly still in the gully between the front and back seats, peering over the back to watch Wesley's final approach. Gripping the gaff, he watched through the tinted glass as Wesley unlocked the driver's door, inches away. There was no one around. Not that it would matter much. Oskar crouched behind the driver's seat on the floor, holding the passenger door shut in case Wesley decided to put his bag onto the back seat. The front door opened and the bag landed on the passenger seat in front. Wesley stepped up into the leather seat behind the steering wheel and closed the door. The key went into the ignition.

Now. Before the truck started.

Oskar sat up. Wesley heard the movement and began to turn, and Oskar hit him across the temple with the gaff. The skin of Wesley's skull split but his eyes remained open. Oskar hit him again. This time he went down.

Oskar locked the driver's door and quickly put tape across Wesley's mouth. He then pushed the front passenger seat forward and dragged Wesley toward him. By the time he got the dead weight into the back seat, he was sweating heavily in the closed compartment. He put the pillowcases over Wesley's head.

He checked the carotid artery and got a pulse. Good, he thought. He did not want Wesley's murder on his head, or he'd be as good as dead himself.

He secured the pillowcases by wrapping tape around Wesley's neck. Then he moved into the rear storage area, reached over the back seat, grabbed the hooded figure by the shoulders and hefted him into the back. Wesley groaned.

Oskar had to move fast. He quickly taped Wesley's wrists, hands in front, and then his knees and ankles. Then he went to work. Kneeling beside Wesley, he reached for the suitcase and dragged it into the back compartment with them. He opened it and removed twenty kilo bricks, which he stacked beside him. He lifted Wesley's taped wrists, and when the hands fell open he placed the brick against Wesley's left palm. He then put the brick back in the suitcase. On the next brick he pressed Wesley's right index and middle fingers. Then, into the suitcase. On the third, the right index and thumb. It took less than two minutes to do all twenty.

Wesley was still out of it, moaning occasionally, but no risk. Oskar was pretty sure he wouldn't have a clue what had happened.

He zipped up the suitcase and threw it onto the back seat, then followed it and reached over to grab Wesley's gym bag. He may as well make it look like a robbery. He put the gaff in the gym bag and pulled the nylon off his head with relief. He checked his hair in the dim rear-view. It would do.

He looked around the parking lot. It was still light out at 7:40. But there was nobody nearby. He got out of the truck, carrying the suitcase and the gym bag, and closed the locked door behind him. He walked slowly to his rental and opened the trunk. He peeled off the medi-gloves and stuffed them into the side pocket of the suitcase. Then he tossed the suit-case and gym bag into the trunk.

Oskar got into the car and eased out of the parking lot. He drove slowly past a green Suburban, a few spots down from where he'd been parked—empty, so far as you could tell.

He drove the speed limit, lights on, for a few miles until he reached Wesley's house. This part of the plan required speed and boldness.

The house looked deserted, as he'd expected. He drove up the driveway and into the carport and turned the car off. He quickly removed the suitcase and shovel and carried them to the back of the house. Deserted. He returned to the car and took out the garbage bags and work gloves and shut the trunk.

Carrying the suitcase, he ran through the dusky back yard in the direction of the playhouse. He left the suitcase outside of it, on the far side, then ran back to get the garbage bags, shovel and work gloves. He left them with the suitcase and ran back to the car. He was roasting. The overalls were an unwanted layer with all his activity.

He reversed out the driveway and drove down the street. At the end of the block he turned and parked just inside the lane. He got out of the car, hands in pockets, whistling quietly, and headed back toward the house he had just left.

Dusk was gathering, darkening the trees and garages along the lane. Oskar slipped into the hedge. Once through, he could see the house. Still no lights or signs of occupancy. He ran past the playhouse toward the carport, just in case. Wesley wouldn't be home for a long while yet, but he didn't want to take any chances on unexpected company. The carport was still empty.

He ran back to the playhouse. It was a two-level number, built on a wooden pallet. The downstairs had solid walls of plywood and the upper floor was open-air, framed with two-by-fours and topped with a peaked roof. He was counting on it not being too heavy.

He reached through a side window and tried pulling the structure toward him. It was fucking heavy, but it moved. He pulled again, exhaling hard. It gave again, but was hooked on the lip of grass. He would have to lift and pull. He braced himself and gave it a heave. It came. Slowly he worked the playhouse sideways about three feet. There had been no action from the house or neighbours.

He took the cocaine out of the suitcase, put the bricks into two garbage bags and tied them off. He lined the suitcase with another garbage bag and sat it on the grass. Then he picked up the shovel and began digging. He put the soil onto the garbage bag in the suitcase. It was slow work.

Once the suitcase was full, he knew there was more than enough room for the coke. He placed the two garbage bags containing the coke side by side in the shallow grave and covered them with a couple of inches of dirt, making sure a bit of plastic showed through. He didn't want them to be missed. He then went to the other side of the playhouse and pushed it back into place. In the darkness, he was pretty sure the playhouse was repositioned properly and the grass that it had rested on for half an hour wasn't suspiciously damaged.

He placed the extra garbage bags in the suitcase, then zipped it up and lifted the heavy bag. He picked up the shovel, and with one last look at the peaceful house, he walked back toward the thick hedge and the lane.

• • •

Frank Wesley couldn't breathe. He came to, knowing he was suffocating. He tried to open his eyes and then, with horror, realized that they were open. It was blacker than he had ever seen. Now he knew what people meant when they said black was an absence of light. He tried not to panic.

He thought he knew what had happened: he'd been buried alive.

Oh, fuck. He'd heard those stories—sickos burying people and then squirrels or pine cones blocked the airways. Oh, fuck.

Why hadn't they killed him? He wondered if it was too late for God. For the first time he could remember since being an adult, he was scared.

Panic won't help a thing, he thought. Try to stay calm and inventory the situation. What did he see? Blackness. What did he smell? His own sweat and aftershave. He felt a surge of encouragement when he remembered he had been at the gym. What did he hear? Nothing. Maybe traffic a ways off. Where could he be? Buried in a culvert?

Fuck. Who'd done this? It occurred to him that he wanted to see his kids again. What did he feel? His head ached. He almost recalled being hit. He was sure he'd been hit. His mouth was bone dry and he couldn't open it. Taped. His wrists, knees and ankles were taped, too. He felt a little bruised, but apart from his head there were no significant injuries he could feel.

As he calmed down, Wesley realized he was hooded. Maybe he wasn't buried. He began to regain a sense of control.

He wondered if his captors were watching him. He didn't want them to know that he was conscious. The fuckers had had the first surprise; he wanted the next one. He lay still. He was lying on his back. The floor was firm but comfortable, and he could feel with his left hand that it was carpeted. What was their next step? If they had wanted to kill him, they could already have done it. That was good. On the other hand, if it was an extortion attempt, he was fucked. The club would never do something as weak as giving in to blackmail, and they sure as shit wouldn't go to the cops over it. They would take it personally and avenge his death, but that was small comfort. He decided that the best way to get the ball rolling was to let them know that he could communicate.

He moaned and rolled, expecting a boot in the head or chest. Nothing. He rolled again, moaning. His head bumped into something firm but soft. He tried stretching his legs but couldn't. By moving around he calculated that whatever room he was in was about four feet by three feet. He was growing more and more confident that he was alone.

Wesley listened, hard. He could hear a couple of women laughing not far away. He moaned. Not loud enough.

He was counting on them being passersby, not connected

with his abductors. He had to hurry. He manoeuvred his body perpendicular to how he had been lying before and stretched out as far as he could. Now he was certain he was in a van, parked somewhere but perhaps only briefly. This opportunity might not come again.

He raised his legs and bashed his feet at what he hoped was the van wall. His calves came to rest, hard, on the back of the rear seats. Puzzled, he pulled himself up and felt the surface. It wasn't a van, he realized. It was some kind of station wagon or sport utility.

He had to get out before they came back. But how far could he get, taped like this? He'd need a knife or scissors: unravelling would take forever. He didn't have forever. He needed those broads' attention. Now.

He scrambled into the back seat and moved his torso between the two front captain's chairs, swinging his legs after him. It crossed his mind that the interior of this vehicle was similar to his Chevy. He leaned on the horn as hard as he could for a full minute, then he reached for the door handle. It didn't give.

That brought back a memory. He reached his hands toward where the lock release would be in his truck. It was the same in this one, and he heard the door locks release as he pressed it. He pushed the door wide open and leaned forward against the horn. Now he heard at least two people approaching. He hoped this wasn't how he was going to die. He kept pressing the horn until he heard a woman scream. She screamed again. He pushed himself away from the steering wheel and leaned back against the soft driver's seat and moaned.

"Are you all right?" It was a woman's voice.

He nodded and moaned. Then he heard three number keys being pressed on a cellular phone. He moaned again, shaking his head, but he was ignored. He heard her say "police." And then he heard the rest: "We've found a man, hooded and tied up in a vehicle in the Muscles Unlimited parking lot. Corner of 144th and Scott Road." He knew the rest then, before she described the vehicle in which he'd been found—"a dark green Chevrolet Suburban," with a BC licence number he knew by heart.

When they ran that one, he thought, they'll come running.

He felt hands on his chest. "Just lean back, I'm going to take this hood off." The screamer's voice was soft and pretty.

"Judy, you'll never be able to unravel that," said the one with the cell phone. "It's duct tape. We'll have to cut it off. Why don't you go back to the gym and get some scissors."

He heard her go off at a run.

The cell phone owner repeated the licence plate number. Wesley smiled under the tape. "It'll be okay," she told him. "The police are on their way." He just bet they were.

He heard the other woman returning at a run.

"Thanks." Miss Cellular was going to do the cutting. "Lean back and tilt your head back." He did as he was told. She gathered the fabric at his throat, above the tape, and cut a slash across in the first pillowcase, missing most of the second layer.

"Thorough," she said.

He liked her cool. "Uh huh," he grunted.

She repeated the cut. Now he could see light. Next, holding both layers, she cut straight up from his Adam's apple to mid-brow, like a tent flap, continuing until the pillowcases split and fell like a cowl around his neck.

He blinked hard, adjusting to the dim light.

Miss Cellular and Miss Scissors were both in their early forties and both a bit plump. He thought they were beautiful.

"With that beard, I think you'll want some solvent for that tape," Cellular said, pointing to his mouth.

He shook his head no.

"All right," she sighed. She pulled and cut as gently as she could, and about half the job was done when the first police car arrived. Sergeant Falkner, a local Mountie, took over and the tape was off in less than a second. Wesley glared.

"Well, well, well," Falkner crowed.

Wesley knew how to wipe the smile off Falkner's fat face. "I want my lawyer," he said.

"But Mr. Wesley, you aren't charged with anything. Not even suspected of anything—specific to tonight, I mean."

"Fair enough," said Wesley. Cellular was being permitted to cut the tape at his wrists and legs now that they'd been photographed by the police exhibit man, who was hovering around waiting for each shred of tape and fabric. "But I'm not still not going to say a f—" She looked up at him. "I'm still not saying a thing until Tony's here. And since I'm the victim, not the suspect, you can't hold me."

"We're taking you to the hospital for observation," Falkner said. "You probably need stitches. And then questioning."

"All I need is to be left alone. I'm not looking for charges to be laid against anyone. And you know I won't be testifying if they are. Go home, Sergeant."

There was little the police could do. "Fine," said Falkner, "but I'm seizing the vehicle for evidence."

Wesley sighed. "Seize away, but I doubt you'll find anything of use. Can you call me a cab?"

The sergeant offered to give him a ride. Wesley didn't speak a word during the seven-minute ride from the gym parking lot to his dark, quiet house.

• • •

Jackson Cole was brutally tired.

He'd been on the move almost constantly since the wire-tap installation four nights ago. As the file co-ordinator he had been assigned four top-notch, tight-lipped investigators to assist him in the methamphetamine trafficking investigation. Cole had assigned one investigator to try to quietly identify where the chemical precursors for the methamphetamine lab had come from. Someone somewhere in the chemical industry had to have heard about shipments of massive amounts of safrol and ephedrine to Canada, even if apparently ordered by a pharmaceutical company.

Because of the concern that overt inquiries would alert the club of police interest, it was slow going. So far they had come up with nothing.

One of the other investigators assigned to Cole was reviewing Canada Customs port of entry lists, reading the names of people who had been checked when arriving in Canada. The idea was that he might be able to identify the American experts coming up to help the club do its setup, by checking the names against a list of known professionals in the field of meth cooking. It was a lot like looking for a needle in a haystack.

The other two new arrivals to the project were working with Peter Grant, developing profiles on the people expected to show up at the clubhouse. Each profile included the person's club history—how long the person had been a member, his position in the club, his criminal record, his known associates, informers who had given information about him, any computer entry indicating contact with the police—as a suspect, victim, witness or lead—and any pertinent information about his general background that might make him susceptible to a police approach or more dangerous to police than other members. It was time-consuming work, in light of the two large branches involved.

Cole had helped where he could first thing Monday

morning, but then club members had started showing up at their new clubhouse and the wires started picking up conversations. He and Grant had then joined Pearce in the monitor room in an effort to identify people at the new house, by voice, conversation and video photograph picked up by Winter's video camera in the front hall light fixture.

The club used wannabes as their movers, ordering them around like serfs. These servants were of almost as much interest to Cole as the club members, in that they had less to lose and were easier to relocate in the Source/Witness Protection Program if they co-operated with the police. They weren't, however, privy to the top end of the conspiracy Cole was investigating.

After listening to the first few intercepted conversations, Cole had left voice identification to Grant and Pearce and turned his attention to trying to put together all of the information obtained by the different investigators on the file. He had spent most of Tuesday and Wednesday in the secure work room across from the monitor room on the second floor of headquarters, reviewing profiles. As far as Cole was concerned the two most interesting profiles related to the two presidents of the target branches: Langley's "Bones," a.k.a. Brian Edward Allen, and Vancouver's "Jojo," a.k.a. Paul Lucci.

Bones was forty-six. His criminal record included a conviction for assault causing bodily harm, possession of a prohibited weapon and wounding. There was a stay of judicial proceedings with respect to a charge of unlawful confinement and another weapons charge, a rape and a robbery. At five-foot-ten, Bones weighed three hundred and twenty if he weighed a pound.

Jojo's profile wasn't much different. He had been Vancouver's president for three years, revered by the branch and members all over North America. His criminal record reflected one conviction for assault and one for extortion, both over twenty years old; the list of charges that hadn't been proceeded with, for one reason or another, went on for two pages and ranged from fraud to murder.

Reading Jojo's profile, Cole felt certain that it wouldn't be complete without charges relating to the three bodies found in the Hedley mine less than a week ago. While the wiretap investigation targetted the methamphetamine lab and the trafficking conspiracy, if the tapes provided evidence of other crimes, the police were allowed to use it. Cole badly wanted to pick up something about the Hedley murders on the wire; the crimes were three years old but the bodies had just been found. The passage of time since the killings just might make someone sloppy and his investigators very lucky.

Bobby Pearce was supervising the monitor room and its civilian monitors. Their task was to listen to conversations being intercepted and identify those intercepts that would be of interest to the investigators on the meth lab investigation, or of interest to the police generally. Cole had asked them to keep their ears open for any chat that could relate to the discovery of the dead witnesses at Hedley.

The monitors were pro's at their jobs and could quickly identify voices and conversations significant to the investigation at hand. They made notes summarizing intercepted conversations in logbooks that were kept in the locked monitor room. From these records they made lists of dates and times of calls which they deemed to be important, flagging them for the investigators.

Cole's job was to synthesize the information obtained by Grant, Pearce and the four new investigators, and to identify suspects, define the kingpins and figure out how the investigation should proceed. By mid-week he had got into a routine of starting his days with a review of the important intercepts, which had been flagged by the monitors during the night shift. If any followup was required as a result of his review, he would assign it to the profilers or customs reviewer, or do it himself. If there was anything left of the day, he would review and make suggestions with regard to the profiles of visitors to the clubhouse. Most afternoons were spent updating his police notebook and writing the ongoing court brief—the narrative story of the investigation, which would eventually be given to the prosecutors' office when the investigation ended. Assuming they turned up a lab, and that it had methamphetamine in it, and that they could connect people to it. A lot of ifs.

Everyone on the project was cautiously optimistic. In only five days of wiretapping, they had Bones and Jojo discussing who would look after what aspect of the meth lab. It was clear that it was going to be huge. They planned on bringing in a steady supply of the precursor chemicals by truck from the prairie provinces. It sounded like they had a contact in the pharmaceutical business who wasn't averse to obtaining big orders for their bogus company, for a small fee. They were planning on having so many loyal middlemen that the operation would be thoroughly insulated. After listening to them Cole didn't like them, but he respected them.

On Thursday he had read the transcript of a call made two nights earlier: Tuesday night at 9:14. Its contents made him sit up straight and read it again. According to the transcript it was an outgoing call from the clubhouse to a telephone number registered to the home of one Frank Wesley. The known voice of the caller had been identified as that of Brian Edward Allen, also known as Bones.

Outgoing call to: (604) 555-6792
Time: 2114:08
Unknown male: "Hello."
Bones: "Yeah, hey, Frankie, it's me."

Unknown male: "Hi, how you doing?"

Bones: "Okay I guess. A bit uptight. Did you hear?"

Unknown male: "Hear what?"

Bones: "They found it."

Unknown male: "Found what?"

Bones: "Our friend. It was in the paper this morning."

Unknown male: "I don't know what you're talking about."

Bones: "Well, it's just that with Parker getting cold feet and now this, I just don't want any heat—"

Unknown male: "Parker is looked after."
Chuckle. "He knows that if he doesn't co-operate, he'll buy more than one farm."
Cough, cough. "The best way to prevent heat is to use your head. Which means not using the phone."

Call terminated: 2114:24.

Cole had picked the transcript off the pile of intercepted conversations identified as inconsequential by the monitors. It had sat there for two days. The names of the speakers alone, assuming that the person Bones was speaking to was in fact Frank Wesley, would have set bells off in every cop who had ever investigated organized crime in this part of the country.

He found the tape and located the call. Without a doubt, the voice of the unknown male referred to in the transcript was the voice of Frank Wesley. When he told Bones he didn't know what he was talking about, Wesley's voice was hard ice. Something was up.

Someone had found their "friend," and Wesley's quick termination of the call told Cole that the finding related to something illegal. Then there was the reference to someone buying the farm, or a farm. It definitely tied into Morrit's description of how the meth lab was going to be set up in a barn, insulated from nosy neighbours and police surveillance. Surrounding farmland would be a good buffer.

Cole had come across Wesley before, always apparently on the periphery of whatever was being investigated. Cole knew that he was not a club member but that he had a reputation of not being averse to helping them out. He'd even heard a rumour about Wesley being on retainer to the club. One thing he knew for sure, from personal experience and from speaking with other cops, was that ordinarily co-operative, law-abiding citizens became violently unco-operative and hostile to the police when they became witnesses to any of Wesley's alleged crimes. Cole's instincts told him that Wesley was extremely bad news. He was certainly not above taking care of witnesses who could hurt the club. But if Bones's call related to the discovery of the bodies at Hedley, why say that only one "friend" had been found?

Cole could not help but feel a twinge of excitement. Wesley was wily, always aware of surveillance and suspicious of wiretaps. Cole had read transcripts of his conversations from other wiretaps and had seen how Wesley arranged physical meets outside, rather than inside where bugs could be planted. He never talked business on the phone. A call like this was rare.

The monitors had been right: the call did not appear to relate to the meth lab they were investigating, nor did it jibe with the details of the witness murders. But Cole was convinced that someone in the police community would be interested in the call. As well, he wanted to find out about this "Parker," presumably a person. He kept listening to the tape. Two and a half hours after that first call, Bones called Wesley again.

The mechanical voice of the automatic dial number recorder identified the call as an outgoing call from the club-house to area code (604) 555-6792; the time of the call was recorded as 2358:22.

Cole leaned forward to listen.

"Yeah, hi, it's me again." Bones.

Wesley's voice was cold. "What do you want?"

"S-s-sorry about earlier. I w-was a little agitated."

"Uh huh," said Wesley. "What's up?" Cool.

"W-we should talk."

"Why?"

"I ju-just need to talk to you about a couple of things."

Wesley sighed. "Bones, you are such a schoolgirl. I'll meet you at that bar you like so much in twenty. You know the one I mean." Smart, thought Cole.

"Yeah, I know," said Bones.

"And, hey," Wesley hissed.

"Yeah?"

"No more phones, you fat fuck." He hung up.

Cole knew there would be no more phone calls between the two of them. Too bad. Wesley was known to be the club's most effective persuader and money man, focussing more on the latter as the years passed. Cole would have loved to listen in on the financing arrangements of the club, even if these calls weren't about anything of specific interest to the police.

After finishing his review of the transcripts for the day he left the monitor room and let himself into the secure work room, where Grant worked quietly at a desk. He looked up when Cole entered.

"How's it going on the wire?" Grant asked.

"Everyone who's anyone in organized crime is in that place," Cole responded, "but the hard evidence is coming slowly, as expected. Although I did come across an interesting, possibly unrelated call between Bones and Frank Wesley."

Grant whistled. "Wesley doesn't talk on phones."

"I know," said Cole, nodding thoughtfully. "Bones is agitated, talking about the recent discovery of a 'friend.' That, I'm going to look into. Then Wesley refers to someone by the name of Parker 'buying the farm.' The way he said it made me think that Parker had actually made a purchase, as opposed to being offed, in the vernacular. Have you come across someone by the name of Parker in your travels with the bikers?"

"Sure I have," Grant laughed. "Rickie Parker, the wheeler and dealer of the Vancouver Stock Exchange. I've had him pegged for money laundering for the club for a couple of years, but I haven't been in a position to put it together. And let's face it, not many people care about a little laundering when murder and rape stats are going through the roof.

"Parker has a brokerage house in Yaletown. He's a securities broker and a realtor, I believe. Last thing I heard he had a pretty good legitimate business going, but he has a habit of setting up shell companies and depositing big cheques into the accounts of the companies and then using company cheques to make purchases. I think most of the purchases were in real estate." He paused, trying to recall. "I did a few company searches a year or two ago. Parker was always a director of the shell companies he set up, so he could do business. The theory was the companies were actually set up by the club, with Parker as their puppet." He scratched his head. "There was something about bearer bonds, too, but I can't quite remember the scheme. Does that help?"

Cole nodded slowly. "I've got a feeling that if we find farmland bought by Parker, we've found the location of the meth lab. Can you start on a profile for this character first thing tomorrow? Everything you've got on him. Including all real estate purchases he has made, personally or as a corporate director or power of attorney. And get the names of any corporation he's associated with. Can you do that?"

"No problem," the red-eyed staff sergeant replied with a smile. "One thing I can tell you for sure is that the club either trusts Parker like a member, or they have his balls in a vice."

Cole nodded.

"On that note, Jacko, I'm going to take my sorry old ass out of here and find a beer and a burger. Want to join me?"

Cole declined. They said goodnight and Grant left Cole leaning against the desk, thinking.

He felt certain that the farmhouse was their first concrete break in the investigation. He was looking forward to paying Parker a visit, although he would have to wait a while. If the police showed up now, Parker would undoubtedly tell Wesley. Wesley would be savvy enough to wonder how the police had caught on. He would suspect wire. And that would be that.

Cole leaned back and rubbed his jaw. He needed a break. Some exercise and maybe some sleep; then he'd be effective again.

Before either, however, he had to make a call. He had received Janine's page the day before, when he had been in a meeting with the other investigators organizing surveillance teams to cover the club members. His pager had indicated a voice message and, never knowing when someone had urgent information, he had listened to the first few words to identify the caller. When he heard Janine's voice, he had groaned inside. She had no doubt heard about the flowers and was calling to give him hell. Right now he felt like the flowers had been a bad impulse.

Anyway, he had not had time for personal calls until tonight. He looked at his watch: 8:25. He picked up the phone and retrieved the page, listening to the whole message this time.

He hung up the phone slowly. Janine wanted him to call Lauren Grey. He couldn't have hoped for a better situation, except for the timing. Still, he was going to take a break now. If she fit into his schedule, he would see her now. If not, it would have to wait until the next gap. Like always.

He dialled the number Janine had left.

• • •

Lauren had had a miserable day.

Rick had stayed in his office drinking and crying until he finally passed out at about three in the morning. She had slipped out of her hiding place and peeked into his office. He was slumped at his desk, face down. The stacks of money were still there, along with a nearly empty bottle of gin. She was at home and asleep forty minutes later.

Her internal alarm woke her up at 8:45 and she showered quickly, with her cellular phone on the bathroom counter. She was dressed and had coffee brewing by 9:00. By 9:15 she had begun flipping through the morning paper, pretending she wasn't clock-watching. She wondered if Fox had transposed some numbers.

By 11:00 she was a wreck, from disappointment and fatigue. She couldn't understand why he hadn't called, if only for the money. She must have misread Fox completely when she saw some kindness in him. This was truly cruel.

She finally stumbled back into the bedroom, clutching the phone, and fell asleep. She awoke close to five, went for a long run and was contemplating the contents of the pantry when the phone rang.

"Hello, Lauren Grey? This is Jackson Cole. We met through Janine Wright, on Robson Street a week or so ago." His voice was deep and cheerful.

"Oh, yes, how are you?"

217

"Just fine, thanks. Listen, Janine asked that I give you a call. I'm not sure that I got her message right, but it sounded as though you were having problems with some man she thinks is trying to blackmail you."

"Well, that's not entirely right. Janine can be a bit over-imaginative at times."

"If you think it would help to run it by a cop, I'd be happy to listen," he said, sounding slightly hurried.

At first Lauren had thought that he was calling her for a date and she was somewhat indignant that he would, after taking Janine out. But now that it was clear that he was calling for another reason, she was surprised to find herself feeling disappointed. He had crossed her thoughts several times since they had met. Impulsively, she decided that she wanted to see him.

"Yes, I'd appreciate that," she said.

"Oka-a-a-ay." He drew the word out, as though he was balancing things in his mind. "I'm mixed up in a file that has a timetable of its own. I was going to take the next couple of hours off for a run and a meal. If it works for you, why don't we discuss it over food?"

"That sounds great. Where are you running?" she asked.

"From the Rowing Club in Stanley Park."

"Okay," she said. "How about the West Coast Café, by the tennis courts?"

"Sounds good," he answered lightly. "An hour?"

"I'll be there."

"'Bye."

She arrived first and chose a table outside on the balcony, overlooking the chestnut trees and the lit-up tennis courts. It was one of her favourite restaurants, with beautiful hardwood floors and warm panelled walls for cozy winter evenings and flowering gardens in the spring and summer.

She ordered a Scotch and sipped it, watching a tennis

match on one of the courts. She wanted to look cool and uninterested, as she usually was. She couldn't believe that her stomach was tingling in anticipation of seeing him. She wanted to retain control of the situation.

Cole stepped out onto the patio and searched the few tables until he spotted her; then, with a broad smile, he moved toward her quickly. There was no doubt about it, he was handsome. Flushed from exercise, he looked healthy and strong, his dark hair damp and curling, pulled back into a neat ponytail. In the shadow she noticed a dimple in his left cheek and could see his biceps and chest muscles through the crisp white shirt as he approached.

And there she was.

He felt like saying, "Hey gorgeous," and kissing her. Instead he put his gym bag on the floor by the table and said, "Sorry I'm late. It appears that I'm not as fast as I used to be."

She laughed. "It's awfully nice of you to do this. I get the impression that you're extremely busy."

"Yes, things are busy. But it's nice to have a diversion." He ordered a virgin Caesar, spicy. "Do you like oysters?"

"Love 'em," she nodded.

"Okay. We'll have an order of the Penn Coves, for two." The waiter disappeared.

Cole looked out at the courts and the gardens. "I love this place. It's one of the prettiest spots in the city, but you can almost always get a table. Great beer and a great setting after seven miles. What could be finer?"

"The great beer?" she asked laughingly, as the waiter put down his drink.

He liked her.

Leaning forward in his chair, into the candlelight, he looked at her eyes and asked, "So, what's up?"

She had been considering what to tell him ever since he

had called, and she had finally decided that an edited version of the truth would work. Assuming that Fox still intended to do his part, she wouldn't mind finding out something about him from Jackson, if possible. She didn't think his proposal was illegal: it wasn't blackmail, yet it wasn't your everyday arrangement, either. But she had no intention of discussing with Jackson the plans that she had in mind.

She had already got more than enough corroboration of Fox's story during her visit to Rick's office. Still, knowing more about the scrawny little man would not hurt, especially after his failure to call, and she had to come up with something to allay Janine's concerns. Who she was really interested in knowing about was the man from the restaurant, the man screaming at Rick in his office. But she would not bring that up.

She took a sip of her Scotch and leaned toward him, hands cupping the candle as if for warmth. "I got a note in my mailbox at home. A postcard, from this man who said that he knew something about my husband's death. I don't know if you were aware or not, but my husband died in a car crash a couple of years ago. The crash was attributed to his being intoxicated. I never believed it. Anyway, I met with this fellow. I got Janine to come with me, to keep an eye on me and make sure that nothing went wrong."

Cole was watching her intently.

If she continued the story truthfully, Lauren was sure that he would check out Fox's name and would confirm that Fox was who he said he was. If that were so, Jackson would probably give some weight to Fox's story, or think he was trying to scam her. Either way, she was sure he wouldn't leave it alone.

"He wasn't lucid," she continued. "It was quite sad, really. He was well spoken and informed in some ways. I'm pretty sure he was in the mainstream at some time, but he didn't have anything to offer. But we got talking and I told him that he could help with cleanup at the gallery if he wanted. I kind of took a liking to him, as odd as that sounds," she smiled, looking down at the table. "I doubt I'll see him again, though."

"What was his name?" Cole asked softly. He wondered why she was lying.

"Dan something," she said. "I didn't catch his last name."

"Well," he said, "there's not much I can do. I can't even see if he's got a criminal record without a last name."

He wasn't going to call her on it. She hadn't really set this up and if she wanted to keep some things private, that was okay with him. He was confident that if the situation got out of her control, she would come to him for help—if she felt comfortable with him. Part of that involved not pushing the issue now.

"It doesn't seem like there's anything you want me to do right now, anyway. Right?" He was looking straight at her.

"Not really." She looked down at her drink. "I suppose I didn't think it would hurt if a police officer knew about the meeting, in case I disappeared or something. It *was* a bit out of the ordinary." She sounded slightly defensive and she knew it.

"Downright weird," he said, letting her off the hook with a smile. "But I'm glad it happened."

"You are? Why?"

He took a chance. "Because if it hadn't, you probably wouldn't be here right now."

She liked the way that sounded.

The oysters were delicious. They ordered salmon and salads and drifted easily away from the topic that had brought them together.

At 10:45 Cole's pager brought him back to reality: a numerical page with 911 behind it. He excused himself and went to a pay phone in the restaurant to retrieve the message. "Someone abducted a Frank Wesley, or something," one of the civilian monitors told him. It was all over the wire; she thought Cole would want to know.

She was right.

He decided that the only person he needed to call was Staff Sergeant Grant. With his background information on bikers, he would be able to make sense of the situation faster than anyone else Cole could think of. He would return to the monitor room and listen to the calls and, with Grant's help, try to figure out what was going on.

The staff sergeant was delighted when Cole called and extended the invitation. He was playing pool downtown and losing money. He would meet Cole at the office.

Cole hurried through the softly lit dining room and out onto the deck. Lauren sat at their table, facing him, beautiful and peaceful-looking in the candlelight. He was sorry their evening was ending.

"I've asked for the bill," she smiled.

"Good instincts." He sat down across from her. "I've really enjoyed tonight, even though I can't do much in the Dick Tracy department for you."

"It's just as well." She pushed a loose strand of hair away from her eyes and looked down at the candle. "I've enjoyed tonight, too."

The bill came and he took it.

"Let's split it," she said.

"Not a chance," he smiled. "It's been a long time since dinner has been this great, so it's worth twice the price of one, if you follow."

"Well then," she said. "Let me even it out. Let me make you dinner." She couldn't believe she had said it. Since Martin, she had not cooked for anyone other than Rick and the odd business associate or girlfriend. She wanted to take the implications of the offer away. "I'm told I'm a hell of a cook," she added quickly.

"I'm sure you are. That would be great."

"How about Saturday. 6:30?"

"Perfect." He stood up and walked behind her to pull out her chair for her. It was the closest he had been to her. She smelled marvellous. Her hair smelled clean and fresh and her perfume was musky. He remained behind her for a fraction of a second longer than necessary.

Lauren liked it. She could sense his body behind her, and its scent of soap and spice. She wanted to touch him as much as she wanted to get away from him.

The waiter brought the change and broke the spell.

They walked through the restaurant without speaking. Down the steps and into the fragrant shadows of the park, toward the parking lot. Cole opened her car door for her and she stepped toward him. Up close, he was almost a full head taller than her. She looked up at him as if to speak. Bending down, he broke all his rules and kissed her gently on the lips. She could taste garlic and spice and his own special taste.

"Drive safely," he said. He watched her drive out of the lot before walking to his own car.

He was at the office fifteen minutes later. Grant was already in the monitor room.

"What's up?" he asked.

"It's the damnedest thing," Grant answered. "I've listened to some of the tapes but can't figure out whether it's connected to the meth lab deal or not. I've got no doubt that he's helping the club put together the meth deal, if only the financing for it. But whether or not tonight's activities relate to that or something else, I don't know."

"So, what happened tonight?" Cole asked, slightly impatient.

"Frank Wesley got cold-cocked and strung like a pig to

market and then locked up in his own truck." Grant was laughing. "Surrey Detachment took the call and our people picked it up from an alert on PIRS."

The Police Intelligence Reporting Service had a computer program that alerted them to any change in status of any of their targets' police files. If Bones got checked by a cop for anything, anywhere in Canada, Cole's group would know about it as soon as the officer checking had made the required computer entry recording police contact.

"Strange," Cole said. "It could be anything. Whatever it is, someone took a hell of a risk playing with that boy."

He sat down to listen to the intercepts. Predictably, Wesley was cooler than the club members. They phoned each other and tried to guess why their brawn and brains had been attacked like this. There was only one call with Wesley on it, an outgoing call from the clubhouse to Wesley's home. Six rings.

Finally, "Yeah?" Cole recognized Wesley's voice.

"Frank, it's Bones." He imagined the speakers, Bones soft and flaccid, Wesley tough and strong.

"Yeah?" Wesley didn't sound particularly interested.

"Listen, that bitch on the front desk of Muscles phoned, saying you'd been kidnapped or something. You okay?" He sounded upset.

"Except for my head feeling like it's been hammered by a sledge, I'm fine. Thanks for your concern." There was a touch of irony in Wesley's voice. It was lost on his caller.

"Yeah, good. Good." Bones paused. "Who the fuck do you think did it?"

"I don't know, Bones," Wesley said, sounding tired. "It wasn't you, was it?"

Bones laughed uncomfortably. "Don't be ridiculous. We're buds; you know that."

"Yeah, yeah." Wesley didn't sound like he cared much.

"Hey, that little fuck Parker . . . I bet it was him, after the other night."

"I don't think so, Bones. Rickie Parker doesn't have the balls for this kind of thing. I'll figure it out when I'm not seeing stars. I gotta rest now. 'Bye."

"I'll send one of the whores over to look after you," the fat man offered.

"Maybe later, Bones. Not now." Wesley hung up.

Cole had barely heard the last part of the exchange. *Parker.* He turned to Grant. "I know we don't have a profile on Parker, but do we have any personal details on him?"

Grant pushed himself out of his chair and walked over to one of his nonexistent filing cabinets, all of which had been brought over to the workroom after the suite at the Sutton had no longer been needed. He spent several minutes sorting through various manila files before he found one labelled Proceeds of Crime Investigation—Section 462.31 Criminal Code. Money laundering. He found what he was looking for almost immediately: a Certificate of Incorporation, presumably of historic value to the file.

"This is all I've got," he said, passing Cole the certificate. "I ordered it from Corporate and Consumer Affairs when Parker first showed up and I got my theory of him as a money launderer."

Cole looked at the document. It was a certified copy of a Certificate of Incorporation describing Martin Grey and Rick Parker as sole shareholders in Grey and Parker, Investment Consultants, Inc. Sixty-five, thirty-five split.

He whistled out loud. Martin Grey was Lauren's Martin. Parker had been his business partner. If Grant was right and Parker was laundering money for the club, it wasn't beyond reason to speculate that Martin's untimely death might be connected somehow.

Going through the file, Cole found documentation dated

about a year after Martin's death, showing a name change in the company, with Parker dropping Grey's name. He wondered why. Ego, maybe. Although there would be good will value in keeping Martin's name on the letterhead. Maybe Lauren. Who knew?

What was clear was that someone connected to Lauren was likely a crook, involved with some very heavy people. He was sure she didn't know. He wondered if Martin had been so inclined.

"The crash was attributed to his being intoxicated," she had said. "I never believed it." Interesting.

He wondered who Dan was. And what he had said that Lauren didn't want Cole to know about. If he was right, so was Janine: Lauren was into something way over her head.

Pete Grant tapped him on the shoulder. "Man, I don't know where you were just now, but that was some deep thought. The monitors have something going on that might interest you, if you can pull yourself away from your reverie."

"What is it?"

"It sounds as if there is an impromptu meeting at the club-house," Grant answered. "Someone's just arrived from the States. They're talking about the recent arrival and storage of hundreds of pounds of safrol and ephedrine. You might want to listen."

Cole and Grant spent the next few hours with the monitors, listening to live conversations taking place in the club-house. As he listened, Cole made notes and gave orders.

It seemed that an unidentified man and woman had sailed up from Friday Harbor, stateside, to Vancouver. The club members called him Doc. He was obviously the laboratory expert consultant. The man was somehow connected to the San Francisco branch of the Warriors and was evidently a long-lost pal of a number of the Vancouver and Langley members.

Watching the video camera images, Grant muttered, "He looks like a bloody doctor, not a biker."

Cole looked at the freeze-frame of two people entering the house. It was true. Tanned and wiry, "Doc" had a neat beard and short hair, greying at the temples, and he wore khaki shorts, a golf shirt and gold wire-rimmed glasses. If Cole were a customs officer, he wouldn't have checked him either. Unless it was to have a longer look at the blonde bombshell with the good doctor.

As they listened, it became clear to Cole and Grant that word was getting around that the club had visitors. Within half an hour of Doc's arrival, four senior members had arrived. They all chatted for an hour or so, very social, discussing mutual friends and associates, until the logbook read like a Who's Who of organized crime.

Jojo arrived just after midnight and they quickly got down to business, leaving the women in the living room to their coke and white wine. Tucked into the den, five of the most senior members talked business while Cole and Grant listened. Someone in the den turned on a stereo. One of the monitors flipped a switch; the speaking voices were immediately enhanced, the music reduced to background noise.

As the club members made their plans, Cole made his own. He had three separate surveillance teams set up on the clubhouse, with enough different cars and different people that they shouldn't be spotted. He didn't want Doc out of sight; when he left the clubhouse, he would have a constant police shadow.

He had paged Pearce and assigned him the task of getting a court order authorizing the placement of a tracking device on the vehicle associated with the chemist. That would eliminate the need for constant surveillance: they would know where his car was at all times. With a little luck, he would tour the lab. With a little more, he would drive to the tour site himself.

The conversation in the den quickly began to sound like a science class, with the scientist lecturing on safe storage of the meth precursors, emphasizing the care required to store the hydrogen chloride gas required to make the drug. He was reassured by voices, believed by Cole to be those of Jojo and Bones, that any accidents up to and including a minor explosion would not attract law enforcement authorities.

Bones mentioned "acreage," and Grant looked at Cole. He nodded, thinking the same thing: the farm purchase.

Science turned to commerce and marketing, as the five men discussed distribution strategies and ways to insulate themselves from detection.

As usual, the club would be involved in the financing, setup and profit sharing; it would not be directly involved in anything else. Distribution and sales would be looked after by associates of the club who would delegate and redelegate until no one on the street knew for sure where the shit was coming from.

Distribution was planned for British Columbia, the Yukon, Alberta and Saskatchewan, Washington state and Oregon, with a cut of the profits going to the San Francisco branch. The beauty of the plan was that most of the risk took place in Canada. Even with a lab of the size being contemplated, chances were good that jail time for anyone caught would be minimal—probably less than two years, whereas the same lab in California would get someone ten years to life.

It was all on tape.

Cole was confident they had enough to charge them with conspiracy to traffic methamphetamines right then. But he wanted more than that. He wanted to hit them when they had spent as much money as they were going to on the project and when they could almost taste the profits of their efforts. Then he wanted to take it down.

He looked at his watch: 2:07.

He had to get some sleep. Get some sleep and sort things out in his mind. He said goodnight to Grant and headed through the silent building, out into the black night for home.

True to his word, Fox's lawyer was at the Pre-Trial Centre by 8:15 with a faxed copy of the police report describing the robbery.

"You should move out of this town, Danny," was Larry's advice as he sat down in the interview room. "There're cops in this town who get a hard-on for you whenever there's a robbery." He slapped the report down. "Go somewhere where not everyone'll believe you're a legend."

"You'd starve," Fox retorted. "What have they got?"

"Nothing. One unidentified informant who won't testify, naming you as the guy, and then three eyewitnesses who all describe the robber as five-foot-eleven, medium build. One guy says 'stocky.' You, my friend, ain't that. The age is wrong, too." He looked at his file. "Prints were lifted off the register. Anything to worry about?"

Danny shook his head.

"Okay. I'll see what I can do," he said. He left the interview room.

He had Fox out in under forty minutes. Fuck.

Fox walked a couple of blocks until he found a pay phone with a receiver. He dropped the quarter. He was shaking.

She answered on the third ring.

"H-h-hello," he stammered. "It's Danny."

"You're about a day late, aren't you?" Her voice was cool.

He went for the truth. "I got arrested right after I saw you in the park. I just got released. I couldn't call you 'cause you're not my lawyer and anyways they would trace the call. I'm real sorry I didn't call. If I could of, I would of."

She had no reason not to believe him. And he had been smart not to connect them. "What were you arrested for?" she asked.

"A gas station holdup. They got me confused with some six-foot fat guy. It happens all the time."

She smiled. "Have you had breakfast?" she asked.

"No."

"Me neither. We've got some things to talk about. Can you meet me at the Denny's at Thurlow and Davie, in an hour?" It was a good middle ground, in the West End, with lots of street people mixed with old people, gay people, crazy people and everyday people. She and Fox wouldn't be the oddest couple in the restaurant.

"Let's make it an hour and a half." He had a few things to take care of before they hooked up.

"Okay," she said brightly, "see you there."

He couldn't resist. "It's a date."

She laughed and hung up.

Freshly fixed and showered, Fox walked from the mission through the downtown core up to Denny's. He grabbed a booth where they would have pretty good privacy and watched her walk in. White shirt, blue jeans and sandals. She was a knockout. When she saw him, her face lit up. She seemed genuinely happy to see him.

They both ordered coffee and a Grand Slam and talked about the weather until their breakfasts arrived. She leaned into her food with enthusiasm.

"I didn't eat much yesterday," she explained.

He laughed. "I never saw someone your size pack groceries down like that."

Once the eggs and bacon were gone, Fox brought up business. "Have you got the money?"

"Not yet." She shook her head. "But I will by tomorrow morning. Something came up." She described what she had seen at Rick's office. "The man who was yelling, the leader," she said. It was hard to get the words out. "That's who killed Martin, isn't it?"

He looked at her solemnly, liking her. She treated him decently, and she was spunky and smart. He nodded and leaned back in the naugahyde booth.

She leaned back too. "It's okay, I've known since that night, really. I've had time to adjust to the face."

He nodded again.

"I wouldn't have figured it out without you, so you'll still get your money. A deal's a deal."

"I feel like it's too high now," he said. That much money for almost nothing.

She leaned forward and whispered earnestly, "So help me. Earn the rest of it."

"How?"

"You already know." She took a deep breath. "I'm not asking you to do anything. Just get me into a position to do it. I can't keep going unless I take care of this. Rick's not going to do anything—would you? They'll kill him or they'll kill his son, or both. The police can't do anything. You said it yourself, the evidence got buried two years ago. So he gets to get away with it?" Her voice was still a whisper, but high-pitched. "Martin was my best friend in the world." She stopped, shaking.

Fuck, he thought. Fuck. Get up and walk away. Go steal a car or break into a house. Get up now.

He looked down at the table. "The full three hundred," he said quietly.

She nodded.

"And you'll need fifteen hundred for a gun."

"Okay."

"And some practice. And a good plan."

She nodded again.

"Do you know what you're getting into?" he asked. "Even if you don't get caught, you'll have to live with yourself every day, knowing."

"If I *don't* do this, I'll have to live every day, knowing." Her voice was flat. "Let's get the bill and find a bank."

They found a branch of her bank open two blocks west of the restaurant. There she withdrew fifteen hundred-dollar bills and gave them to Fox as they stood by a deserted New Accounts counter. He bent down as if to tie his shoe and stuffed the bills into his sock.

"I'm giving you two hundred thousand dollars tomorrow," she said. "Where do you plan on putting it? The other sock?"

"I've got a stash place in my room, until I go."

"What if someone steals it?"

"No one'll find it. It's where I put my stuff, and the cops missed it when they tossed the place Wednesday."

"What if there's a fire?"

"I don't know," he said. "I've never had this problem before."

"I have an idea," she said. "While we're here, why don't I

give you a hundred dollars more—we'll take it off the total price—and you open up an account and get a safety deposit box. That way your money will be safe and accessible."

"And the bank doesn't know what's in the box?"

She shook her head. "Nope."

"Okay," he said. As he took the two fifties from her, they both had the same thought: the obvious alternate use of the money.

"I won't," he said. "Your idea's smart, long run."

"You're smart, too. I've got to go see Rick. How long will it take to get your shopping done?"

"I'll have it tonight."

"Do you have any plans for tomorrow?" she asked. "Could you start to teach me?"

"Yeah. I don't suppose you've ever handled one before?"

"No."

"Okay. We'll go out to the range off the Barnet Highway. Rifles and handguns. No one'll give what you've got a second glance."

"What will I have?"

"The best," he answered simply. He sounded confident.

She insisted on picking him up outside the Auckland at 9:30 the following morning.

When she left the bank, he was speaking with a clerk who had finally appeared behind the counter.

She decided to walk the half mile to Rick's office. She needed fresh air and time to figure out how she would approach him. Her feelings toward him had changed. She understood his vulnerability, especially through Billy, but she couldn't help feeling that their special friendship since Martin's death had been built on a lie. While she agonized over the coroner's verdict, he knew. He must have.

She reached Yaletown too quickly. As she rounded the corner and approached Rick's office, an ambulance pulled away from the deli across the street, siren off. A patrol car and two unmarked police cars were double-parked in front.

Rick stood in a small crowd of onlookers. His shoulders were slumped and he had huge bags under his eyes. She couldn't help but feel sorry for him. He spotted her as she approached and managed a smile. They kissed cheeks.

"What happened?" she asked.

"A young kid killed herself. Hung up the Closed sign and went in the back and drank until I guess she got enough courage to slash her wrists. That's the neighbourhood gossip, so far." He sounded sad.

Lauren felt icy fingers crawl up her spine.

"What did she look like?" she asked, trying to sound idly curious.

"Gorgeous," he responded. "Young. Great legs. Great smile. Man, I'd have thought she didn't have a care in the world. What can be so bad to make you want to die at twenty? You know, I thought about asking her out myself, except for that asshole boyfriend of hers."

"A little young, don't you think?" Lauren tried to sound light. She was sure she could smell booze on him. "What was wrong with the boyfriend?"

"He was a creep." He looked away from her. "A real biker type."

She instinctively pulled away from him. Alcohol, bikers, Rick. And a "loose end across the street." She felt sick with certainty that she knew what had happened.

She looked at Rick, wondering if he had any idea that he might be connected to this death scene. "What's the matter, Rick, don't you like bikers?"

He seemed to whiten. He changed the subject. "What brings you to this neck of the woods, Lauren?"

"I need to convert some paper," she said, trying to sound normal. "Come on, let's go upstairs and you can work your magic." She put an arm around his shoulders and steered him away from the crowd and death.

The main floor was brightly lit and busy. The two assistants were on the phone and the den mother-cum-office-manager was banging away at her keyboard. As they climbed the stairs to Rick's office, Lauren felt like they were climbing away from normalcy. She felt almost dizzy as they passed the armoire.

They walked into his office, neat and empty. No stacks of money to be seen. Rick went to the window and looked down on the street they had just left. Lauren headed directly for the bar.

Pretending not to see the half-empty glass on his desk, she pulled out a bottle of Scotch and poured two glasses. She handed him one. "It's a bit early," she said, smiling, "but you look like you could use one."

He nodded and took the drink gratefully.

Lauren decided that business could wait. "You look terrible, Rick," she said gently.

"I know." He pushed himself away from the window. "Kid, I'm in trouble. I'm doing business with some very bad people." He remembered the telephone bug and realized that there could be others in the room.

"Why don't you go to the police?" she asked.

"Oh, it's not like that," he said lightly, scribbling on a note pad. "When I say bad, I don't mean crooked, I just mean really aggressive. I can handle it, I'm just getting old."

He passed the paper to her. "That's a lie," she read. "This place is bugged. They're DANGEROUS." The last word was underlined three times. Lauren pocketed the note and nodded.

"Maybe you just need a vacation," she said. "Why don't you slip down to San Diego for a week?"

"Maybe I will," he smiled, flashing her a thumbs-up. He

gulped down half his drink. "Now, about you. It sounds like you're actually here for money."

"I am." She felt far warmer toward him than she had since she had first realized he was involved with Martin's killers. She was certain that if he didn't think they were being listened to, he would have told her his suspicions. "Rick, I need three hundred thousand cash. Fast."

"Three hundred *thousand*," he sputtered. "Jesus, Lauren, why?"

She was ready for him. "There are a couple of paintings coming up for sale in Europe. Private dealers. Believe it or not, some of them aren't even satisfied with cash—some insist on bullion—so I'm getting off light."

"So," he said, "three hundred US?"

Smart question, she thought. International dealers worked in US dollars or Swiss francs. Not Canadian currency. "Canadian's fine. I'll wire it over and deal with the exchange as I make the buys." It sounded reasonable.

"Okay, Lauren, let's just look at your file." He pulled it up on his computer screen. "You've made a killing on Sessnex," he said, referring to a gold company in the north. "You'll have tax implications, but it would probably be a good time to get you out of that." He sounded more like himself, calmed by familiar tasks and excited by the victories of the market. "Buyers won't be a problem. When do you need the money?"

"Tomorrow." She took a breath. "I actually need two hundred today, but I would imagine that's a little unrealistic." She looked at him, inquiring.

"Jesus, you don't want much, do you? The market closes here at 1:30. The New York and the TSE are already down for the weekend. I'm leaving for Calgary in a couple of hours for a meeting tomorrow."

"Can you do it?"

"I can try," he said, not wanting to let her down.

"That would be super. I'd really appreciate it."

"Okay, but if I can't swing it, it will have to wait until Monday. Will you be home tonight?"

"Yes."

"Okay. If I can unload two hundred, I'll courier a cheque to you tonight."

"Thank you, Rick." She finished her drink and stood up. "I think you'll like what I'm getting."

She kissed him on the cheek and left.

He buzzed his assistant and told her to rearrange the airport limo. He would spend as much time on the phone for Lauren as he could. He would pack what he needed from the closet here and leave for the airport from the office.

• • •

Oskar entered his third travel agency of the afternoon, with his third fake passport and set of credit cards in a third different name. Once again he purchased tickets for Vancouver-Los Angeles-Mexico City, return. Once again, they were open-ended, both ways. He had no intention of returning. Or of staying in Mexico City for more than a couple of days.

A great believer in solicitor-client privilege, he had asked for and received from his lawyer a current list of countries that were parties to Canada's extradition treaty. Belize was not on the list. It wasn't going to be a complete breeze, but with luck and good planning he would fly Vancouver-LA on one passport, toss it, fly LA-Mexico City on the second, and use the third to obtain accommodation in Mexico so that he would have time to make the arrangements for the final leg of his journey.

After he reached Belize he would be more or less unrecognizable: hair dye, coloured contact lenses, the works. At least for the first few months. How long he stayed away would depend on how he liked it and how he felt about his safety in Vancouver. He had given his lawyer power of attorney with instructions to wire him money on request.

He would be free of the motherfucker in a matter of days. Wesley would be fucked, and he would be drinking beer on some beach watching chicks in micro-bikinis. Life was looking up.

He would arrange for a call from Donna tonight and another in the next couple of days and pop, that would be that. He approached the agent, smiling and relaxed, and introduced himself as Erik Jorgensen.

As much out of boredom as curiosity, he asked to borrow the white pages as the agent checked and rechecked her computer for flights. He thumbed through the *P*s to Parker and found the Yaletown address he had seen on the scrap of paper under Rick Parker, Investment Brokers. That was interesting. Below that was a residential listing for Rick Parker. A luxury high-rise downtown. Oskar watched the woman across the desk from him without really seeing her. He was thinking.

If Parker was a drug dealer or gang muscle, Oskar would have heard of him. Had the note been a plant, intended by whoever put it there to be found by Oskar? He didn't think so. What would be the point? What would anybody think he would do just because he saw a name and address?

On the other hand, it had his interest.

Mike had thrown Rod-dee the shorts. They were too long for Roddy, would likely have fit Mike. Mike was obviously muscle for the Warriors. If they were his shorts, the note could mean that the Satan's Warriors were somehow connected to this investor, Parker. Which could mean a civilian link, which could mean a weak link. Which could mean an opportunity to hurt the fuckers.

Or it could mean that Mike was smart with his money and invested it professionally.

Oskar did not think so.

He smacked the packet of tickets against his left palm and walked toward his car, parked near the door of the travel agency. He had decided to go take a look.

•   •   •

The black Porsche moved slowly along the curb in front of the brokerage house. It was a two-storey job, with a big balcony and French doors on the second floor. It looked to Oskar like an old house done over. He liked modern.

The lights were on on both floors and he could see people downstairs. He pulled out his cell phone and punched in the number he had seen in the phone book.

"Parker Investments, may I help you?"

"Rick Parker." Oskar kept it short.

"He's with someone right now," the woman responded. "May I have him return your call?"

"No," Oskar replied simply, and pressed End.

He pulled the car back into the stream of traffic and headed for Rick Parker's residential address. Parker was not a member of the Warriors, so what was the connection? The club was either extorting something from Parker or using him to launder their money. Or both. Either way, it was not a bad bet that a non-criminal type involved with the club would try to get something on them, if only for his own protection. The most logical way to do that would be to amass information about the deals you were involved with and the deals you heard about. Information could be power.

Oskar was betting that some form of record existed and that Parker kept it close to his chest. At home. If he was wrong, he would have wasted nothing but time. He felt the adrenaline pumping.

He parked the car in the alley behind the high-rise and grabbed a pair of latex gloves and a small set of tools from the glove compartment. He walked around the block to the front of the building.

It was a pleasant place to wait. The outside foyer was tiled and walled in marble and a large fountain splashed noisily in its centre. The security intercom was set in a statue by the fountain. There was no list of tenants and codes: it was clear that you knew what you were doing here, or you did not get in.

As he waited, he pulled a small roll of electrician's tape from the tool satchel, tore off a one-inch strip and rolled it into a ball between his gloved hands. Just as he finished this task, he saw a woman inside, walking slowly across the lobby toward the front doors. Oskar guessed her to be in her eighties. She wore a pale blue dress, a matching hat and white gloves. She carried a cane.

As she approached the locked glass door, a cab pulled up at the curb. Oskar walked swiftly to the door and waited with a smile for her to open it. When she did, he took the door's weight from her and opened it wide.

"Thank you, dear," she said in a crusty voice.

"You're welcome," he replied, charming.

As she stepped past him, he took a step toward the building and stuffed the ball of tape into the lock latch. He then joined her at the top of the stairs and extended his arm to her. She took it and they walked slowly down the steps to the waiting cab. Once she was in the cabbie's care, Oskar raced back to the building. He did not want any alarms going off because of the door having been ajar too long. He took a small file from the satchel and flicked the ball of tape out of the latch hole. As he walked to the brass elevator banks, he heard the front door close securely.

Once inside the elevator Oskar saw that 18 was the top floor. That suited his purposes: penthouses usually had fewer suites, which meant fewer neighbours to pop home in the middle of Oskar's entry. Not that he expected to take long to get in. He would have been surprised if the locks on Parker's door were trickier than standard fare, given the security downstairs.

The elevator ascended noiselessly and landed gently at the top of the building. Oskar stepped out into a darkly panelled corridor. Muzak was being piped in from somewhere. A quick scan confirmed his hopes: Parker's apartment was one of only two on the floor.

Oskar moved quickly across the thick carpet and listened at the door of 1802. He heard nothing. As he had expected, the locks were straightforward hardware crap, in brass. He was in in less than a minute, closing the door quietly behind him.

He stood on the threshold for a moment, surveying the place. It was impressive. The threshold was raised four feet above the living room, and gave onto a marble catwalk that ran around the back of the huge room toward what Oskar presumed to be the kitchen and bedroom areas.

The living room was huge—seventy by a hundred feet with sixteen-foot ceilings and windows of floor-to-ceiling glass. Sheer drapes hung the length of the windows, fluttering in the breeze. An oak bar occupied one corner of the room and cream-coloured leather sofas defined two separate conversation areas. There were several oak end tables with large vases and huge sprays of flowers. Whoever Rick Parker was, he lived well.

Oskar ran silently along the catwalk through a modern kitchen, and checked the bedroom, den and two bathrooms. Satisfied there was no one in the apartment, he returned to the living room and pulled apart the sheers. The balcony provided a stunning view of early afternoon in English Bay. It was tiled in terra cotta and decorated with huge pots of flowers. It was unoccupied.

He considered briefly where to start. Anything of interest was sure to be found in an unusual hiding place. He was certain that Parker would not put such a sensitive document in an obvious spot like a safe. Assuming that such a sensitive document existed. His guess was the kitchen or a bathroom.

He walked through the master bedroom to the ensuite bathroom. It was starkly simple, painted white with black accents and towels. There were no pictures on the walls and no countertop clutter. He checked the sink cupboard and behind-the-counter mirrors, unable to find anything out of the ordinary. There was almost nowhere to conceal things in the room.

In the kitchen he examined the fridge and freezer, tossing most of their contents on the floor. He opened the oven and took apart the Jenn-Air range, and found nothing.

It would be easier if he knew what he was looking for.

Once he had gone through the kitchen cupboards, he moved to the second bathroom. It was decorated in antique white and green with clusters of small prints on the walls and toiletry ornaments all over the counter. After checking the backs of several of the prints, Oskar realized that the room's style was the exact opposite to that of the bathroom off the master bedroom. It was hard to believe the same person had chosen both styles. He left it without touching another item and ran back to the austere bathroom he had already searched. He went directly to the only unsearched place in the room where an object could be hidden and lifted the lid of the toilet tank. Inside, resting on the bottom of the tank in a sealed freezer bag, was a computer disk. Pay dirt. Oskar reached into the cold water and grabbed a corner of the bag.

He dried off the bag and his hands on one of Parker's

black towels, removed the disk from the bag, placed it in his shirt pocket and tossed the bag in the sink. He left the tank lid resting on the toilet seat. He still had lots of time.

He walked back to the den and straight to the computer. He turned it on and inserted the disk. He found the right drive and opened the document: "If you are reading this, I am probably dead," it began. It went on to lay out Parker's work for the Warriors over the last two years, detailing the purchase of huge tracts of real estate, including a farm that Parker understood was going to be converted into an illicit laboratory. It detailed who had supplied him with the purchase money for the farm as well as dozens of share acquisitions, shell companies and off-shore companies. They were all listed there, along with Wesley's name. Lucci. Scofield. Allen. It was fucking dynamite.

Oskar turned to the writing desk next to the computer terminal and found Parker's supply of stationery in the top drawer. He helped himself to a large envelope. He found a phone book in the bottom drawer of the desk and thumbed through it, then dialled the non-emergency number for the RCMP, Vancouver Headquarters, and asked for the officer in charge of outlaw bikers. He was transferred.

"Staff Sergeant Grant's office," a woman said. Oskar wrote the name down on the envelope.

"Yeah," he said. "I've got some interesting reading material for the staff sergeant. I need your postal code."

She gave him the number and he wrote it down below Grant's name and the RCMP address. He then took Parker's last stamp, licked it and stuck it to the envelope. Finally he placed the computer disk in the envelope and sealed it. He turned the computer off and returned to the living room. He stood quietly at the door, listening for noise in the hallway. Hearing nothing, he opened Parker's front door and left. In search of a mailbox.

● ● ●

Cole wrapped things up at the office just after 6:00 and stopped for takeout sushi and a six-pack before heading for home. He would be back in the office first thing in the morning to review the night's events on the wire, but now he needed a break to maintain his effectiveness. There was a Mariners game on the tube, after which he planned to crash. He couldn't remember the last night he'd spent like this.

It didn't last.

His pager went off halfway through the third inning. He recognized the number, which he hadn't called in over a year. A woman named Diane; a few nice times, but a bad fit for both. They had more or less agreed on the split. So he wondered why she was calling him at 8:30 on a Friday night. He dialled the number.

"Hi, Jackson." She sounded upbeat.

"Hey, Diane, how are you doing?"

"Just great. Listen, I don't know if you'll be interested in this or not but I've been volunteering with Crime Stoppers once a week for the last few months. At about twenty to eight tonight, I got a call from a tipster about Frank Wesley. I remember you mentioning him a couple of times as someone important. I thought you might want to know. I know the city police will get the information, but I'm never sure how much you guys get."

"Not much," he said wryly. "But you're right, I'm very interested in this guy. Is this the first call on him?"

"No. I pulled up the sheets and there have been six calls in total, four from a female and two from a male with an eastern European accent."

"Okay," Cole said. "Let's not talk about it on the phone. Could you meet me somewhere, or could I come by?"

"Sure. I copied the sheets, just in case."

"You're a doll. I'll be there in fifteen." He hung up.

• • •

He sat at her kitchen table and read the reports, and when he was finished he rubbed his jaw thoughtfully and looked at her, shaking his head slowly. "Diane, this is dynamite. Will you get in trouble if I take these?"

She shook her head. "I'm sure the city police have the information, and there's not really anyone I can call on the weekend, so if you need it, I think you should have it."

"How about if I refer to the information contained in these reports in a search warrant affidavit?" He didn't want her to get in trouble, yet he desperately wanted the use of these tips.

"I don't think so, Jackson. My understanding of the program is to ensure confidentiality, while assisting the police to prevent and solve crimes. Well . . ." She stopped, tilting her head as if to think. "I'm not breaching any confidentiality and the fact that you're a Mountie and not a city cop doesn't seem relevant to me."

"I like your logic, Di." He stood up and tucked the papers into his jacket pocket. She walked him to the door and they said their goodbyes.

Cole drove straight to his office and began drafting the amendment.

On Friday, June eighteenth, at eight-fifty p.m., I was advised by a confidential and reliable source and do verily believe the following:

1. The said confidential and reliable source is a volunteer worker at Crime Stoppers, Vancouver. In this capacity s/he receives and

records telephone calls received in the Crime Stoppers office.

2. Crime Stoppers is a non-profit organization aimed at citizens assisting the police in preventing and solving crimes.

3. The said confidential and reliable source also retrieves Crime Stoppers records of incoming calls as part of his/her duties.

4. Now shown to me and marked Exhibits A through F, inclusive, to this my affidavit, are six Crime Stoppers records with respect to incoming calls received at Crime Stoppers, Vancouver, relating to Frank Wesley.

5. I verily believe the contents of Exhibits A through F to be true.

Exhibits A through F were six summaries of phone calls from two concerned citizens, identities unknown, regarding Frank Wesley and his trafficking in cocaine. Judging from the woman caller's intimate knowledge of Wesley's house and lifestyle, Cole guessed that she was either a girlfriend or a hooker. Hooker was more likely, since any girlfriend of Wesley's would know which side her butter was on. And what he was capable of.

The male sounded more knowledgeable about coke than the woman. Competition trying to ensure Wesley got taken out of the game? Cole wondered. It didn't really matter. If the calls were accurate, Wesley had been actually dealing for more than six months, and the Mounties hadn't had a sniff. He knew people on the street were afraid of Wesley, but he would have expected to hear something about Wesley physically moving product. As far as he knew, this hands-on dealing by him was unprecedented. According to the woman's call tonight, he was bragging about getting fifty kilos in the next couple of days.

Cole finished up his affidavit and left a message on Felix Blackburn's home phone, saying he had another affidavit for review, pronto. He then put the document in the office safe and headed home to bed. The Mariners game had ended hours ago.

Saturday, June 20, 1998

"I t's going to have to be a separate wire order. Different investigations," Felix Blackburn said, putting down Cole's draft affidavit.

"Even though he's showing up on calls on the wire we've got going?" Cole asked.

"Yes," Blackburn nodded. "I'd say so. You'll have to refer to that in this new affidavit, but yeah, I think we're looking for procedural problems down the road if we just tag this onto the first wiretap order."

"You're the boss," Cole said, crossing his long legs at the ankle and stretching against the upholstered chair.

They were in Blackburn's office overlooking Georgia Street from twenty-two storeys up. They had met at 7:30. It was now 8:45.

They discussed what exactly was necessary for a few more minutes, then Cole left to meet a trusted paralegal at his office to make the necessary changes to the document. They had an appointment with a Supreme Court judge for twelve noon that day.

• • •

Lauren had awoken before six, without the alarm clock, full of nervous energy. She went for a long run under the fresh morning sky and stretched on the deck by the sea. On the way downtown she stopped at a bank machine and deposited the cheque for two hundred thousand dollars that Rick had couriered to her the night before. While parked in the bank lot, she put down the convertible top. It was going to be a beautiful drive.

She parked curbside in front of the Auckland Rooming House and waited for Danny with the engine running. A beautiful early summer morning and there were already—or still—street hypes walking down Main Street. Skinny white legs and arms with blue tattoos and bruises. Danny's home was bizarre: three-dimensional faces poking out of the building's facade, laughing or scowling at passersby. They were remarkable. She could tell, even from this distance, that they were hand-cast. Odd faces with pointed noses, chipped, arched brows, all cobalt blue, staring out from the wall. She was still engrossed in them, wondering who the artist was, when Danny turned around the south corner of the building at a run, panting.

"Sorry I kept you waiting," he gasped. His hair was wet, flat against his head and he was out of breath.

"I'm not. These are fascinating," she said, pointing to the tiles. "Where were you?"

He jerked his thumb backward. "At the mission. For a shower. This place has great art but lousy hot water. Look, I just gotta scram upstairs for a second, I'll be right down."

He was back in moments, carrying a nylon fanny pack.

Lauren leaned across the passenger seat and opened the door. He got in beside her and closed it after him. As she eased the clutch out and moved them into the early morning traffic, he leaned back, touching the leather seat.

"Jeez," he said.

They said nothing more until they hit a red light five minutes away from the rooming house. She pulled over, popped the trunk open and hopped out, all in one motion. She returned with a navy crew-neck sweater, which she tossed to Fox.

"Here. Put this on."

They continued toward the rifle range in silence as Danny rolled up the sleeves on Martin's favourite sweater.

"You've never handled one of these, right?"

"Never."

They were standing outside at the range, at the target farthest from the entrance and from any nosy employees or onlookers. This early in the morning, off hunting season, it wasn't likely to be crowded.

On Danny's recommendation they had parked the car a few blocks away in a residential area and walked in: no vehicle to identify her, no evidence of their pre-planning.

She had tucked her hair into the tam he had insisted she wear and she had put on Martin's sweater under her light jacket to bulk her up. She hadn't removed her sunglasses until they had paid their fee and reached the field. He had dealt with the man at the counter.

"Okay." Fox took a deep breath and continued. "This is a Gloc 9 mm handgun." He produced a lethal-looking gun, flat silver grey, about ten inches long. It was real. "They're mostly plastic, so they're good and light. They're pretty accurate at a distance, but we don't really care about that." He looked at her, searching for a sign of weakness. "They're also pretty fu—pretty darned effective. That we care about."

She nodded.

"You're going to have to get close to him. Eight to ten feet, max. It's going to be a man you're shooting; this ain't CNN. It's the real thing. You want to be just far enough away that you don't get splattered with his blood. Are you sure you want to do this?"

She nodded again.

"Okay. Here we go."

He held the gun toward her and she reached for it.

"Never!" he hissed.

She jumped. "What?"

"Never touch this gun without gloves. You want to kill this asshole, not ruin your own life, right?"

"Yes. Yes," she said. "I wasn't thinking. That's smart advice, except a little late. I didn't bring gloves."

"You can't afford not to think."

She nodded, chastised.

He pulled out a couple of pairs of translucent surgical gloves from the fanny pack and they put them on.

"Okay." He began with a review of the clip, inserted into the butt with fourteen rounds. "It's a semi-automatic, which means that once you've engaged the clip like this," he pulled the spring on top of the barrel back toward himself, "it's a matter of very little trigger pressure, and you're happening."

He had her remove and insert the clip more than twenty times. She didn't complain. She understood detail and appreciated that she would be a better shooter if she really knew her weapon.

Next they practised removing the safety, again and again and again, a quick and simple move.

"I want you to be able to do this in your sleep," Fox said. "If you freeze with this guy, you might as well give me all your money now, 'cause you're not going to live to spend it."

She nodded and did it again. When Fox was satisfied, they left the bench they had been sitting on and walked ten feet to the practice line. The circular target was thirty-five feet away. Fox pressed the button control and brought it forward another fifteen.

"We'll start with this distance while you get comfortable with the gun. When we're almost done, I'll bring it in closer. Close up with a handgun will look weird. A bit of distance is the norm out here and since you're a woman, twenty feet isn't all that odd. It doesn't matter how far away you are from your target as you get used to the sitings and kick. You'll only be better, closer. Unless you freeze."

"I'm not going to freeze," she said matter-of-factly.

He took the gun from her. "Two hands, always." He reviewed the stance he wanted her to use, repeating that she would be close enough to feel his breath when she wasted him and did she really want to?

Lauren concentrated on shooting and did well. The gun was pretty accurate at twenty feet, and she became more steady and confident. She couldn't miss his chest if he was ten feet away from her. She could do this.

"You're doing good," Fox said. "Let's take a break."

He went to the office and brought back two Cokes and more rounds. They drank in silence, enjoying the late morning sunshine and gentle breeze.

Halfway through her Coke, Lauren spoke. "You know, I don't know anything about you."

"There's not much to know." Fox looked pale and out of place outside the city.

"I don't believe that." She was quiet for long enough that he thought she was going to leave it. "Do you have family in Vancouver?"

He looked at his can. "I got a kid somewhere." He stood up and downed the last of his soda.

"Sorry," she said. "I shouldn't have pried."

"It's okay. I'd be curious too. I've got a kid that I ain't seen in forever and a couple of ex-old ladies, but what I got most of all is a habit. No one can compete with that. There's always three in the room."

There was nothing to say. "What's next?" she asked.

"You use these rounds up on the target after I move it closer, and then we pack up and go home. You're there now, but a little more practice close up can't hurt." He picked up the gun and handed it to her, safety on, handle first. She accepted it with familiarity.

He moved the target ten feet closer. "How does that feel?" he asked.

"Like it's on top of me," she answered.

"That's how it's gonna feel, lady. He's gonna be closer, probably." He waited a moment. "What do you think?"

"I think he was closer when he killed Martin," she said evenly.

"Okay," he nodded.

She fired the three clips, unloading and reloading expertly. The bull's eye was shredded when she was done.

"You're ready," he said. "Let's go." He took down the target and pushed the board back out to a respectable distance. They took off their gloves and stashed them in the fanny pack with the gun. It was quarter to twelve.

They walked in easy silence to the car. No one noticed them.

As they pulled onto the highway heading back to the city, Fox spoke. "I'll keep the gun with me. I'm not going to let you approach him alone for three hundred thousand. We'll do it together, but it's your hit." He tried to sound hard at the end.

Relief flooded through her. She had been willing to do it, but she was terrified. With Danny's support and wiliness, she knew she could do it. She looked at him quickly. "Thanks," she whispered.

"It's okay," he muttered. "I know where we'll do it. I'll get wheels—your car and licence plate can't be anywhere near the scene. I want you in a big hat again, big glasses and baggy clothes. I don't want any snoopy neighbours identifying you in a police lineup."

"My God," she said, "could it get to that?"

"Lady, anything can happen when you murder someone." She said nothing.

"I'm gonna see about a silencer for this thing," he said. "It won't make any difference on how it handles, but we won't be as noticeable."

"When are we going to, going to do it?" she asked. Her palms were sweaty on the steering wheel.

"I'll let you know when we're ready. If I tell you now that we're gonna do it a week Thursday you won't sleep the nights before and you'll be a basket case on D-Day. I've got your cell number. Keep the phone with you. It'll happen in the next month. Just be ready. I don't want to go through my end of things and find out you're not available. Okay?"

"Okay."

"Are you sure you want to do this?"

Lauren was silent, thinking of the man from the restaurant, bashing Rick against the wall, forcing alcohol into Martin, watching the car go. She thought of the girl at the deli. "I'm sure," she nodded.

She put on a Van Morrison CD as they flew toward the city.

"Hey," Fox said as Lauren drove past Main Street, "you missed the turn."

"I'm taking you to your bank."

"My bank," he laughed.

She pulled up in front of the bank a few minutes later and reached into her jacket pocket. She passed him a white envelope. "Don't spend it all in one place," she smiled.

"We'll be talkin'." He took it and walked into the bank as she drove away.

He opened the envelope while he was standing in line.

Inside were ten cheques, all payable to Mr. Danny Fox, each in the amount of twenty thousand dollars.

• • •

They were in front of the judge at noon and had a sealed order authorizing the wiretapping of Frank Wesley's home telephone before one o'clock. Cole shook Blackburn's hand and almost ran to his police car to drive a copy of the order out to the installers. They'd be hooked up on Wesley's phone by sundown.

It was a huge breakthrough. Even though Wesley was notoriously cautious on phones, he might let something slip when talking to a friend, on his own line. It was different than talking on the Warriors' line, when he had every reason to believe the cops were listening.

• • •

12:20. Lauren had been remiss in her attention to the gallery. She had the whole afternoon free, except for picking up things for dinner, and it was on the way home. She pulled into her parking spot, smiling to herself at how frightened she had been in her first encounter with Danny. Funny how things turn out.

She entered the gallery through the rear entrance. Her assistant, Terry, was in the front arranging a new display.

"My God, look what the cat dragged in!" Terry said. "Where in heaven's name have you been?"

"I've been busy," Lauren said. They hugged briefly.

"I can see that." Terry nodded toward Lauren's office.

Lauren looked toward her office. "Wow," she said.

"That's what I thought," said Terry.

On her desk sat a huge basket of flowers in a riot of colour—roses, lilies, carnations.

"You should have seen them when they first got here," Terry murmured.

It was clear that they had been there a while. Some of the leaves had begun to brown at the edges and curl, and the blooms were beginning to wilt. "When did they arrive?"

"Sunday night, just after six. I happened to be here working on the Tremblay mailouts when the florist dropped them off."

"Is there a note?"

"Yes," Terry said. "And you'll be proud of me. I didn't open it."

"How very restrained of you," her boss said sarcastically, with a smile and a sideways glance.

She opened the small white envelope that rested among the stems and leaves. "It was a pleasure . . ."

Lauren felt her legs buckle. She grabbed for the desk. A Sunday delivery. She had met Frank Wesley on Saturday. He had to know who she was, had to know she had been married to a man he had killed. Was that somehow attractive to him? He was even sicker than she had thought. Lauren tasted stale metal in her mouth.

Terry had rushed to her side. "Lauren! God, Lauren, are you okay?"

"Yes." She stood up, leaning against the desk. "Sorry, Terry. These are from an old flame I thought had been properly extinguished. Why don't you take them home? Please. Or courier them to a hospital," she said frantically. "Just get them out of here. I've got to get out of here. I'll be back in tomorrow and we'll have a normal day. Sorry about this."

She raced out of the gallery. The lilies smelt like death.

She needed to feel normal and to feel safe. She hadn't really let herself think about dinner, but now she let it consume her thoughts. She would make a fabulous meal, let shopping and preparation fill her time and her mind, and she wouldn't be alone. She enjoyed Jackson's company and it would be wonderful to have conversations that didn't deal with shooting ranges or murderous psychopaths. She drove to the farmer's market at Granville Island, a crowded open-air shopping area full of fresh food, the smell of baking and the sounds of laughter and seagulls and buskers. Her spirits were lifted by the colourful sights and activity as she strolled through the market. She bought fresh oysters for the appetizer, salad greens, lamb for the entree, and then she cheated, buying a croque en bouche for two for dessert. By the time she had picked up the wine, she was feeling better.

By 3:45 she was unpacked and organized in her kitchen.

• • •

The telephone security people had bugs on Wesley's phone lines within minutes of receiving a copy of Cole's wiretap order. A lot of people associated with law enforcement had been waiting a long time for this day.

The technician assigned to the job had been installing bugs on phones for seventeen years. He knew who was who in the zoo and when he heard from Cole that the wiretap was forthcoming, he drove out to the substation nearest Wesley's residence with a portable security-cleared fax machine. As soon as he received a faxed copy of the order, he hustled into the substation and made the installation. In his mind there was no point in missing any calls unnecessarily.

The monitor room had been put together in a hurry. All four monitors were Top Secret cleared; two were cops' wives. It couldn't hurt.

Cole had been in the monitor room since hookup, listening to Wesley's line ring and ring until the answering machine picked up incoming calls, listening to the message, analyzing the calls, checking the caller's number in the crisscross directory. One of the calls was from Bones, talking about money.

Cole predicted that Wesley would be furious about the call, which was clearly incriminating if anyone was listening.

Wesley got home sometime before 4:40. He made a call to a cell phone and then one to the clubhouse. Cole listened as Wesley blasted Bones, telling him never to call his home again. Smiling, Cole left the monitor room.

• • •

He showered and dressed carefully. White mandarin shirt, black wool jacket and black dress pants. He made a couple of stops on the way and parked his truck in front of her door at 6:32. He had decided to let himself go.

Lauren opened the door as he raised his hand to knock.

"I heard you coming a half block away. What is that thing?" she asked.

"A '67 Land Rover," he said, smiling with exaggerated pride. "Guaranteed to leave oil stains on your driveway."

She laughed. "Come on in."

She ushered him in. The foyer had a vaulted ceiling, with stained glass light filtering through a window in the peak.

"This is for you," Cole said, handing her the basket he'd brought.

"How intriguing," she said, accepting it. "Let's go into the kitchen where there's more light—not to mention martinis— and I'll open this."

He followed her into the kitchen, an airy room with light wood and tile and a magnificent view of the ocean. She put the basket on the counter.

"Do you like martinis?" she asked him.

"Love 'em," he answered.

"Can you make them?"

"With the right ingredients, I can make magic." His eyes twinkled as he smiled at her.

She took the gin and glasses from the freezer and pointed to the vermouth and olives, already out. He got to work. In the closeness of the kitchen he was taller than she remembered. His thick brown hair was tied back and he was freshly shaven, and she could see the nape of his neck and his left profile, with its strong cheekbone. His shoulders were broad, like Martin's had been. Lauren wondered for a moment whether she would ever be able to look at a man again without comparing him to Martin.

Inside the cellophane-wrapped basket she found a pound of Earl Grey tea, a bottle of Grand Marnier, a bottle of Amaretto and a CD.

"'The Art of Tea'?" she asked.

"There's an art to everything. And that guy has the art of saxophone down very well." He shook the mixer. Ice rattled.

"And the other items?"

"Blueberry tea," he said with mock horror. "You can't tell me you've never heard of it?"

"I don't get out much." It could have been funny, but it wasn't. They were silent for a moment.

Cole poured the martinis into the two frozen glasses and handed her one. "To getting out." He proffered his glass.

She stood within a foot of him. She looked up into his strong face and touched her glass to his. "To getting out," she said quietly. She felt slightly guilty.

They took a sip. It was delicious: icy and strong. Lauren stepped back.

"All right," she said, all business. "We have oysters, which I can pan fry or whip up a quick Florentine. Your choice."

"Do you have Tabasco?"

"Yes."

"It's a gorgeous evening. Why don't we take our drinks and oysters to the beach. I'll shuck them and we can eat them as they're meant to be eaten."

"I'd love that."

As he held the door open for her and she stepped out onto the deck with her drink, she felt a stab of nostalgia.

"I'll refresh the music," he said, handing her his martini, "and bring the oysters."

She made her way to the rocks and waited.

The sound of a saxophone drifted out of the speakers as he reappeared on the deck. The breeze pushed his jacket open and Lauren could see the taut lines of his belly and chest. She looked out at the ocean toward where the sun would set.

Cole shucked half a dozen oysters and lined them up on a large rock, on the half shell. He squeezed lemon on them and sprinkled Tabasco sauce liberally.

"Ready?"

"Absolutely."

He took up the shucking knife, dislodged the oyster from the shell, then put the shell to her lips and tilted the oyster in. She chewed and grimaced and swallowed and reached for her glass, all in one motion. He did the same and they both laughed.

He refilled their glasses, and they finished their oysters as the wind came up. "Let's go in," she said, shivering slightly.

Inside the house, the kitchen smelled wonderful. Lauren lit the candelabra on the chopping block and passed Cole a bottle of wine and a corkscrew. She lit a couple of candles on the counter and turned off the overhead light.

"What can I do now?" he asked. He had taken off his jacket and rolled up his sleeves.

"Dinner's almost ready," she said. "Why don't you light the candles in the dining room and pour the wine?"

"Done." He moved away easily, leaving her alone with his scent.

She was unnerved at how aware of him she was, and at how much she was enjoying the evening. After Martin's death, she had not expected ever to want anyone else again, and she hadn't. Up until now.

And now she wished desperately that she had someone to talk to. What she had set in motion with Danny Fox was terrifying. She couldn't just back away, knowing that Martin's killer was walking around freely, living days that he had stolen from Martin. But now she was aware that she might actually want to walk away, in large part because of what future there might be with the man in her and Martin's dining room. The deal with Fox was stoppable, if she wanted to stop it. But she felt certain that it would be impossible to live a new life happily, leaving so much undone from this one.

When Cole walked back into the kitchen, Lauren stood staring at the candles on the counter, her head bowed.

"Are you okay?" he asked quietly.

She turned and looked at him, almost not recognizing him for a moment. "Yes, Jackson. Sorry." She smiled, pushing her hair away from her face with a backward motion of her hand. "Sorry about that. I have my occasional reveries."

He nodded without speaking.

Lauren welcomed familiar tasks again. She moved quickly around the kitchen, taking the lamb and potatoes from the oven and placing them on a platter, dressing them with steamed vegetables.

"Voilà," she said, more brightly than she felt.

When they sat down, Cole raised his wine glass. "To the hostess."

"Thank you for coming," she said. Their glasses touched.

The meal was wonderful. Afterward, Lauren put on water for tea and they stood in the candlelit kitchen, waiting.

"Whatever made you think of blueberry tea as a hostess gift?" she asked.

"Well, knowing who you are, I figured you would have lots of wine and lots of knowledge about wine, so I couldn't win there. And I knew you had already received flowers this week. So I figured music was a good place to start, and this is my favourite CD. Since it's about tea, the next items were obvious."

She laughed. "You make it all sound so logical."

As they returned to comfortable silence, she realized something he had said didn't fit.

"How do you know I got flowers this week?" she asked him.

"I sent them."

"Those were your flowers?" she whispered.

"Well, yes. I know I didn't sign the note, but I figured, how many new men could you meet in one day?"

"Oh, Jackson. One too many!" Lauren covered her mouth with her hand and laughed out loud. "Oh, God, I met an absolute creep on Saturday, in addition to meeting you. I thought he had sent the flowers. I had my assistant send them to a hospital! They were gorgeous, too." She was laughing so hard she had tears in her eyes.

"So you liked them?"

"Loved them."

"Well, that's all I care about. Even if it was a fleeting enjoyment," he said wryly.

The tea was ready. Cole poured Grand Marnier and Amaretto into two brandy snifters and topped them off with hot tea. He picked up one glass and took it to Lauren. Standing close, he put the snifter in her hand and bent down, brushing the nape of her neck with his lips.

"Let's go outside," he said.

He put his jacket around her shoulders and they settled in the Cape Cod chairs on the deck. Clouds were scudding across the moon, casting shadows and revealing and hiding stars. The waves lapped at the rocks nearby. They talked about their childhoods and their work, carefully skirting the subjects of past relationships and dead husbands. Lauren realized that she didn't want the evening to end.

Oh, Martin. She felt off balance.

They went back in the house as it grew cooler, and Lauren flicked on the gas fireplace and turned on a small stained glass lamp. Cole put on a CD and Shirley Horne's voice was planed through the flickering light of the room.

> *No complaints*
> *and no regrets*
> *I still believe in chasing dreams*
> *and placing bets . . .*

"Do you like to dance?" Cole spoke the words quietly.

"I haven't for years," she said stiffly.

> *But I have learned*
> *that all you give*
> *is all you get,*
> *so give it all you've got . . .*

"Will you now?" he asked.

She looked at him and nodded. He put her drink on a table, then took her in his arms.

> *I had my share*
> *I drank my fill,*
> *and even though I satisfied,*
> *I'm hungry still,*
> *to see what's down another road*
> *behind the hill*
> *and do it all again . . .**

She could feel his muscular hardness against her as he pulled her close. She couldn't help responding. It felt like they were melting into each other.

They danced slowly around the room, the firelight flickering gently.

Cole looked down at her dark eyes and pushed a few loose strands of hair away. He bent his head and kissed her. Softly first, and then their tongues met. He could taste her sweetness and feel her warmth.

They pushed into each other, closer, kissing lips, necks, cheeks, learning each other's scents and textures, moving slowly to the music.

When the song ended he stopped moving and held her close, resting his face in her soft hair. He pulled back and, cupping her face in his large, strong hands, searched her eyes with his. She looked up at him and couldn't help herself; she could feel the hot sting of approaching tears. She couldn't remember when she had felt so good. Or so awful.

"Are you free anytime this week?" he whispered.

"It's pretty open." Her voice was throaty.

"How about tomorrow night?"

She pulled away and turned on another lamp. "You're not exactly playing hard to get, are you?"

"It's taken me this long to find you," he said. "Why waste more time?"

She didn't say anything.

"Come on," he said. "Walk me to the door and turn the alarm on after me."

They walked to the dark foyer, leaving the room where the firelight kissed the photographs of the dead husband, who looked unseeing at the empty room.

Sunday, June 21, 1998

"Come on, baby. One more call and that's it." Oskar watched Donna sulkily flipping through a magazine at the kitchen table.

"Where've you been all week?" she whined.

"All week? I don't see you a day and you think I'm gone somewhere." He walked behind her, reached down into her blouse and pushed his cock into her shoulders. "Where've I got to go but here? You're the best I've ever had. I love you." He had never said that before.

She squeezed his hand through the fabric. "I love you too."

"And I'm going to make you so fuckin' high you're gonna love me forever," he murmured, checking his watch.

11:18. The plane left at 1:50, with a check-in of 11:50. He wouldn't make the check-in time, but catching the flight wouldn't be a problem. He didn't have much luggage.

She swivelled quickly in her chair. "You are?" she giggled.

"Yeah, baby." She made him sick. "Right after the call."

"Let's get it over with. What do I say this time?"

He told her and punched in the number. "Crime Stoppers," said the distant tinny female voice as he passed the phone to Donna.

"H-h-hi. It's, I'm tipster number 31982. I've, I've talked to you guys before."

"Just a moment." There was a pause. "Yes, okay, I've got your file up on the screen."

"Okay, well, I've just been at Frankie's house. I stayed overnight and he's nuts. He spent most of the night doing coke and packing up kilos and digging under a playhouse in his back yard. He says he's got at least fifty kilos buried there and he's going to deliver them to his customers tonight sometime." She hurried the last words, watching Oskar chop up powder on a mirror and divide it into four thick lines.

He mouthed the words "Describe it."

She nodded. "I s-s-saw the coke. It's packaged in bricks and wrapped in plastic with little Coca Cola bottles all over it. He gave some to me. It's really excellent."

Oskar had been through the courts enough to know that the more details there were in a search warrant application, the more likely the cops were to actually get the warrant. He decided she had given them enough. He gave her the thumbs-up signal.

"Th-that's it." She hung up with relief and slid across to the coffee table where Oskar was working.

He rolled up a hundred-dollar bill into a tube and handed it to her. She inhaled the first two lines greedily and then stopped, pinching below the bridge of her nose. She shook her head and dove into the next line, and she had almost finished the fourth when she saw the drops of blood on the table.

She croaked in disbelief, looking at Oskar wildly. Blood filled her throat and a frothy pink bilge poured out her nose.

She reached toward Oskar for help. He gently took the hundred-dollar bill from her hand.

He was at the airport at 12:03.

• • •

The Crime Stoppers dispatcher called the Vancouver city detective's pager number at the top of her screen. He called back less than a minute later and she read back the conversation she had had with Tipster 31982.

"I'm going to need a copy of that summary to get a search warrant."

"I thought you might," the dispatcher said. "When?"

"I'm twenty minutes away. I'll be there in fifteen."

He arrived at the Crime Stoppers office with a laptop and banged out the search warrant application with boilerplate phrases. Then he added the seven Crime Stoppers reports as Exhibits A to G, stating that he believed the contents of all of them: detailed information from someone who had stayed the night on the property, that there were fifty kilos of coke under a playhouse. He was sure it would be grounds for a warrant.

He had already phoned his sergeant and described the situation, and the sergeant was organizing their squad to be ready for the search as soon as the warrant was authorized. If things didn't screw up, they'd get the warrant and execute it before Wesley moved the cocaine.

The officer finished the affidavit and hurried to the courthouse to find a justice of the peace to grant him his search warrant.

At 2:35 he emerged from the courthouse with judicial authority to enter the asshole's house, along with eight of Vancouver's finest, in search of enough cocaine to fill an exhibit locker. He was high.

He ran down Main Street half a block to the police station and into the squad room where they were planning the entrance strategy.

•   •   •

Lauren awoke with a slight headache. Feeling it made her smile, recalling the evening before. She stretched diagonally across the king-size bed and listened to the ocean, thinking about the coming day: a shower and coffee, then a long over-due stint at the gallery. Then a workout, and tonight, Jackson. She decided that she was looking forward to it all.

She jumped out of bed and stripped as she headed for the bathtub.

•   •   •

The meeting in Calgary had been a bust. The guys Parker had gone to meet had been lightweights, taking all of Saturday to get nothing done. He would be surprised if they ever got their financing in place. It certainly was not a com-pany he wanted to have anything to do with promoting.

He had begged off dinner and tried unsuccessfully to get a flight out that night. As it was, his 2:00 Sunday afternoon flight was delayed an hour and a half by bad weather. Eventually he gravitated to the calm of the airport lounge to wait.

By the time they took off he had had a couple of Scotches, to keep a good-looking redhead company at the bar. They had continued on board, and by the time they reached Vancouver they were both half cut. It wasn't a bad flight. Still, she had said no to his invitation of a limousine ride to anywhere in the city, and he had arrived home alone.

Now he was looking forward to a really good Scotch, a

long shower and an hour or two stretching out in a lounge chair on the balcony with the paper. He opened the door and dumped his leather carry-all on the marble floor. He walked down the steps and into the sunken living room to the bar, and poured himself four fingers.

He carried his drink across the room and stepped out onto the balcony. It was the end of a beautiful afternoon, warm with a light breeze. The sun was still sparkling a trail for late-day sailors on the waves of English Bay, as it headed for a bank of dark clouds building on the horizon.

Leaning against the balcony railing, Parker took a sip and felt the familiar burn. It was good to be home.

He finally tipped the last amber drops onto his tongue as the clouds eclipsed the sun. The afternoon had turned dark. He decided to have one more drink and a bite to eat out on the patio before showering and before the rain fell. He refilled his glass at the bar and walked toward the kitchen. He froze at the threshold of the room as icy fingers ran up his back.

The kitchen was a mess. Someone had been here. *They* had been here.

His mouth was sticky dry. He wanted desperately to run out of this place they had violated, but he had to know. He ran to the master bedroom, saw the light in the bathroom burning and ran toward it. When he saw the toilet tank lid resting on the bowl, he gagged.

Sagging against the bathroom wall, Parker vomited into the sink in terror. When he saw the plastic bag, he threw up again, hard.

They had it.

He could hardly stand. Raising his eyes to the harshness of the brightly lit mirror, Parker saw that he looked hollow-eyed and sunken in the stark white room. He had sealed his own death with his cleverness. He was looking at a dead man.

He put the tank lid back on and ran water into the sink, slapping it around to rinse out the vomit. He watched the movements of his hands detachedly, as if they belonged to someone else. Leaning into the sink to cup water into his mouth, he started to sob. The cold water hit his hot face and mixed with his hot tears and mucus. He was freezing.

He finally pushed himself away from the sink and dried himself with a black towel. He could taste terror.

He staggered dizzily through the dim bedroom back through the kitchen. Melted ice cream and daiquiri mix had congealed on the floor in a sour mess. He stepped around it, wondering why he was still alive, given that they had broken in some time ago. Probably that was all part of it: scare the Jesus out of people before you kill them. He wondered if they were coming now, now that he was home. He went up the catwalk and double-bolted the door.

As he returned to the living room down the threshold stairs, Parker tripped on the last step. He fell heavily into an end table, sending it and the vase of flowers on it crashing.

"Fuck," he said in a strangled voice. The fear had eaten his speech. He needed another drink.

He walked heavily to the bar and filled a fresh glass, emptying the bottle. He drank hungrily as he stood by the bar thinking. They would have to punish him for making the record of his activities for the club. Just thinking about it made him shake. But they had to figure that if he had made one copy, he had likely made others. If so, and if a copy were available to the police, there would be real heat on the bikers. They would be aware that the risk existed, and they would know that killing a kid could be an extremely bad public relations move at an extremely bad time. While he would have to be made an example of, for making the record, the possibility of other copies floating around would likely save Billy from their revenge. Parker was banking on it.

His fingers trembled as he unwrapped the seal on a fresh bottle of Scotch. How he had fucked things up! At least Martin had died knowing he had standards; Parker was left with nothing. Sobs racked his body as he poured the liquor. His ex would love this, he thought bitterly. She always wanted to see him fall. Billy would miss him. So would Lauren. Who else? He could not think of anyone. It made him cry harder.

He wished he had ice.

He drained his glass, walked unsteadily to the bar fridge and fished a couple of cubes out of the tray. He placed them in his glass carefully and then topped it up and took it to the balcony and the fresh air. Stepping out onto the tile, he could smell the sea. The traffic sounds were clearer than they had been earlier that day—cars honking, people yelling, sirens. And not one person who really gave a shit if the fuckers came in right now and castrated him before offing him. He was crying again.

He slumped against the railing, drink in hand, and took a good last pull. He dumped out the ice cubes. Then he reached into the evening air, extended his hand over the empty garden below and let the glass go. He was sure he could hear it shatter.

He then rested his upper stomach against the railing and leaned his head over and down into the empty space. He gripped the outside of the railing with his hands above his head. He felt dizzy. He took a couple of practice tries, kicking his feet off the balcony tiles, donkey style.

On the third try, he kicked high and briefly achieved a perfect handstand outside the eighteenth-floor balcony, before releasing his grip and plummeting down to the pavement.

• • •

By 4:30 Lauren had reviewed the gallery inventory, responded to all her correspondence and prepared a tentative guest list for an evening of art and cocktails in support of cystic fibrosis.

Her cell phone rang. "Hello."

"Pick me up in front of Safeway, Guildford, in an hour." It was Danny Fox.

She gasped. "Today?" He had caught her completely off guard.

"You said you were free all month. Let's get it done." His voice was rough.

"Yes, but—" she stammered. Had last night changed something? She hadn't had time to think it through.

"No more phone. Now or never. Guildford, 5:30." He hung up.

She stared at the phone in her hand. A noise in her temples was thundering. She realized, guiltily, that she had barely thought of Martin today. But she thought of him now: if it had been Lauren who was killed, he would never have hesitated.

4:32.

Frank Wesley had killed Martin. Taken away their future and dumped it like it was garbage, without a thought to what he was doing or who was affected by it. No one had stood up for Martin. And now this man was still walking around and handing out his own brand of terror. He had murdered Martin and victimized her and got away with it, scot-free.

Bugger that, she thought.

She stood up and grabbed her purse and phone, yelling to Terry that she would be back tomorrow as the door closed behind her. She had forgotten Jackson.

She resisted the impulse to speed. Guildford was a large shopping mall in Surrey, a city east of Vancouver that had metamorphized from rural quiet to suburban sprawl in just a couple of decades. The mall was about forty-five minutes from her office. She didn't know the mall layout but she knew where it was. If she got there in forty-five or fifty minutes, she would have a few minutes to drive around and find the Safeway store.

She let her mind float back to her wedding day, rerunning it as the miles fell behind.

She spotted Fox just before 5:30. He smiled and waved quickly, like a little kid, and got in the car.

"You okay?" he asked.

"Yes." She looked at the package in his lap.

"I added a silencer, like I said. It won't make a difference in handling."

She nodded, looking for an exit. "Where to?"

"Where's your hat and stuff?"

"In the trunk."

"Find a parking spot away from crowds and grab them."

She did as she was told.

"Put 'em on. And here." He passed her a pair of gloves.

She put on the tam and tucked her hair up into it, and put on a pair of large, over-the-counter reading glasses. She rolled up the towel, wrapped it around her midriff and pulled down her sweater. Then she put on the gloves.

"Okay, let's go," he said, pointing to a far corner of the lot. "You've never looked better."

"Thanks a lot," she said with sarcasm.

"Well, you look good for this. No one would recognize you at a distance," he said. It was true: gone was the svelte, sophisticated brunette. In her place was a long-legged, barrel-chested woman with thick glasses and very short hair. The disguise was quick and effective. They got out of the car.

Fox led her to a 1994 Crown Victoria and opened the passenger door. She got in.

"Where'd you get this?" she asked.

"A downtown parkade. I'm pretty sure whoever owns it won't be looking for it until the offices close. We'll have just about finished with it by then. And even if it's broadcast pronto, it'll probably just go out on the city police channels, not the Mounties." He gave her a crooked smile, easing the car out of its spot. "And we're in Surrey and Surrey's Mountie territory, so minimal risk."

"You're pretty smart," she smiled back. She felt like she was in a movie.

Fox was a bit jittery, but was enjoying himself. "Here," he said, passing her the package. "Have a look and feel. You'll see what I mean—it's no different with the silencer."

She pulled out the gun, which was folded in fabric. It was the same gun they had practised with the day before, but attached to the barrel was a silver cylinder about four inches long. She held the gun in proper position. It didn't feel much heavier.

"It's loaded," he said. "But check it anyway. It's your show."

She did, removing the clip and checking the rounds. She reloaded.

"When did you decide we'd do it today?"

"Yesterday. You got good with the gun and you were confident. If we left it, you'd lose faith in yourself."

"Why didn't you tell me yesterday?"

"How rested would you be right now if I'd done that?" He looked at her. "Listen, any time you want, we stop this. Right now, we're just looking at theft of an auto and possession of a prohibited weapon. Two years, tops."

"Very amusing," she said, looking out the car window.

They stopped at an intersection and a young man and woman crossed in front of them, holding hands and laughing.

"I want to do this," she said. It was almost a whisper.

A few minutes later they drove into a neighbourhood of ranch-style houses, and Fox pointed out a grey and white one with a well-kept lawn, set back from the road.

"That's it," he said.

A green Chevy Suburban sat in the driveway and a beat-up pickup was parked at the side of the carport.

It was happening so fast.

"It looks like he's home and he don't have company. Are you ready?"

"For what?" she asked in a whisper.

"We're going to go in, get him to step out of the house. You're gonna blast him and we're gonna get back in the car and get the hell out of here." He signalled his turn into the driveway. "It's gonna be quick and it's gonna be over. Are you ready?"

She spoke the word *yes*, but no sound came out. She nodded.

He pulled up into the driveway.

• • •

The phone rang.

"Hello."

It was his ex-wife. Wesley could feel the venom on the line almost before she spoke.

"Listen, Frank, I've just come from my lawyer's and if you think you're going to get away with that bullshit about no assets—"

• • •

Cole sat in the monitor room, listening. He had been there all day, hoping to glean something useful for the file. So far it had been a lot of nothing: a couple of calls to doctors, one to his brother. A couple to a stockbroker about penny stocks, all amounting to zip.

He leaned forward now. If the ex got into the subject of his assets, they might get a basis for looking for hidden proceeds of his suspected criminal activities. That meant criminal charges and court-ordered forfeitures.

• • •

"Listen, Linda, why don't we talk about this the next time I pick up the kids?"

"No," she shrieked, nearly hysterical. "We talk about it now. How am I supposed to live on three thousand a month?"

"I don't want to talk about this on the phone." His voice was hard.

"I don't care what you want," she screamed. "You got your way for nine years."

"Calm down." His voice was ice. It seemed to register. "Somebody's at the door, I'll be back in a second."

He put the receiver down on the table in the entrance hall as she yelled "Fuck you!" and hung up.

Looking out the window, Wesley saw a weird-looking broad and a skinny little guy. What the hell could they want? He'd get rid of them in a second and then deal with Linda.

• • •

Fox had parked the Crown Victoria right behind the pickup. They had got out of the car and walked along the brick path leading to the front door. Lauren took the glasses off and put them in her jacket pocket. Fox walked ahead of her a couple of feet.

When they were fifteen feet from the door, Wesley opened

it, filling the doorway. "I don't want whatever you're ped-
dling," he snarled.

Lauren took two steps toward him and then stopped, raising the gun in both hands, aiming directly at his chest. Blood
rushed in her head. She knew if she squeezed the trigger now
she would hit him perfectly.

"Oh, fuck!" he bleated, laughing. "What is this? The Odd
Couple does Clint Eastwood?" Recognition flickered across
his face. "What the fuck are you doing here?" He moved
toward her.

She found her voice. It was surprisingly strong. "Stay
where you are."

• • •

Her words filled the monitor room. Cole sat up straight in his
chair and stared at the tape machine. What was going on?

• • •

Lauren took the safety off without taking her eyes off Wesley.
It crossed his mind that he might have made a mistake.
Maybe he should have closed the door on this crazy bitch
and dialed 911 for the second time this week. He wondered
if the scarecrow and the bitch had had anything to do with
the incident outside the gym. And if they had, then Parker
was involved too.

"Why did you kill Martin?" Her voice was shaking with
emotion.

Fuck, he thought. This was Martin Grey's old lady. Well,
what do you know. He could tell she was unravelling. Get her
talking and let her really fall apart and he'd stuff that fucking
9-mil down her throat. What did she think she was gonna do,
kill him?

He let out a snort.

• • •

It was Lauren's voice that filled the monitor room, picked up by the phone bug, still active with the receiver off the hook. What the hell was she doing there? Didn't she know how dangerous this man was? If she knew, or believed, that he had killed her husband, wouldn't she figure out that she wasn't safe talking to him about it?

Cole picked up the phone in the monitor room and punched in the number for the Surrey RCMP detachment. "It's Sergeant Jackson Cole, headquarters, Undercover Unit. Put me through to dispatch." He spoke quickly, with authority. The call was transferred immediately. He described what was going on.

"We have an Emergency Response Team going to that address right now," the dispatcher advised him, "accompanying a Vancouver City Drug Squad search."

"What do you mean?" Things were getting out of Cole's control.

"Vancouver City's got a Narcotic Control Act warrant for that residence. They should be there any moment," the woman said.

"Radio them that there's an innocent civilian female at the address," he said, thinking fast. "Don't for God's sake let a hostage situation arise."

"Got it, Sergeant. I'll relay your message immediately."

He hung up and returned his attention to the sounds in the room.

• • •

"Listen, little lady, you put that thing down and we'll talk." Wesley reached toward Lauren.

She pulled the spring back. "Don't you come any closer." She was crying.

He kept walking. "You stupid bitch, I'm gonna take that thing and you're gonna find out what it really does."

What was she doing? she thought to herself. He was horrid. He was huge and hairy and laughing at her and laughing at Martin and she couldn't do anything. She couldn't do it.

She could barely see him approaching through her tears. She couldn't swallow.

"I'm going to kill you right here," he said, laughing, "since you got it all figured out. And I'm going to call it self-defence. It sure ain't my gun."

She believed him.

• • •

Cole was trapped. He could do nothing from here but listen. She was forty miles away, but she might as well have been a million.

He couldn't bear to stay and listen, but he couldn't leave. He stood at the desk, staring at the tape recording machine.

• • •

Danny Fox had never really understood hunting big game. Big, pretty animals with plaintive eyes and spirit and life. Setting them in your sights a hundred yards away and blasting them to kingdom come didn't seem much like sport to him.

Lauren reminded him of a deer now. Kind and beautiful and helpless and nearly dead. He wouldn't be far off that mark himself, if he let Wesley get the gun.

He stepped up beside her, gently took the weapon from her and, holding it in his right hand, completely contrary to his instructions to her the day before, shot Frank Wesley, one-handed, first in the right temple, then in the chest. The first shot threw Wesley's head back. The second brought him down.

It was like hitting one more fish over the head.

• • •

"Come on."

In the monitor room Cole heard another male voice, not Wesley's, at some distance from the phone.

Lauren was crying.

• • •

Fox carried the gun to the car and slid it under the front seat. Lauren got in beside him. He released the emergency brake and slipped the car into reverse. He had just reached the end of the driveway when a plain grey ghost car blocked his way.

"Oh, fuck," he said, mostly to himself. He shifted gears and drove back up to the pickup, giving them fifty yards' distance from the cops. In his rear-view, he saw four more cars and the Emergency Response Team van.

"Put your gloves in the glove compartment," he instructed Lauren calmly.

She did. "What's going on?" she asked.

"Trouble," he said. "Take the hat and stuff it down the back seat. Throw the towel on the floor in the back. No disguises, the cops are here."

"The police?" she squeaked.

"Yup. And we've got a body and a gun with bullets that match. Give me the glasses." He put them in the breast pocket of his shirt.

He checked the rear-view again. Two cops were coming up the driveway in full Emergency Response Team gear. He opened his door to stall them. It worked; they backed off.

"Okay, Lauren, what're you gonna tell them?" he asked her, not taking his eyes from the street.

"I don't know," she stammered. She was on the verge of throwing up.

"Nothing. You ain't gonna tell them a damn thing except your lawyer's name. Or my lawyer's name. Can you do that?" His voice was intense.

She nodded.

"Okay, this thing's going to mean life for me, Lauren. I'm not going anywhere, so just do me a favour and don't say a thing. If you don't say anything, they can never trip you up. Remember that. They got no evidence on you and it'll be easier for me to sort out a story if I don't have to worry about what you're saying, okay?"

She nodded, uncomprehending.

He leaned out of the car and yelled, "I've got a hostage!"

He grabbed her by the front of the sweater and under the arm and dragged her across the seat and out the driver's door, shielding his body with hers. She was amazed at his strength.

• • •

The male voice yelling was vaguely familiar. Cole racked his memory. Who was the hostage? He did not want to guess.

Then an amplified voice: "This is Corporal Roberts of the Royal Canadian Mounted Police!" Cole recognized the name. The Emergency Response Team always included a trained negotiator, in case an arrest or search went awry and citizens came under risk.

He stared at the wall and tried to picture what was going on. What was happening to her.

• • •

The world was spinning. Lauren struggled to get away from Fox.

"What are you doing?" she asked fiercely.

"It's gonna work out okay," he said into her ear. "We did the world a favour getting rid of him. I've finally been useful to society." He laughed harshly.

He had his left forearm across her chest, up to her throat and was waving his right hand around. She realized he was holding the gun. And she realized she was frightened. What would desperation make him do? Was he really taking her hostage?

He was yelling now. "I fucking killed him. Popped him good in the head and then—boom—in the chest." He laughed like a maniac. "Went down like a sack of shit."

He didn't have any more time. He couldn't let them do it half right.

He shoved Lauren away, hard. She cried out and skittered on the concrete, landing on her hands and knees, scraping her palms. Why was he being so mean to her? She pushed back her hair and looked back at him through tears.

He looked back at her, mouthed the words It's okay, put the barrel of the gun into his mouth and pointed it upwards.

"N-o-o-o-o!" she screamed.

The negotiator prattled on. Fox pulled the trigger.

• • •

For a few seconds there was an odd silence from the transmitter.

Then Cole could hear her sobbing and male voices consoling her. Someone said, "Get a blanket."

He could hear no one arresting her for murder or advising her of her rights. They seemed far more concerned for her than the stiff on the doorstep, or the other one, whoever he was. It occurred to him that Lauren had that effect on people.

There was discussion of calling an ambulance to deal with her shock. Someone thought to radio for the coroner and the Serious Crime Unit. All in all, it sounded like they were buying the hostage thing. With the dead guy's admission, unless there was physical evidence around or unless she talked, who would know that she was the reason two people had died today?

Cole wondered who the hero was, and then recalled Janine's concern over the guy in the park. It had to be him. Lauren had said his name was Dan.

And then the penny dropped. How many Dans were there in the city's criminal element? The voice in the monitor room had been familiar to Cole because he had bought a pound and a half of heroin from the man less than two weeks ago.

He cursed himself for not pursuing it with Lauren further. If he had pushed her to discuss the meeting at the Aquarium, she might have come clean and realized the insanity of what she was planning—before it was too late.

He walked over to the monitor room door and locked it. He fast-forwarded the master tape to near the end, let it record dead air for a few minutes until it was full, then switched to a new tape. He inserted the full tape into a stand-by machine, rewound it for a minute and then hit play. He heard Wesley's voice, ". . . somebody's at the door." Too far back, but close. He pressed the fast forward button for a couple of seconds. Her voice: ". . . kill Martin?"

He felt old and tired.

He rewound the tape for a second and listened. As she asked her question, he hit play/record. The question and Wesley's responding threats were gone. He played the tape to hear how it would sound. It was okay. With the other big break of nothing recorded at the end, it just sounded like the machine had screwed up. There was nothing else on the tape that could hurt her.

He was relieved by a regular monitor at 7:00. The hour couldn't come fast enough.

He walked down to his office and called the Surrey detachment. He was advised that Lauren had been released without charges having been laid against her; it seemed that she was being treated as a victim.

Cole got in the Land Rover and headed for the North Shore fast. It took discipline to control his fury and ease off the accelerator. Staring straight ahead, he drove hard through the leafy causeway toward the Lions Gate Bridge, noticing nothing but the road.

He slowed down as he approached the hedge and dipped down the drive to Lauren's house. All the lights were off. He got out of the truck and rang the front doorbell. He could hear it chiming deep inside the house. He rang it three more times before she finally peered out through the living room curtains. He could hear her steps on the slate tile as she walked to the door.

She dreaded opening it. In a few short afternoon moments she had traded in her present and her future to take care of part of her past.

As she had driven to Guildford to meet Danny Fox, she had realized that she was kidding herself that she could possibly begin a life involving Jackson, knowing that she had been too selfish to ensure justice for Martin's death. But when Fox had pulled the trigger and blood had poured out of Frank Wesley, when Wesley's head hit the brick path and made a sound she'd never heard, when his throat gurgled, and when it hit her that he would never, ever feel the wind or hear laughter, solely because of her, she knew it couldn't work with Jackson this way either. She was the monster. And now he was here, forcing her to face him.

If she could just get through the next few moments that she owed him, she could shut out the world and surrender to the darkness that she could feel edging in on her.

She opened the door.

"Hello, Lauren." His voice was hoarse.

"Hello, Jackson." She looked into his eyes briefly, and then looked away, leaning against the door for support. She did not invite him in.

Neither spoke for a moment.

"I know about this afternoon," Cole said finally.

She nodded. "It was awful."

"No, Lauren," he whispered. "I know about it all. About Danny Fox and your plan and Frank Wesley killing Martin. I know that the police think things are awfully different than they actually are."

She looked at him strangely, her dark green eyes red-rimmed and open wide. She was shaking her head back and forth. "But how would you possibly . . ." Her thin voice trailed off.

He watched her, aching. "There was a bug on the phone at Wesley's. It was off the hook the whole time." He looked up at the stained glass window. Purple wisteria. "I happened to be the listener in the monitor room today. I heard everything that was said out there."

Her eyes filled with hot tears as his words sunk in. "I'm so sorry, Jackson. I'm so, so sorry. I had to finish it before I could start something else."

He nodded. He thought he understood. But the field had changed. The night before, they had both thought there was only the two of them. Cole realized now that he had been an intruder, even though neither he nor Lauren wanted it to be so.

"I'm sorry too," he said. He wanted to take her in his arms and make it not matter, make the clock go back to their first moments together. To the beginning of nothing. But that would just bring disaster for them both. He looked away.

Silence.

She had to ask the question. "Is there a—a recording of—" She searched for the right word. "It?"

He shrugged. "There should be, but something screwed up, technically. Some of the conversation didn't record properly."

"Oh." She didn't know what else to say. She didn't want to ask whether he had had a hand in the technical problem. She couldn't stand knowing that her actions might hurt him further.

"I just came by to see that you were okay," he said quietly. "And to say goodbye."

He couldn't read her silence.

"I like clean finishes, too, I guess." It was a jab. Protection. The minute the words were out he relegated them to the pile of things he wished could be undone that day.

She started to cry. "Will I see you again?" she asked.

He shook his head. "I don't think that would be very fair to any of us, do you?" Not to you, not to me, not to Martin.

He had been careful not to touch her up to now. If he held her, he knew he wouldn't let go. Now he bent down and quickly brushed her cheek with his lips. He could taste her tears.

"Look after yourself, won't you?"

She nodded mutely.

He walked stiffly to his beat-up truck as she retreated into her darkened house.

Sleep had been impossible Sunday night, and Cole had taken Monday off to exhaust himself in the mountains. He had driven forty minutes out of the city to the base of a glacial mountain and had half-run, half-walked up the steadily ascending switchback trails. There was still snow at the top, which was fine for his purposes: it made movement even more strenuous. When he got home that night, his body finally took over his mind and let him sleep.

He awoke early Tuesday morning, almost rested, and was at his desk before 7:00. No one at the office knew of his connection to Lauren, but she, along with Fox and Wesley, were still big news.

As was Parker. His body had been identified, and with his connections to the Warriors and evidence of a struggle in his apartment, everyone had pretty well concluded that Wesley had had a hand in the fall. Not that it mattered now.

Cole found himself thinking that Lauren had avenged more than she'd anticipated. He shook it off. He had to make himself stop thinking about her. He returned to the stack of intercept summaries that Corporal Pearce had brought him earlier. Halfway through, there was a knock on the door. He looked up to see Pete Grant standing in the doorway, grinning.

"Hey, Jackson, I got something from the mailman that's gonna turn that glum mug of yours upside down." He was almost bouncing with excitement.

"What's up?"

"You've got to come see."

Cole followed Grant to his office. Once there, Grant closed the door and unlocked his computer screen. Cole read Rick Parker's opening paragraph and whistled.

"Son of a bitch, eh?" Grant was enjoying himself.

Cole nodded and kept reading. It was all there: bank account numbers, summaries of investment activities, offshore accounts, shell companies, transfers of title, land purchase agreements. All set up to hide, move and clean the Warriors' money. The third to last entry related to the recent purchase of acreage. In Langley.

"Who've you got preparing the warrant?" Cole asked.

"I thought I'd do it, after showing you this," Grant replied.

"Sounds good." There was no one more qualified. "I'll get the search team together. Let me know when you're ready to go."

"We'll need the fire department there," said Grant. Meth labs were flammable.

Cole was already moving toward the door.

"And the lab boys, and ERT. It should be quite the show." He looked at his watch. 10:17. "Do you think you'll have the paper by 4:00?"

He couldn't see why not.

"That should be no problem. Let's aim for that as entry time. If it looks like there's going to be a delay, I'll page you."

"Okay."

Grant headed back to his computer. Cole walked quickly back to his office to start making arrangements. Normal life was taking over.

● ● ●

The property covered twenty acres. The old farmhouse sat on top of a rise at the end of a rutted dirt driveway about a quarter of a mile long. Pale yellow wild grass swept the yard from the front porch down to the ditch alongside the quiet country road. Anyone at the farmhouse could see everything going on down on the road below.

A couple of hundred yards behind the house stood the outbuildings: a low-lying hen house, a repair shop and a huge barn. Beyond them lay field gone fallow, beyond that, a wire fence, then Zero Avenue and beyond that a stand of evergreens that were in the United States of America.

In the field, about fifteen feet from the fence, stood a small pump house, its wooden siding silvered by weather. Its wooden flooring was new and could be pulled up easily for access to a tunnel, recently dug, which headed due south under the fence and Zero Avenue.

The first of the chemicals had been delivered over the weekend. Doc had overseen the careful storage of the containers in separate areas of the barn. The repair shop had been rewired and the ventilation jacked up. It was the kitchen, and the fortified hen house was the storage site for finished product ready for distribution. Doc had spent Monday and Tuesday tutoring eight lab technicians in the art of methamphetamine production. There was already product in the hen house, generated by his lessons.

Jojo and Bones had come out a couple of times to talk to him in person, but they had to stay out of sight of the lab workers, for insulation. The science part of the operation was the Doc's show anyway; there wasn't much for them to do once they'd arranged adequate security and countersurveillance setups. But earlier that day, Doc had called them to say that his students were ready to take over. It was time for him to go. Out of respect, the two branch presidents had driven out to the farm to say goodbye.

Bones was just opening the bottle of bourbon he'd brought when the phone in the farmhouse rang. It was the sentry in the rental house a mile down the road. Six police cars, an ERT van and two fire trucks had just turned onto the quiet country road, less than three minutes away.

Bones turned to Jojo and Doc. "We're busted." He spoke to the striker who had appeared in the kitchen doorway. "Get rid of all of it." The man was already moving.

For a fat man, Bones could move surprisingly quickly. He began wiping down the glasses he had handled and every surface he could remember him or Jojo touching. Fuck. Good luck on getting them all.

Jojo and the scientist were moving toward the back door. "Don't waste your time, Bones," Jojo snapped. "Let's move."

"Go ahead. I'll be right behind you." He opened the front door with a cloth and wiped the outside knob, then wiped the bathroom door knobs, then decided to fuck it. Sweating freely, he ran out the back of the farmhouse. He could see strikers and lab rats running between the outbuildings. A few of the strikers carried red jerry cans. It would be quite the show.

Bones laboured away from them and toward the field. Jojo and Doc were already at the pump house. By the time he reached it, they had already dropped down into the tunnel and begun moving toward the border.

He stuck his head into the dark hole. "Jojo?" There was panic in his voice. He could hear a muffled noise. This was a fucking last resort that he hadn't planned on using, so he hadn't paid attention to the details when the tunnel was built. He wondered how they were breathing in there. He looked at the entrance. The hole looked fucking small.

He heard sirens and looked back toward the farmhouse. The barn was on fire. He had to move. He lowered himself into the hole in the floor and leaned his head into the tunnel. It was fucking black. He wondered if the other two had had flashlights; he remembered hearing someone say lights would be stashed here. The fuckers. Every man for himself. Like always, in the end.

He pushed himself in, head and elbows first, then dragged his body into the dirt tunnel. It was tight. He realized he wasn't going to be able to get his elbows underneath his chest to push himself along, and he might not be able to back out, either. He dug the heels of his palms into the dirt on either side of his head and pushed hard, which pushed him back toward the opening. He did it again, wiggling his knees, trying to get purchase with anything he could to propel him back toward light and air and space.

Finally he sucked in open air and peeked out the pump house door. Every building was aflame.

Two fire trucks had stopped near the house and people were running around the yard. Stupid.

He hesitated for a moment, then turned and walked the rest of the way across the field to the fence. He climbed over it, crossed Zero Avenue and headed for the cover of the trees. There could be motion sensors at this part of the unmanned border, but maybe not. He'd take his chances.

The quiet of the forest was ruptured by the sound of a

huge explosion, followed by three lesser ones. All four made the earth shake. Bones took one last look back at the inferno. He could make out a dozen people standing outside its perimeter. Then something else caught his eye: dust rising from a faint seam joining the pump house to Zero Avenue. Cave-in.

Wednesday, June 24, 1998

Oskar read about the kill in a courtesy newspaper as he ate breakfast in his suite in the Mexico City Hilton. It was one of the stories in the International section, a small item headed Satan's Warrior Mourned. The story was all about the funeral, with reference to a news story the day before about one Frank Wesley being killed by a gunman named Danny Fox. That name rang bells. An old con, a real killer. Oskar liked the irony.

But more than that, he liked the fact that Wesley was out of the picture without Oskar being responsible for it. Without Wesley, there'd be no one to tie him to Dovee's death, and without that, the Warriors had nothing on him. He could be a free agent again in the town of his choice.

Fuck Belize.

He put the paper down, picked up the phone and booked a flight to Los Angeles for later that morning, with a connecting flight to Vancouver at 6:00 local time.

He made both flights without a problem. No Frank Wesley. No Donna. No Warriors. No loose ends. He loved it.

The plane touched down at 9:10 and he walked to the luggage area with the rest of the lemmings. Standing with his back to a pillar, he saw two men in sports jackets approaching him. Definitely cops.

The tall one spoke. "Oskar Kalnins?"

He nodded, cool. No one had a thing on him.

"You're under arrest for the murder of Dovee Federov. You have the right to remain silent . . ." He had his gun out and trained on Oskar, and the little cop was putting handcuffs on him. Oskar was stunned.

"You have the right to an—"

"Yeah, yeah. I know all that. This is nuts. I didn't kill Dovee, he was my cousin, my best friend. This is nuts."

"Have you ever heard of Frankie Wesley?" said the tall cop.

"Sure," Oskar nodded. "Everyone has. I heard he's dead."

"He sure is. But it isn't entirely a situation of dead men telling no tales. When we were searching his place, we came across a shotgun with your prints all over it. Ballistics did a match with the shots from your best friend's body—or what was left of it—and bingo."

"So what?" Oskar asked haughtily. It meant nothing. He could have handled the gun sometime after the murder, after it had been wiped clean. Prints meant almost nothing. "So I touched a gun. Didn't Frankie have a permit for it?" he sneered. "Talk to my lawyer."

He loved it. Both cops looked disappointed.

Then the tall one brightened. "Oh, and there's this."

He held up a photograph for Oskar to see. It was a picture of Dovee kneeling in the woods and Oskar, back and left profile, pointing a shotgun at his head. Fucking Wesley had taken a picture.

"It was in an envelope taped to the shaft of the gun," the short cop explained.

Oskar kept his mouth shut.

Thursday, October 22, 1998

"**A**re you sure I can't give you a lift to the airport tomorrow?" Don Edwards asked.

Cole shook his head, watching the clouds roll toward the mountains. "No. Thanks. I've made arrangements to drop this off at the airport." He nodded toward the rental car he was leaning against. "You should be relieved—the flight leaves at an ungodly hour."

They stood in the parking lot of the dojo for a few minutes longer, in silence. They both knew they wouldn't see each other again for a long time.

Cole had taken an indefinite leave of absence from the force, needing urgently to replace his surroundings with unfamiliar sights and faces. He had decided to try Greece and Turkey for a start, after a good long visit with his son.

"It'll be good for you to see Michael," Edwards said, somewhat uncomfortably, not wanting to refer directly to the shooting incident with Lauren Grey. It had changed both of them—Cole, imperceptibly; Lauren, vastly. Cole had become even more of a lone wolf, declining all social invitations unless they were from Edwards, and then it usually involved karate and a meal. And no discussion of Lauren.

The wiretap order on the meth lab had expired in August and resulted in a number of arrests. There was an outstanding arrest warrant for Bones, and Jojo and the good doctor had been reburied by professionals. The trial of the minor players was set to start in a year. Cole would come back to testify if they did not plead guilty. All in all, there was no reason to stay. So he'd rented out his flat, put his truck and a few belongings in storage and bought an open-ended ticket to London. Why not.

"Where is she?" Cole asked finally, looking squarely at his friend. He had driven past the beach house and seen it deteriorate, the hedge untended, the lawn grown long and seedy. The last time he had gone by, there had been a For Sale sign on the property.

"She's at their—her—place at Whistler. Listen, Jacko, Liz has been up to see her. So has Janine. They both say she's a mess. She won't come back to the city and she won't get help."

"I appreciate the warning," Cole said. "Where is her place?"

Edwards gave Cole directions to the house, which he described as a log house with a river rock foundation and sweeping verandah overlooking the golf course and Whistler Mountain. The distinguishing feature on the house was a set of stained glass panels, one on either side of the double front doors. "Some droopy purple flower."

"Wisteria," Cole said.

"That's it."

"I should get going," Cole said.

Edwards nodded. The two men looked at each other for a long moment and then bowed, deep and low.

"Thanks for everything, Don," Cole said. "Look after yourself, and Liz and the kids."

"You too, Jacko." Edwards's voice was hoarse.

He got into his car and headed for the office.

Cole got into his rented car and headed north. For Whistler.

WHISTLER, BRITISH COLUMBIA

He found her out on the verandah.

He had come upon the house just before 4:00, and when no one answered his knock, he had walked around the big timbered porch that circled the house until he reached the back of the place.

She was standing on the deck with her back to him, dressed in jeans and a woven jacket, holding a paintbrush and stroking blue lines on a canvas. Around her four other easels stood in a semicircle, like sentries. On each easel stood a painting, each one at a different stage.

She didn't turn around at the sound of his footsteps.

He didn't blame her. Her subject was magnificent: deciduous trees in full fall colour cloaked the dropping fall-line below the house, stopping abruptly against the golf course, emerald green in the failing light. Above and straight across towered the mountains. Their peaks were diamond white with early snow and their bases were blackening as the sun melted into the sea behind the coastal mountains.

He walked toward her, his footfalls plain on the planks, and stopped about fifteen feet away, waiting for her to respond to his approach.

"Hello, Jackson." She put her brush down on the palette near her and turned around slowly.

"How did you know it was me?" He held his breath, waiting to see her face again, off-kilter in her presence.

"Everyone else who might have mattered has come and gone. You're the last one." She paused, looked straight at him, then continued, her eyes focussed somewhere past him. "I'd hoped you would come . . ." Her voice drifted off.

Silence.

"Why didn't you call?" It came out strangled.

"For the reason you said, that . . . afternoon." She could feel her emotions swell from the mere reference to the events that had so shaken them both. She didn't want tears with Jackson this time. Struggling to hold them back, she continued. "It wouldn't have been fair." She looked at him evenly and smiled thinly, gesturing to the paintings around her. "I'm still in therapy." Her voice held a twist of sarcasm.

Jackson nodded.

He watched her push away a strand of hair that the wind had played across her face. He wanted to do it.

He had come to satisfy himself that she was fine. And to make peace with their goodbye. Now, being with her, he wasn't so sure that was what he wanted at all.

The afternoon deepened. Silence.

She breathed in the cold mountain air and asked, finally, "You're going away, aren't you?" She looked at him steadily, trying to memorize every detail of him.

"Yes," he said. "I'm going to spend some time with my son. In Europe. I don't know how long I'll stay."

She nodded.

The coastal mountains behind him were beginning to block out the light, extinguishing the brilliant green of the golf course, and causing shadow to creep up the mountainsides across from them. Toward the snow. Lauren shivered.

The wind picked up, rattling dead leaves across the wooden deck. They watched each other from a distance as the wind touched their hair and tugged gently at their clothing. There was nothing either of them could do.

"Goodbye, Lauren," he whispered at last, turning away.

"Goodbye, Jackson."

She stayed where she was, listening to his footsteps retreat. When she heard his car on the gravel, she turned back to her paintings.

Above her, in the last breath of sunlight, the wind picked up winter's early diamonds and crystals and ashes and dust and gave them brilliance.